The Ones They Buried

An Agent Victoria Heslin Thriller, Book 8
Jenifer Ruff

Greyt Companion Press

ALSO BY JENIFER RUFF

The Agent Victoria Heslin Thriller Series
The Numbers Killer
Pretty Little Girls
When They Find Us
Ripple of Doubt
The Groom Went Missing
Vanished on Vacation
The Atonement Murders
The Ones They Buried
The Bad Neighbor

THE FBI & CDC Thriller Series
Only Wrong Once
Only One Cure
Only One Wave: The Tsunami Effect

The Brooke Walton Series
Everett
Rothaker
The Intern

Suspense
Lauren's Secret

The Ones They Buried

The Ones They Buried is the eighth book in an award-winning series of standalone mystery thrillers featuring FBI Agent Victoria Heslin. They don't have to be read in order. A list of the Victoria Heslin books and others by Jenifer Ruff can be found at the end of this novel.

CHAPTER 1

One Year Ago - Phoebe

Phoebe Watson's social media posts went viral, reaching millions of views within a matter of days. The surge would have thrilled her, if only she'd been alive to see it.

Hours before her death, she was counting down seconds on her watch. The gym reverberated with the music she'd chosen. The beats and her encouragement drove her athletic conditioning class participants to push their limits. Floor-to-ceiling mirrors lined one wall, reflecting determined faces and bodies glistening with sweat.

Phoebe moved with strength and grace, performing each movement with precision as men and women gasped and grunted around her.

"And...done!" she finally said on the last repetition, clapping her hands. "Excellent work, everyone!"

A man in the front row shouted, "You tried to kill us, didn't you?" which might have been morbidly ironic, though no one, not even Phoebe's killer, knew what would soon unfold.

Phoebe only laughed with appreciation as she kneeled to roll up her mat.

From the back of the room, a man weaved around bodies to reach her. Appearing to be in his mid-thirties, he sported closely cropped black hair and a tanned complexion. Phoebe had noticed him earlier. He wasn't one of her regulars, though something about him seemed familiar.

"Your class was hard," he said.

"I take that as a compliment," Phoebe responded with a grin. For those who attended her classes consistently, hard and good were synonymous when it came to their workouts. She'd designed her routines for the dedicated fitness enthusiasts who pushed themselves until they were drenched in sweat, gasping for breath, and feeling the fire in their muscles. The man standing before her wasn't one of those people. Throughout the routine, he'd found it difficult to keep up.

"Was this your first time taking one of my classes?" she asked.

"First time, yes. I haven't joined the gym yet. I got a guest pass to try it out."

"Oh, that's great. Welcome." Phoebe stood with her rolled-up mat tucked under her arm and pressed an errant strand of red hair behind her ear.

He smiled and said, "I've seen you at Mrs. Catherine's house. I didn't know you worked here, too."

Catherine was one of Phoebe's personal training clients and perhaps the wealthiest, based on her luxurious home and lifestyle. Phoebe drove to the estate three times a week to give private sessions whenever Catherine was in town. Last Christmas, she rewarded Phoebe with a generous bonus, and the gold barbell pendant that never left Phoebe's neck. Catherine Bower was a dream client. How did this man fit in with Catherine's life?

"I take care of her yard, and her house," he said, as if he'd read Phoebe's thoughts. "My name is George."

"Oh, right." Often, on her way to and from her car, Phoebe noticed George at Catherine's place. Perhaps if he'd worn the cap he usually wore, she would have recognized him right away. He'd always seemed nice enough. Phoebe smiled at him now and said, "You're the reason her yard always looks amazing."

George's eyes lit up. "Thank you. I certainly try. It's an honor to take care of a special property like Catherine's."

"I bet. I enjoy being her trainer. Well, glad you came." Phoebe gave a little wave before turning away. She unplugged her phone from the stereo system and took a quick peek at her messages.

We need to talk.

It was from her ex.

No, we don't, she thought, without answering the message. He'd been trying to speak to her ever since she ended their brief relationship. He couldn't seem to accept that she wasn't interested. The more he texted and called, the less she wanted to have anything to do with him. She glanced toward the doorway, worried he was waiting for her. He was a fanatic about going to the gym most nights. Fortunately, she didn't see him.

Phoebe pulled on her hoodie and left the studio, reminding herself never to date anyone from the gym again. Her busy schedule centered around work, leaving little opportunity to meet people elsewhere. That's why she had accepted an invitation to have a drink later that evening with a new guy…not from the gym. He'd intrigued her with his charm and confidence. She hoped her decision wouldn't lead to regret.

Darkness had descended during her class, but the parking lot was well lit. Phoebe hurried to her little Toyota waiting in a space designated for staff. She was reaching for her door handle when a man's voice startled her.

"Good night, Ms. Phoebe."

George stood two spaces away, in front of a familiar blue pickup truck. The door of the truck proudly displayed a magnetized sign that read *George's Landscaping*.

Phoebe waved. "I hope to see you again in one of my classes."

"Yes. You'll definitely see me again soon," George answered.

CHAPTER 2

Present Day - Deja

On her first day of work with the agency, Deja Torres stood by the reception area at Atrium Gardens, an assisted living facility inside a gated country club community. Fidgeting with nervous energy, she absentmindedly chipped away at her gel polish, ruining a nail before realizing what she'd done.

It's just the uncertainty of it all. Meeting your first client, she reminded herself, stuffing her hands into the deep pockets of her white uniform. *You've got this.* And she did. There was no way her new job could demand as much from her as her previous gig with a large online retailer. Package delivery work entailed long shifts with no bathroom breaks and carrying heavy items onto front porches. Furniture crammed into boxes weighed more than she'd ever imagined. She still had the muscles to prove it. Thankfully, her delivery days were behind her. She hoped her new position would prove more satisfying and less strenuous.

A young-looking twenty-three-year-old, Deja frequently received compliments on her stunning appearance. She had shiny hair, smooth dark skin, a slender frame, and big brown eyes accentuated by false lashes. People told her she could be a model. Her beloved grandmother, a significant influence in Deja's life, had discouraged her from modeling. Deja had immense respect for her grandmother's wisdom and values. Gran believed Deja's true beauty didn't reside in her outward appearance, instead with an internal gift possessed by too few people—the gift of compassion. "Nurtured properly, it flourishes with life's experiences, and never fades away," Gran said.

Guided by Gran's insight, Deja had recently completed a course for certification as a caregiver. Soon after, the Senior Specialty Concierge Agency hired her. Deja's first assignment was with a wealthy client in a very fancy place. Obviously, the agency didn't say those things, not in so many words, but the signs were unmistakable. A one-month stay at Atrium Gardens costs more money than Deja would make in half a year.

As she followed a nurse's aide named Jasmine through the long, carpeted hallway, Deja marveled at her surroundings. They passed a glass-enclosed space containing small, colorful birds. A sitting area had plush couches gathered around an impressive stone fireplace, and a formal dining room featured elegant, upholstered chairs and neatly folded cloth napkins. The vacant rooms made Deja think of a luxury hotel preparing for a grand opening.

They rounded a corner and arrived at a central desk area. The luxury-hotel ambiance faded away, and reality set in. The smell of disinfectant permeated the air. A few residents sat around the desk in their wheelchairs. They seemed disconnected from the world around them, offering no acknowledgment as Jasmine greeted them with friendly hellos.

Jasmine turned down one of the many hallways branching from the central area. Room 104 was near the end of the corridor, two rooms away from the emergency exit. A copper plaque on the door announced the name of Deja's client. *Mrs. Catherine Bower.*

While most of Atrium Gardens' residents were elderly, Catherine was not. One year ago, she'd suffered a terrible accident. Deja didn't know what happened exactly. She understood the accident had led to an anoxic brain injury—a trauma caused by lack of oxygen to the brain, similar to a massive stroke. Catherine couldn't walk, get dressed, or feed herself.

At only forty-nine, she depended on caregivers for even the most basic functions.

Jasmine tapped her knuckles against Catherine's door, not bothering to wait for a response before entering. Deja trailed behind her, stepping into the private room. Sunlight flooded the space, casting a glow on exquisite furniture and tasteful décor, though several items provided clear reminders of the room's purpose and the occupant's vulnerability: grab-bars and a sturdy shower chair in the bathroom, and safety rails on the full-sized bed.

In the center of the room, Catherine sat in a high-tech wheelchair, facing a television, her back to the door.

"Just talk to her as if she understands you. They probably told you, right?" Jasmine said. "Come on, I'll introduce you and then I have to get home and take care of my kids."

Jasmine stepped in front of the wheelchair. "Catherine? You awake? Your new caregiver is here. Her name is Deja. She's here to take care of you and whatever you need."

Deja moved to Jasmine's side and could barely contain her surprise when she saw Catherine for the first time. She looked so put together, her black hair styled in a sleek bob, not a strand out of place. A hint of blush swept across her pale cheeks.

"She's so beautiful," Deja blurted, embarrassed as she immediately realized she'd spoken as if Catherine wasn't there.

"She just got back from the beauty shop," Jasmine said.

With a smile, Deja introduced herself to Catherine.

Catherine's expression remained neutral. She gave no sign she'd understood what anyone had said.

"Sometimes she says things or tries to. None of it makes sense as far as I can tell," Jasmine said. "Don't worry. She has a way of letting you know when she's unhappy or uncomfortable. She'll twitch and frown, things like that."

"Is there a list of things she likes or doesn't like?" Deja asked.

"No. You'll figure it out. Just talk to her about whatever comes into your head. Feed her. Keep her clean. Let her watch television. Okay? Well, good luck. I have to go. You'll be fine," Jasmine added, perhaps noticing the way Deja twisted the edge of her uniform between her fingers.

Jasmine left the room, and Deja was alone with Catherine.

"It's nice to meet you," Deja said. "I'm glad to be here. I hope I can help make things more comfortable for you. If you can be patient with me while I work it all out, I think we'll be good. I promise you'll get to do a lot more than just watch television when I'm around."

Deja placed her hand on Catherine's shoulder. Not something she would normally do with someone she'd just met. Yet if Catherine couldn't understand her words, a gentle, firm touch, a universal form of communication, seemed important. Deja had to start somewhere.

She looked out the window at the manicured lawn, and bird feeders hanging from tree branches just outside the window. "We could go for a walk since it's a nice day. Would you like that?" To her own ears, Deja's cheerfulness sounded forced. Adjusting to one-way conversations would take some practice. Catherine didn't appear to be paying attention, anyway. With her gaze fixed on the television, her eyes widened and her perfect eyebrows lifted.

Deja turned to see what had caused Catherine's response.

A flashing red ribbon emblazoned with *Breaking News* scrolled across the bottom of the screen. The camera swept out, revealing a dense expanse of woods. Stark yellow crime scene tape crisscrossed from tree to tree, forming a perimeter.

The reporter announced, "Just a few hours ago, authorities in Rutherford County discovered the body of a woman in the remote area you see behind me. I'm told local residents refer to the area as Madison Creek Woods. At this time, law enforcement is not releasing information about the discovery, and the victim has yet to be identified. We will keep you informed as further developments emerge."

Deja felt an immediate surge of compassion. She understood the profound sorrow that would consume the woman's family.

"Want me to change the channel?" Deja asked. "The news can be so depressing."

Catherine jerked her head, which surprised Deja. She'd asked a question, and Catherine seemed to have responded with a definitive, non-verbal answer. Deja couldn't say if the response was a yes or a no, but it was something. Maybe Jasmine and the agency were wrong about Catherine. Maybe she understood people and could communicate in her own way.

Still staring at the television, Catherine croaked out the sounds, "Ee-bee."

"What's that?" Deja asked, leaning closer.

When Catherine repeated the sounds, Deja focused on the first consonant and heard it clearly. "Phoebe."

"Phoebe?" Deja asked. "Is that what you said?"

"Phoebe—Watson," Catherine said with great effort, her face contorting and her eyes squeezing shut.

"Is Phoebe a friend of yours here in the facility?" Deja asked. "Or a family member? Or someone from before you were…uh …someone from before you lived here? Do you want me to find her for you?"

Catherine shuddered. She clenched her hands together and held them against her chest. Soon her whole upper body shook so fiercely it rattled her wheelchair.

Fear gripped Deja, rendering her temporarily helpless. This was not good. Not good at all. She wrapped her hand around Catherine's trembling arm to steady her. Deja didn't know if Catherine's behavior was a regular occurrence or an emergency. No one had mentioned anything about seizures. This was not how Deja imagined her first hour of her first day on the job. She was about to run into the hallway and call for help when Catherine's shaking subsided. Her eyes opened and tears rolled down her face.

Deja grabbed a tissue from the nightstand and dabbed Catherine's cheeks.

After Catherine's troubling reaction, Deja hoped the name Phoebe Watson would never come up again.

CHAPTER 3

Present Day - Victoria

FBI Special Agent Victoria Heslin sat beside her colleague, Agent Dante Rivera, waiting to learn why their boss had called them into his office. Whatever he presented them with, Victoria felt confident she and Rivera could handle it. They'd faced years of challenges together. Rivera always had her back, and she had his.

Special Agent in Charge Larry Murphy entered his office carrying a mug embellished with the Georgia Bulldogs mascot, a not-so-subtle nod to his passion for college football. His military-style posture added to his commanding presence, and his stern expression conveyed the weight of his responsibilities. He was a good, fair boss who appreciated his agents.

"I've got a new assignment for you," he said. "An hour ago, we got pulled into the Jane Doe case from Rutherford County. Are you familiar with it? The woman's remains that were found buried in Madison Creek Woods."

Victoria nodded and leaned forward to learn more.

"Jane Doe's murder might be connected to a crime in another state," Murphy said. "Last year, officers in North Carolina stopped a man named Dan Sullivan for a traffic violation. Luckily, they had a K-9 unit. The dog alerted them, leading to a search of the vehicle. They discovered the body of a twenty-six-year-old woman in the back. The mother of twin toddlers. She'd been sexually assaulted, beaten, and strangled. Sullivan's DNA was all over her body. The traffic stop and subsequent search were conducted properly. The evidence was solid."

Placing his mug on the desk, Murphy crossed his arms and continued, "Sullivan was convicted and sentenced to life in Virginia. Just a few days ago, he said he wanted to offer authorities additional information."

"What information?" Rivera asked.

"He wanted to give them the location of another woman's remains, and he did, implicating himself in Jane Doe's case," Murphy explained. "Her body was found exactly where he directed the police to search in Madison Creek Woods. Now, he claims to possess knowledge about the location of additional victims and wants to negotiate."

"What are his terms?" Victoria asked. "What does he want?"

Murphy frowned. "He wants his sentence reduced."

"Why do we need to be involved?" Rivera asked.

"Sullivan hasn't disclosed Jane Doe's identity, presumably as leverage. The detective who interviewed him believes Sullivan doesn't know her name. He thinks Sullivan could be lying. We need confirmation that Sullivan is indeed responsible for Jane Doe's death." Murphy directed his gaze at Victoria and said, "You'll take the lead on this, considering your growing expertise in serial killers."

Rivera gave her a slight smile.

"Jane Doe's remains are less than a year old," Murphy continued. "There are no local women missing, so detectives are checking neighboring cities and states. Assuming normal circumstances, we should identify her soon."

"Our job will be easier once she has a name," Rivera said.

"Yes," Murphy answered. "If Sullivan's story proves credible, he serves less time in exchange for the rest of what he knows. The victims' families deserve closure, but we have to confirm beyond any doubt that Sullivan is responsible for Jane Doe's murder before any deal is made."

"Got it," Victoria said. "And if Sullivan didn't kill Jane Doe?"

"I trust you'll uncover the truth," Murphy answered. "Someone out there knows who the poor woman is and what happened to her. Find that person."

CHAPTER 4

Present Day - Victoria

Victoria and Rivera settled inside one of the FBI's conference rooms, preparing to watch a recently recorded video featuring the notorious Dan Sullivan. In the video, Sullivan, his attorney, and two detectives sat inside a small room with concrete walls.

Though shackled, Sullivan dominated the space. Broad chested and bulging with muscles, his victim stood little to no chance. He had full sleeves of tattoos, ink covering his neck, and a cleft lip. He was intimidating and unforgettable. As the video played, his deep voice filled the room, each sentence punctuated by a guttural grunt.

"I'm not giving you any more information until I get my deal," he said.

After watching the video to its end, the agents dug into Sullivan's arrest file, starting with details surrounding Diane Johnson, the woman found in the back of his van.

Diane's routine was well-documented—an early morning drop-off of her twins at their grandparents' house, followed by a short drive to the nearby Top Shop Diner, where she worked breakfast and lunch shifts. According to the reports, Sullivan's frightening mugshot triggered recognition among Diane's coworkers when the police interviewed them. They vividly recalled his crude advances and lingering stares.

"Guy was a stalker," Rivera said. "He followed her for two months, and acting stealthy wasn't his strong suit. That should work in our favor when it comes to proving he killed Jane Doe."

Victoria nodded in agreement. "Yes, though it won't help us until we know who she is."

Delving deeper into the files, the agents could trace Sullivan's propensity for violence to a turbulent and abusive childhood. Hospital records and domestic violence reports substantiated his father's brutality. Sullivan had witnessed those horrors and endured his father's abuse firsthand.

"Like father like son," Rivera said. "It's a shame how frequently we witness that pattern, especially when therapy and positive role models could make a difference. In Sullivan's case, he really took the abuse to a whole new level."

"He knew right from wrong," Victoria said. "He understood what he was doing when he took Diane Johnson's life, leaving her twins motherless. Now, in exchange for information on other potential victims, he wants a lesser sentence. This is like a no-win situation. The whole thing makes me sick."

She hoped Sullivan wasn't responsible for Jane Doe's death. Victoria didn't want him getting any special deals. But if he wasn't the killer, a dangerous murderer remained at large.

CHAPTER 5

Present Day - Victoria

The agents entered the brightly lit autopsy room and breathed in the sharp scent of bleach. Pathologist Dr. Rebecca Boswell was singing as she peeled off a pair of gloves by the sink. Over her pink scrubs, she wore a white coat with her name embroidered on the left side. Rebecca had a self-assured, glamorous allure that made her stand out wherever she went, and especially in the autopsy room.

Rebecca dropped her gloves into the trash and looked sideways toward the door. She ended her verse with a smile, removed earbuds from her ears, and tucked them into a case.

Rebecca had never made a secret of her fondness for Rivera. Victoria understood the appeal of his chiseled jawline and dreamy brown eyes, his blend of quiet strength, determination, and genuine sensitivity. Not to mention the hours spent on the basketball court that gave him a trim, muscular physique.

"Hey, there," Rebecca said. "To what do I owe the pleasure? No, let me guess. You're here about our Jane Doe."

"Yes, that's right," Victoria answered.

"Excellent. I finished her exam, and I sent debris and fibers to the lab. I knew someone was going to come in and ask about her this morning. She's still on a table," Rebecca said, grabbing a new set of gloves from a box over the sink. With a fluid practiced motion, she slid two gloves over each hand, covering her bright pink nails, a perfect match to her scrubs and the tiny beads in her long braids.

Victoria grabbed a set of gloves for herself. She was mostly a rule follower, unless she needed to break the rules for the greater good, something she had no problem doing when necessary. She slid the gloves on. The plastic hung loose in three places, where a surgeon had amputated her frostbitten fingers at the knuckles.

"Right this way," Rebecca said, leading them to a stainless-steel table on the right side of the room. Her foot pressed a button on the floor, activating an overhead light with an adjustable arm as she lifted a sheet off the corpse. "Here she is. Washed clean, she's a lot easier for you to look at now. Someone buried her directly in the earth, so her soft tissues are gone, leaving us with bones and a trace of her organs."

Victoria scanned the unidentified woman's remains and said, "Tell us everything you know."

"Caucasian female," Rebecca answered. "Approximately twenty-five years old. Reddish hair. Not colored. From the state of decomposition, deceased for nine to twelve months."

"Cause of death?" Rivera asked.

"Manner of death is easy. Homicide. Cause of death, that's hard to say. I'm fairly certain she was strangled because her hyoid bone is broken." Rebecca motioned to the victim's neck. "I can't say that's what killed her."

Rebecca moved to the end of the table and touched her gloved fingers to the victim's skull. "She took several blows to her skull and torso. The indentation in the skull fracture here suggests a heavy, sharp-edged object. A shovel or hoe, perhaps. The same instrument might have caused a fracture in her left arm and collarbone."

"Those traumas occurred around her time of death?" Rivera asked.

"They did. There are no signs of healing in those areas. In contrast, she had one old tibia fracture. Probably happened when she was a teen. She also had a beautiful set of teeth. Bonded in the front to lengthen them."

"With the healed fracture and the dental work, she shouldn't be hard to identify." Victoria said. "Someone must be missing her."

CHAPTER 6

Present Day - Victoria

Inside the forensics lab, the evidence team lead, Henry, sat on a stool hunched over a microscope. Rivera knocked on the outer door. Henry remained engrossed in his work and oblivious to the agents' presence. After scanning their badges and retinas to gain access, the agents entered the lab, still unnoticed by Henry.

"Hello, we're here about the Jane Doe they found in Madison Creek Woods," Victoria said as they approached Henry.

Finally, Henry swiveled his seat around to face them. "Long time no see. It's been a few months, hasn't it?"

"Yeah, it has," Rivera said.

"I was working up the evidence on Jane Doe. Just haven't written the report yet," Henry said.

"Can you share what you've found?" Victoria asked. "We need evidence to support the confession of the person claiming to have killed her."

"Somebody confessed?" Henry asked.

"Yes. A convicted killer. But there are doubts about his truthfulness," Victoria answered.

"Intriguing," Henry muttered, removing his glasses and heading toward a nearby computer. "I'll pull up the data so I can give you accurate information."

As they waited, the room fell silent until Henry said, "Alright, here's what I have. The burial site was a remote private property, far from any homes or stores. Without the tip, Jane Doe might have remained hidden forever. Buried four feet underground, more of a deep hole than a grave."

"Was there anything in there with her?" Victoria asked.

"Nope, she was completely naked. No clothing, no identifying items. Dr. Boswell found some trace evidence in her hair, though," Henry said.

"She mentioned that," Rivera said. "Any leads from it?"

Henry kept his eyes glued to his computer. "They were navy and white fabric threads. I'm still waiting for further analysis."

"If we get you a sample of carpet from the suspect's van, can you check for a match?" Rivera asked.

Henry turned to face the agents. "Based on what I observed under the microscope, I can rule out carpet fibers. It's more likely they came from a high-end blanket or an expensive towel."

"Maybe we already collected something similar from Sullivan's house," Rivera said. "If I give you a case number, can you cross-reference your fibers with previously collected evidence from our guy's trial?"

Henry nodded. "Send me the case number. I'll take a look."

"Did you uncover anything else we can work with?" Victoria asked.

"There were some unusual substances in her hair—eucalyptus and neem oil, onion and garlic spray, and salt," Henry told them.

Victoria ventured a guess. "Cooking ingredients?"

Henry gave her a look that said, *you obviously don't cook.* He was right; cooking was not her area of expertise. Most of what she ate at home came from a food service that delivered healthy, locally sourced meals. Victoria knew almost nothing about cooking except for the homemade crock pot meals she prepared for her dogs.

"No one cooks with neem oil," Henry said. "Those substances have something in common—they're all organic pesticides used by conscientious gardeners to eliminate insects, weeds, or fungi."

"Sullivan didn't strike me as a gardener, or conscientious about anything," Victoria said. She exchanged a look with Rivera, who shook his head in agreement.

"It's clear Jane Doe's death occurred elsewhere, given the lack of evidence at the burial site," Henry concluded. "Unfortunately, that's all I can provide you with at the moment."

"Alright, it's a good start. Please contact us when you have more information about the fibers or anything else," Victoria said.

"I have your numbers," Henry said. "I'll send a link to my written report once I finish it."

The agents left the evidence lab, focusing on their next course of action. Wanting a quick pick-me-up, Victoria guided them toward a Starbucks kiosk, where she indulged in a London Fog latte. With the warm cup between her hands, she and Rivera retreated to a quiet corner of the building.

"We should find out if Sullivan ever owned organic gardening products," Victoria said, taking a sip of her sweet concoction.

"Consider it done. I'll make sure Henry gets the evidence collected from Sullivan's van and apartment to cross-reference with the forensic findings from Jane Doe."

"Excellent. I'm going to scour the VICAP database for potential connections, and then coordinate with the local police on missing person cases that match up," Victoria said.

With their plans laid out and their collective expertise in motion, they were on their way to figuring out what happened to Jane Doe.

CHAPTER 7

Present Day - Deja

In room 104 at the Atrium Gardens Facility, Deja's work went smoothly. No worrisome incidents had occurred since her first day, when Catherine had become visibly distressed and said, 'Phoebe Watson.'

Taking a moment to observe her surroundings, Deja's gaze settled on the portrait hanging above Catherine's bed. Enclosed within a dark wood frame, it captured Catherine's beautiful family on a beach with white sand and shimmering turquoise water.

Catherine served as the picture's focal point. Toned and tan in a white sundress, she looked relaxed, radiating sophistication and elegance. Diamonds graced her ears and her neck. Her serene brown eyes sparkled, beckoning Deja into the scene.

A handsome man with dirty blond hair, a square jaw, and crystal blue eyes sat on a bench beside Catherine. Behind them stood a younger man and woman. They sported Catherine's narrow face, dimpled cheeks, dark hair, and brown eyes with heavy lashes. Yet there was no hint of a resemblance to the man by Catherine's side.

Catherine's daughter, slender to the point of concern, possessed a striking beauty reminiscent of her mother, and looked to be in her late twenties. Catherine's handsome son had the confident aura of a college athlete.

Deja could not take her eyes off the beautiful picture and wished her family had a portrait like it made before her mother died.

Everyone in Catherine's family looked perfect, and Deja wondered what they were really like behind their gleaming smiles. The photographer must have enhanced the image. Maybe, in reality, their eyes weren't as bright, and their skin didn't have that gorgeous, healthy glow. Deja didn't know for sure because not one of them had visited the facility. Not since Deja started her job. She'd even checked the front desk's registration log to see if they came after her shifts ended. They hadn't. According to the records, Catherine's only visitor for the past two weeks was someone named George Martin.

"Does Catherine's family come to see her?" Deja had asked Jasmine that morning.

"I've seen her son," Jasmine said. "Handsome fellow. He goes to college somewhere out of state."

A college boy. Just as Deja suspected. Though she had yet to meet him or anyone else in Catherine's family, that was about to change. In less than an hour, Deja and Catherine were headed to Catherine's home, where she lived before Atrium Gardens, for the occasion of Catherine's fiftieth birthday.

Deja turned away from the portrait and smiled at Catherine. "Let's finish getting you ready."

From the stacks of designer clothing inside the closet, Deja had chosen a soft blue cashmere sweater and long gray skirt that draped over Catherine's thin legs. The house would have air-conditioning, and Catherine seemed perpetually chilly. Tiny goosebumps pimpled her arms and legs when they weren't covered.

"I'm going to put your makeup on now. When I'm done, you're going to look just like you do in your family picture," Deja said, assuming that was how Catherine wanted to present herself to the world.

After applying makeup, Deja added the finishing touches, fastening diamond studs into Catherine's ears, and surrounding her neck with a diamond pendant necklace. The same jewelry Catherine wore in the portrait.

Deja got the hand mirror from the dresser and held it up for Catherine to see her reflection.

Sometimes Deja was sure Catherine knew what was happening around her. This was one of those times. The corners of Catherine's mouth turned up ever so slightly. Just enough to make Deja feel good about the special care she'd taken.

As Deja was putting the makeup away, her phone rang. The agency only permitted personal calls during her breaks, and Deja usually turned off or silenced her phone at work. She'd forgotten to do either of those things, and now her heart leaped. The distinctive ringtone meant her grandmother was calling, and Gran wouldn't call unless something important had happened.

Deja answered quickly. "Is everything okay, Gran?"

"Yes. I'm sorry to bother you at work, honey. I have a quick question about an important matter. Well, it might be important."

"Oh," Deja said, relieved her grandmother was okay. "No problem. What is it?"

"I got an email letter from the bank. The letter says there's a problem with my account, and I have to verify some information as soon as possible or they'll close it permanently. There's a link to click. Everything looks real, yet I'm not sure if it is. Something about it just doesn't seem right to me. I think someone might be trying to trick me."

"Look at the address the email came from. What does it say?"

"Let me see. I have to put my glasses on first. It says no reply and then numbers and letters are gobbled together with no spaces. I don't think they spell anything. That means it's not really the bank, doesn't it? I see now. What is wrong with people? Someone was trying to trick me. How could they be so terrible?" Gran asked.

"Some people can't help being terrible. It's in their blood. Glad you didn't click the link," Deja said.

"Why did this come to me?"

"It's not personal, Gran. Probably millions of people got the same email. I have to go. I'll see you later. Remember, I won't be home for dinner tonight."

"I remember. Good luck with your trip. I hope it goes well," Gran said. "Oh, did you give Catherine your gift yet? The book you're going to read to her?"

"Not yet."

"Well, when you do, tell her I said, happy birthday."

"I will. I'll see you tonight. Love you."

"Love you too, baby."

As Deja slid her phone back into her pocket and looked up, she caught Catherine smiling. A slight smile, maybe even a sad one, yet it was there. Perhaps she'd understood Deja's exchange with her grandmother and was thinking about seeing her own family. She must miss them.

Deja patted Catherine's chin with a washcloth, where a thin line of drool started trailing through her makeup. Deja had gotten better at anticipating Catherine's needs and better at keeping up one-sided conversations.

"You look beautiful," Deja said. "Definitely ready for your party. You must be excited to see your husband and your children, right?"

Catherine scrunched her nose and squeezed her eyes shut; an expression Deja had come to know well. It was a telltale sign of Catherine's deep displeasure.

Deja recalled many instances when she had witnessed the same expression on Catherine's face. It appeared during moments of frustration or pain, when Catherine was tired or uncomfortable and had no other way of letting Deja know.

Why now?

Either Catherine hadn't understood, or she wasn't happy about going to see her family.

CHAPTER 8

Present Day - Deja

As they neared the end of Catherine's seemingly endless driveway, Deja's eyes widened in astonishment. In front of her towered a majestic white-brick mansion, an imposing symbol of wealth worlds away from her own humble upbringing. Every detail of the building left her in awe. Catherine's room at Atrium Gardens was lovely, but nothing compared to this architectural marvel.

When the van stopped, Deja unhooked Catherine's wheelchair and grabbed the bag with their supplies.

As the driver lowered Catherine and her wheelchair to the ground, he must have noticed Deja's nervous expression. "Don't worry. They won't bite," he said.

Deja laughed. "I certainly hope not."

"They're very lucky to have you taking such good care of Mrs. Bower."

Deja swallowed and nodded. She needed that little boost of confidence. Her stomach was turning, and because she was so on edge, she had to use the bathroom. Not the first impression she wanted to make. She couldn't help worrying. The people inside that house were her bosses. The ones who hired her, the ones who could fire her. She wanted them to like her. She wanted them to know she was doing everything she could to take excellent care of Catherine.

Once inside, Deja expected them to grill her with questions. They'd want to know who she was, where she came from, her opinions and beliefs, what she talked about with Catherine, and other details. Deja understood their curiosity. If someone in her family had a full-time caregiver, she'd want to know everything possible about the person.

The house itself was imposing. Until Catherine, Deja didn't know anyone else who lived in a place like that. The people who lived there probably had everything they could ever want and nothing to worry about. Naturally, they would have high expectations for their mother's care.

As she approached the house, pushing Catherine's wheelchair across the smooth, interconnecting stones of the driveway, Deja reminded herself they'd already chosen her. Someone in Catherine's family had viewed Deja's employment history, her photograph, the background check, and the two paragraphs she'd written and rewritten and revised a dozen or more times about what she offered as a caregiver. After reviewing all that, they'd selected her and not someone else.

"I'm looking forward to meeting your family," Deja said as she pushed Catherine up a ramp, heading to the front of the house.

Through the enormous glass and iron front doors, Deja could see in—stone floors, a grand piano, a massive staircase with black iron railing, soaring ceilings, so much open space—and straight through to an incredible backyard on the other side.

As the van drove away, Deja rang the doorbell. They waited.

The home appeared empty. No signs of activity. Maybe the people inside were hiding and would soon jump out and surprise Catherine. That's when Deja realized she didn't know who was going to be there. Catherine's immediate family from the portrait, she assumed. Who else? A fiftieth birthday party was a big deal, a reason to gather with extended family, friends, and neighbors. Yet there were no cars in the circular driveway.

Each side of the house had an attached garage with three polished wood doors. Six spots in total. Maybe the guests had traveled together and parked inside as part of the surprise.

At least a minute passed. Deja peered through the glass as she rang the doorbell again.

A blur of movement came from a doorway near the piano. A woman appeared. The young woman from the family portrait. In a silky top, yoga pants, and bare feet, she seemed to almost tiptoe toward them, her eyes focused on Catherine. Tossing her straight hair over one shoulder, she flung the door open.

"Happy birthday, Mom!" she exclaimed as she stepped outside, accompanied by the faint smell of cigarette smoke. She wrapped her arms around Catherine and gave her a quick squeeze. Just as quickly, the woman straightened and walked around to the back of the wheelchair.

Deja stepped aside as the woman grasped the wheelchair's handles and said, "I've got her."

Without a hello or an introduction, she pushed Catherine into the house, leaving Deja behind.

Deja closed the door and followed them into a large, bright kitchen. In the center of a marble-topped island sat a cake and three presents, each wrapped with different paper.

"Mom is here!" the woman yelled.

The handsome older man from the picture entered the kitchen from a different corridor. "Honey, don't you look beautiful," he said, picking up Catherine's hand and lifting it to his lips. "Absolutely as stunning as ever. Happy birthday, darling."

Deja heard footsteps as someone ran downstairs. The last of the family of four joined them, confirming Catherine's family looked as beautiful in person as they did in the portrait over her bed.

Catherine's son hugged her for several seconds and whispered something into her ear. When he let go and took a step back, he said, "Sorry I haven't been to visit in a few weeks. I've got exams. Just a few more left and I'm done. They've been brutal. Intentionally. To weed some of us out. But I wasn't going to miss your big day."

With a smile that deepened his dimples, he turned to Deja. "And you must be Deja."

Deja offered a professional smile, though she was thinking he couldn't be more handsome if he tried. "It's nice to meet all of you," she told them.

"I'm Will," he said, then pointed to his sister. "That's Taylor." His gaze moved to the older man. "And our stepfather, John. I better warn you now, Deja. Things might get a little *interesting* around here."

"Oh," Deja answered, wondering what Will's comment meant. She set her bag of supplies next to the island, then wrapped her arms around her body.

Will had already turned back to his mother. "We've got your favorite takeout food from Flower Child. I'm starved, so how about we get right to eating?" He turned her wheelchair around.

Surrounded by family, Deja expected Catherine to be happy. Her expression said otherwise. Perhaps seeing her loved ones together, in the home where she no longer lived, was not an easy thing. Maybe she didn't recognize anyone or understand where she was.

"I hate it at Clauss and Steinman," Taylor told her mother when they were seated around the kitchen table. "I'm not staying there much longer. The hours are awful. Someone always needs something, and it's definitely not fun. But you know, some of us have to work." With that last comment, her gaze shifted toward her stepfather for a few seconds before returning to her mother. "Oh, did you hear Stacy W. got engaged a few months ago? Some guy she met at her mother's house in the Bahamas. I'm going to be a bridesmaid. She wants us to wear a hideous dress. You would die if you saw it. I think she's trying to make us look bad, so she looks better." Taylor snorted. "She's gained weight since college. Not a ton, but too much. I'll try to find you a picture." Taylor took out her phone and started tapping the screen. "I'm sure she'll lose a few pounds before the wedding, though. She'd be completely insane not to."

Deja cringed as she listened to the way Taylor talked about her friend. Someone who'd asked her to be a bridesmaid, no less. Maybe Taylor was nervous too, babbling without really stopping for a breath, because her mother's condition was still new to her.

While Taylor searched her phone to prove her friend was now overweight, John removed containers from the massive refrigerator. He set them on the counter, where Will peeled off the tops.

Deja got a bib from her bag to put around Catherine's neck, over her cashmere sweater.

Taylor held up her hand. "No. Take that away. I think we should take some photos, and I don't want my mother to have a bib on in them. Though why she's wearing a fall sweater in late May, I can't imagine." Taylor gave Deja a piercing look. "Did you pick it out for her?"

"She's usually cold," Deja explained. "I have another shirt in her bag." One she'd brought in case the sweater got dirty.

"No, just…whatever," Taylor said with a wave of her hand.

"Food's ready," John announced. "It's buffet style."

Deja made a plate for Catherine. After cutting the food into small pieces, she returned to the table. She needed to sit next to Catherine to feed her. But John sat on one side of Catherine and Taylor sat on the other.

"Would one of you mind switching places with me?" Deja asked.

"I'll feed her," Taylor said, taking the plate with Catherine's food.

Empty-handed, Deja sat down at the end of the table.

"Grab a plate for yourself, if you're hungry," Will said.

"I'm fine. Thank you," Deja answered. She'd already decided she shouldn't join them for dinner, though there was enough food for at least ten people.

"I'm opening a special wine," Will said, holding up a bottle with a French label. He smiled at his mother. "One of your favorites."

"Maybe that's not a good idea," John said.

"Why? Because it's a three-thousand-dollar bottle? Is that why you're against us enjoying it?" Taylor asked with a sneer. "Because there's no risk of her having a drinking problem anymore, right?"

Deja regretted overhearing that comment. The information seemed private, something Catherine might not have wanted people to know.

Will expertly uncorked the bottle and poured the wine into five glasses. One for everyone, including Deja.

"A toast to our amazing mother on her half-century birthday," he said, raising his glass.

John picked up the wineglass in front of Catherine. He swirled it around and sniffed it before bringing it to her lips and tipping it forward.

Deja scooted to the edge of her seat, ready to move between the others and wipe up liquid that dribbled down Catherine's chin. It wasn't necessary. Catherine opened her mouth and drank, gulping down every drop until John tipped the glass away.

Deja settled back into her chair, preparing to taste the most expensive liquid she had ever encountered. She took a small sip, allowing the wine to linger on her tongue. Good, she supposed, though she didn't know if it was three-thousand-dollars good. She took another sip and tried to commit the taste to memory.

Meanwhile, John dug into his meal, while Taylor forked a piece of chicken and brought it to Catherine's lips. Catherine refused to open her mouth.

"Maybe her caregiver could do a better job of feeding her, if you'd let her," John said.

"I think I can handle feeding her," Taylor snapped. "You're the only one here who thinks it's too much to ask of someone."

The tense exchanges occurring between Catherine's family members left Deja deeply unsettled. She turned away from them to look out at the backyard. A white brick building, a smaller version of the main house, stood alongside a long, in-ground pool. A tarp covered the pool.

"Come on, Mom," Taylor said. Her sharp voice pulled Deja's attention back to the table, where Taylor pressed a forkful of something against her mother's lips.

"Don't force her to eat," John said.

"I'm not *forcing* her," Taylor shot back.

"I can take her plate with us when we leave and see if she's hungry later tonight," Deja suggested.

"That's a good idea," Will announced, sliding Catherine's plate to the center of the table.

Taylor held the wineglass up for Catherine, who finished the drink.

After the cake, which Catherine also refused, they opened her presents. A silk scarf and lotion from Taylor. An expensive-looking necklace and earrings from John. Three audiobooks, earbuds, and an iPad from Will.

Taylor, who hadn't eaten a single thing, went outside to smoke, while Will told Catherine about his summer travel plans in Europe.

Without being obvious about it, Deja scrolled through her phone. First her personal messages, then news highlights. An earthquake had destroyed villages in Turkey and Syria. A pop star and his model wife were getting divorced. In local news, the police still hadn't identified the deceased woman they found in Madison Creek Woods.

Everyone started getting up from the table, a sign the party was winding down. Deja wanted to check on Catherine in private before they made the drive back to the facility. "Is there a bedroom I can take Catherine into for a few minutes?" she asked John.

He pointed to a door on their right. "Down the hall. Second door."

Deja wheeled Catherine to the bedroom and closed the door partway behind her. She spread out a pad on the bed and maneuvered Catherine from the wheelchair onto the bed to change her.

Through the crack in the door, the family's conversation reached her from the main room.

"So, the new girl you hired, how is she doing?" Taylor asked.

John answered. "She must be doing a good job because your mother looks well, don't you think?"

"I doubt Mom would agree," Taylor said with a loud huff. "Whatever. She probably won't stick around much longer."

Deja's mouth dropped open. *Who* wouldn't be around much longer? Was Taylor talking about Deja leaving? Or was she referring to Catherine's death?

"Just think about all the people who abandoned Mom over the years," Taylor said. "Didn't her last caregiver leave without telling anyone? And last year, when everything fell apart, George quit doing the yard stuff. Before that, Mom's fitness trainer, Phoebe. Remember, she just disappeared without a trace, never to be seen again?"

The name Phoebe captured Deja's attention. Phoebe Watson was the name Catherine had spoken aloud, the name that seemed to stir up her emotions. If Phoebe had disappeared, perhaps that was the reason Catherine got so upset thinking about her.

"I think Deja is great, so let's try to be nicer and more welcoming so she doesn't quit," Will said. "Mother needs a full-time person. Otherwise, the staff leaves her in front of the television for most of the day."

"If those of us who don't have to work visited her more, rather than golfing all day, that might not happen," Taylor said, her voice rising.

"I'm there almost every day," John said.

Down the hall, Deja's eyes popped at his claim, which wasn't remotely true. She stopped moving, straining to hear what might come next.

"Try to be civil until your mother leaves, can't you?" John said.

"Don't worry. Once we're gone, you can get back to whatever it is you do with your little friend in *her* house," Taylor shouted back. "God, it's no wonder our mother didn't want to deal with you anymore when she found out about her disease."

That last comment made Deja's head spin. She didn't know Catherine had a disease. And it sounded like she'd planned to divorce John before her accident. But why?

CHAPTER 9
One Year Ago - Catherine

Everything had changed, and Catherine wasn't happy about it.

With her hair still damp from the shower, she opened the fridge and removed ingredients for a post-workout smoothie—blueberries, kale, and wheat germ.

She used to eat from a range of foods she somewhat enjoyed; ones that kept her hunger pains at bay without sabotaging her figure. The recent confirmation of her diagnosis—early-onset Alzheimer's—had changed all that. Meal choices no longer revolved around taste, and her figure could no longer be her top priority.

Applying her usual determination, she now avoided foods that caused inflammation or disease. Every morsel entering her body needed to give her the best chance of winning the war, or at least of prolonging the battle. She was fighting the disease with everything she had at her disposal, including her robust bank accounts. She had superior doctors and treatments, and each morning, a brain-boosting drink of super foods and supplements. Her diet had become a primary weapon in her arsenal against early-onset Alzheimer's. Would any of it help? She couldn't say and had nothing to lose by trying.

After scooping spirulina into the blender, she glanced out the back window at the large lap pool and the pool house. Her fitness trainer, Phoebe, held a side plank on her mat in front of the pool. A small tripod held Phoebe's phone a foot or so above the ground to record her exercise routine. She'd said she was calling this video: *Twenty Minutes to a Toned Core*. Surely all she had to do was include an attractive photo of her defined abs and hourglass shape and she'd get a million views. Or maybe it wasn't that easy. Because few things in life were. No matter how attractive one was. No matter how wealthy. Life could be difficult. Catherine knew that well.

Near the pool, carrying an edging machine, George stood talking to his brother-in-law, Christian. George motioned to the side yard before trudging off in that direction. The untied laces of one work boot dragged through the lush grass with each clopping step. He seemed to pay more attention to Catherine's property than to his own appearance. He treated each plant like a nugget of pure gold. Which reminded Catherine, she still needed to head out to the area behind the pool house and check out the pollinator garden George told her he'd created.

George was out of sight. Christian remained. He was a good-looking man. Neat and compact in appearance. Much more attractive than George, with far less work ethic. How often had Catherine seen Christian lounging shirtless near the pool or taking a break on the front steps? Often enough it didn't surprise her. Last month, she'd come outside for an afternoon swim and caught him napping.

He was still standing there watching Phoebe, though she didn't know it.

Catherine couldn't blame the man for wanting to stare, though it was going on for quite some time. Phoebe's sports bra and workout pants fit like a second skin, revealing the toned curves of her beautiful and finely tuned body.

Oh, to be young and healthy, to feel invincible again.

Catherine didn't have to go back far in time to feel that way. A few months ago, her primary worries were Taylor's future and what to wear for an evening out with friends or to a fundraiser. That was before she started experiencing subtle yet unsettling changes in her personality, outbursts of anger and frustration. Before the minor yet unprecedented mix ups with language and the slightly blurred vision, all early signs of her disease. Before the notion of her husband's infidelity crept into her thoughts and dug in.

He made up excuses for nights away from home. When he returned, he went straight into the shower. On the flip side, he occasionally acted more attentive toward her. A few times, he'd actually skipped golf, his obsession, to hang around at home with her. He constantly asked her questions about her health. *How are you doing? How are you feeling?* As if she could sum up her fears and frustrations in a neat and brief response.

Catherine shook away her troubled thoughts and turned her attention back to her smoothie. She'd lost track of the ingredients. Had she added the turmeric powder yet? An extra bit wouldn't hurt. She added a pinch, pressed the blend button, and poured the antioxidant concoction into a glass. Taking a sip, she grimaced at the taste, but drank it anyway.

In the backyard, Christian finally took his eyes off Phoebe and moved on, walking behind the pool house and disappearing from Catherine's sight. Soon after, the rumble of the giant lawnmower started. Catherine wondered if the noise would mess up Phoebe's video. Apparently not, because Phoebe kept going, moving from her hands to her elbows in a plank with her back straight and those fabulous abs scooped in tight as a board.

Catherine finished the last foul sips of her smoothie as Phoebe folded up her little tripod, gathered her belongings, and headed toward the house. They waved at each other from opposite sides of the kitchen window, and Phoebe came in through the back door. Her cheeks were rosy from the early summer sun, her skin dewy with perspiration.

"Did you have to stop because of the yard noise?" Catherine asked. "I can tell them to hold off until you're finished."

"No. I'm good. I don't speak while I'm filming. I'll do a voiceover for the video later. Thank you so much for letting me record here. With the pool and the backyard as the backdrop, it's going to look super."

"It's not a problem. Anytime. How is it going with your videos? Are you hearing from advertisers or sponsors yet?"

Phoebe clutched her bag against her body. "It's going well. I'm earning a little from advertisements and I got my first two sponsors this month. I've been paying to boost my videos so more people will find them. It's just all taking a lot longer than I imagined."

"Be patient. Once people discover you, I'm sure they'll love you as much as I do. Maybe tell them how much I pay you and they'll realize what a deal it is to workout with you online for free."

Phoebe laughed. "I designed your classes especially for you and your body. You know that, right?"

"Of course," Catherine said.

"I should have been recording and posting classes for years. I didn't." Phoebe made an oh-well sort of expression, raising her brows and twisting her mouth to one side.

"Your classes are probably better now than they were a few years ago. It's never...." Catherine averted her gaze as she struggled to finish her sentence. She couldn't come up with the words—a specific inspirational phrase. One everyone knew. Something about only missing the shots you don't take? No, not that one. That wasn't it. Tomorrow, you'll wish you had started yesterday? Not that either. What was it? She'd used the sentiment in an argument with John recently, and on the phone during a conversation with Taylor, who had even less drive than John, The phrase wasn't there for her now.

After a few seconds of awkward silence—Catherine still racking her brain for the correct wording and Phoebe politely waiting—Phoebe said, "I'll see you on Wednesday."

"Yes, Wednesday," Catherine answered, relieved to move on from the forgotten phrase.

They walked from the kitchen through the butler's pantry. When they reached the entryway, John's Range Rover appeared in the driveway. Catherine wasn't expecting him home from golfing so soon.

"Goodbye, enjoy the rest of your day," Phoebe said, parting words she always used.

"You have a good day, too," Catherine answered.

Once Phoebe was outside, Catherine turned to the arched mirror by the door and admired her reflection. A few seconds provided a quick boost of confidence before she carried on.

She plucked a less than perfect flower from the arrangement in the foyer and went back to the kitchen. She put away the smoothie ingredients, rinsed the blender, and put her empty glass in the dishwasher. When she finished, John still hadn't come inside. She walked to the front windows to see what was taking him so long.

John's vehicle was still in the driveway, rather than in one of the garage bays.

Catherine spotted him with Phoebe, standing next to her Toyota. His back was to the house. Catherine had a direct line of sight to her trainer's smiling face. Phoebe tipped her head back and laughed, her body language open and welcoming. That's how Phoebe looked most of the time. That was her personality. Right then, however, something about it bothered Catherine. John and Phoebe stood only a few feet apart as if one of them had invaded the other's personal space.

Catherine was about to turn around when John reached his arm out and touched Phoebe's shoulder. His hand remained there for a few of Catherine's rapid heartbeats before moving back to his side.

Phoebe's bright smile faltered. She glanced toward the house.

Catherine had witnessed nothing scandalous or remarkable. Yet the scene had caused her pulse to quicken and her blood to pound behind her temples.

After another brief exchange Catherine couldn't make out, Phoebe got in her car and John walked into the garage through a side door.

Catherine stayed by the window, hands clasped tightly together, preparing for John's entrance and what she'd say to him.

Phoebe's car remained in the driveway.

But the door to the house never opened. Instead of coming in, John walked back out of the garage and got into his SUV.

Phoebe finally drove away. John's Range Rover followed close behind her Toyota.

Catherine watched until the vehicles disappeared from her sight. A heavy numbness spread through her body. On weak legs, she backed up against the wall.

She experienced the same sensations eighteen years ago. Catherine was younger, stronger, and more confident. Then her first husband's infidelities shattered her emotional security. The devastating experience also taught her an invaluable lesson: Trust your instincts. Don't trust anyone else.

Though she'd suspected John was cheating, never once had she imagined him with Phoebe.

This could not happen again. Not now. Especially not now. Catherine wasn't going to let it.

CHAPTER 10

Present Day - Deja

Deja entered her house, exhausted and happy to be home. The storm door snapped shut behind her.

"Deja? Is that you, honey?" her grandmother called from the kitchen.

"It's me, Gran. Missed you," Deja said, dropping her purse on the bottom step of the staircase.

"If you're hungry, I've got a plate waiting for you in the fridge. I can heat it up when you're ready."

"Thank you. I'll have it now. I'm starving," Deja said, realizing she'd eaten nothing since lunch.

Still standing in the small space between the door and the stairs, she looked around, imagining she was seeing her home the way a stranger might. The way Catherine would. The size alone might shock her. Deja's entire home could fit inside Catherine's family room and kitchen.

Everything in Deja's house was clean and functioned properly, thanks to her grandmother and father's efforts. Yet the house looked its age, especially the kitchen, the two bathrooms, and the furniture. With low ceilings, dark paneled walls, and original carpeting, it lacked a modern touch. Her father had the skills to make updates, not the time. Even if he did, he wouldn't spend it remodeling. Not when everyone living there seemed content, including Deja. Sure, a big, beautiful house might be fun, but also a lot of work, and if it came with a family like Catherine's, it was an easy pass. Deja wouldn't trade the people inside her small house for all the mansions in the world.

Four photos in store-bought frames hung on the wall at the bottom of the stairway. Deja's mother was in all of them. She was beautiful inside and out. There was nothing she wouldn't have done for her family. That's precisely what got her killed on their once-in-a-lifetime vacation.

After watching every foreign movie she could get her hands on, Deja's mother longed to visit Europe. Her wish came true thirteen years ago. But it wasn't the joyful adventure they had anticipated. The family's first trip out of the country turned into a tragedy when Deja's mother lost her life there. The devastating and haunting experience remained branded in Deja's mind, though she almost never spoke of it.

The profound tragedy shattered her world, leaving everyone affected to pick up the heavy shards and carry their weight. Deja's father recovered slowly, in a dark place for too many years, struggling with *what-ifs* and *if-onlys*, until he finally accepted his new reality and pulled himself together. Thanks mostly to Gran, they'd reached a new plateau of appreciating each day they had together, while honoring Deja's mother as best they could. They'd crawled out of the darkness, and they were doing okay now.

In contrast, Catherine's family was not in a good place. That much was obvious. Maybe they needed more time to adjust to their loss. Except...Catherine wasn't gone. She'd only changed.

Deja's father lumbered down the stairs, interrupting her thoughts. He gave her a hug and said, "Was today the trip to your patient's house?"

"Yes. My client. Not my patient," she said, though she was already thinking of Catherine as more than just a client.

"Come sit down." He gestured toward the kitchen. "Your grandmother and I want to hear about it."

Deja went into the kitchen with him. She sat where she always did—facing the window, on a chair whose finish had faded from decades of sun streaming in through the glass.

The microwave beeped. Gran removed a plate of her delicious cooking and set it on the table in front of Deja.

"You didn't have dinner?" Gran asked, settling into her own customary place at the table.

"No. But I had a glass of wine from a three-thousand-dollar bottle. So, there's that."

"Ooh," Gran said. "That is something." She clasped her hands under her chin and her eyes beamed. "What else?"

Deja wished she could describe Catherine's family as gracious and welcoming. She couldn't do that without lying. Will was friendly and seemed to care deeply for his mother. Yet there was something unnerving and strange about the Bower household.

Even if Deja hadn't signed a confidentiality agreement, she wouldn't betray Catherine by sharing negative or gossipy details. So Deja chose her words carefully, expressing admiration for Catherine's stunning home. "I feel sorry for Catherine because she can't live there anymore."

"Well, she's very fortunate to have you with her every day," Gran said.

"I looked up the cost of Atrium Gardens," her father said. "It's astronomical what they're charging. With those kinds of fees, her family could easily afford to bring people in and take care of her at home. It sounds like their house is more than big enough for live-in care."

"I'm sure it's wonderful at Atrium Gardens," Gran said. "Maybe Catherine loves it. Maybe she wanted to live there."

Deja's father grunted. "I doubt that."

Deja's father adhered to a stringent code of right and wrong, and held biases against excessive wealth. He seemed to think those with abundant resources got them by exploiting others or through inherited privilege. While his perspective was not entirely fair, it was deeply ingrained in his beliefs.

His bitterness stemmed from a failed business development following the loss of Deja's mother. A prominent local developer had hired him to help with the construction of a new shopping center. Her father hired other local workers and became a contractor. The developer's first payment covered the initial expenses, including supplies and labor costs.

However, there was a delay with the next payment. Then another hold-up. The developer promised the money would come. He insisted everyone must be patient and keep working to make the agreed-upon deadlines. He promised bonus money if they finished on time. Deja's father and his crew kept working.

The "keep working" message didn't change until the day the project officially fell apart. The developer declared the project bankrupt. No one was going to get paid for the work they'd already done. Racked with guilt about bringing the other workers in, Deja's father couldn't bear not to pay them for their hard work. He took care of reimbursing them as best he could, taking out loans and suffering a loss that sunk his own family into debt for years to come.

Now and then, Deja caught glimpses of the developer roaming the town in his imposing SUV, working on new projects under a different business name.

Deja believed it all boiled down to a fundamental truth everyone eventually came to realize; life simply wasn't fair. Catherine Bower would undoubtedly concur if she could.

Deja climbed into her bed and pulled the sheet and comforter up to her chin. She closed her eyes, still thinking about the conversation with her father and Gran.

What would happen if Gran's health deteriorated? If she got so weak, they couldn't leave her alone? They probably couldn't afford to hire someone to come in and take care of her. Deja could quit work for a few years and find some side hustle, some way to make money from home.

Not quite ready to fall asleep, Deja slid her phone off the nightstand and turned it on.

She typed *Will Bower* into social media. She couldn't find him anywhere. Strange. Then she discovered Catherine had a personal account, and one of her "friends" was Will Montgomery. It was definitely her son. His profile photo showed Will and Catherine on a boat. He just had a different last name than his mother.

Deja scrolled through Will's pictures. He'd posted a few landscapes from his travels. Thailand. Morocco. Israel. Iceland. One group photo from two years ago showcased handsome guys in tuxes and striking women in formal dresses. No other women appeared in the photos, which meant he probably didn't have a serious girlfriend. Several times during Catherine's party, he'd mentioned a grueling workload and intense classes. Yet he'd found time for plenty of trips and adventures. It looked like he lived an amazing life.

Still not sleepy, Deja scrolled through her phone. That's when she first spotted the update on the woman's remains found in Madison Creek Woods. The deceased woman was no longer a Jane Doe. She had a name now. The police had identified her as a fitness expert from Virginia, who went missing a year ago.

Deja jolted upright in her bed.

The woman's name was Phoebe Watson.

CHAPTER 11

Present Day - Victoria

After an early morning four-mile run and a shower, Victoria settled into her home office. Light streamed through the tall windows onto a portrait hanging over the fireplace—Victoria sailing over a jump on one of her childhood show horses.

Bookshelves lined one wall, holding an extensive collection of volumes on crime, law enforcement, and psychology. She'd dedicated an entire shelf to some of her favorite crime fiction and mystery novels. More often than not, the authors got things wrong, as if they'd never actually spoken to a real-life FBI agent or detective in their entire lives. Still, the stories usually entertained her.

The house was quiet. Ned, her fiancé, had left early to swim. At the moment, he was probably at his clinic, preparing for his first veterinary clients while Victoria sat behind the hand-carved desk occupying the center of her office. The presence of her seven majestic yet goofy greyhounds, sprawled on plush dog beds nearby, brought her genuine comfort within the space. Their gentle snores mingled with the clicking of her fingers on her keyboard.

The FBI had confirmed Jane Doe was Phoebe Watson, who disappeared one year ago in Virginia. Phoebe Watson's missing persons case had turned into a murder investigation.

Documents from her missing person case file were now spread across Victoria's laptop screen and monitor. She'd received the electronic files late the previous evening. Half the information was around a year old, from the start of Phoebe's disappearance. The detectives didn't have much to go on. Phoebe was gone. No signs of a break-in. Her purse and phone were presumed to be with her when she disappeared. No witnesses. Nothing caught on video.

The rest of the information came six months later. A show called *What Happened to Them?* featured Phoebe in an episode. The popular program generated thousands of tips, all of which led nowhere.

When Phoebe disappeared, Dan Sullivan was a free man living in the D.C. area. Victoria studied the case files, specifically looking for Sullivan's name or description. She found neither.

An internet search revealed Phoebe had posted over fifty exercise videos on YouTube. Dozens of short videos with tips about fitness and healthy eating existed on other platforms. Phoebe's magnetic personality shone through in every image. It was almost impossible to reconcile the vivacious woman with the sad pile of bones on the medical examiner's table.

Someone might have discovered Phoebe online, watched her videos, and become obsessed. Someone like Dan Sullivan, who might have a penchant for murdering attractive young women in their twenties. Victoria needed to find some proof.

After saying goodbye to each of her dogs, she set out to meet with Sharon Watson, Phoebe's mother.

Just a few miles away from her daughter's former apartment, Sharon Watson lived in a modern condo. Victoria took a seat at the dining room table. Sharon sat across from her, dressed in jeans and a white T-shirt. With her fiery red hair, Sharon bore a striking resemblance to Phoebe.

"I'm so sorry about your daughter," Victoria said.

Sharon crossed her arms and sighed. Despite her puffy and red-rimmed eyes, she was steady and composed. A year of coping with her daughter's unexplained absence had probably prepared her for Phoebe's death.

"We have new evidence, and we're analyzing everything from her case again," Victoria said. "So please bear with me."

"Why? Isn't the man who killed her in prison already? Sullivan." Sharon spit out his name through her teeth. "He already confessed. Why would he say he killed her if he didn't?"

Victoria understood Sharon's disgust. "He wants to make a deal with us because he's facing life in prison."

"And he deserves it. No one should take it away. He murdered my daughter and buried her in the woods," Sharon said. "He might have buried Diane Johnson there, too, if the police hadn't found him first. Who knows how many more women he's killed?"

Victoria removed a photograph of Sullivan from her purse. She set it on the table facing Sharon and waited for her reaction. "Does he look familiar? Have you seen him before?"

Sharon glared at Sullivan's image. "He looks like a monster."

Maybe. Yet Victoria knew from experience that monsters came in all shapes and sizes.

Without taking her eyes off the photo, Sharon shook her head. "I don't recall ever seeing him before. Though that means nothing. Phoebe was an adult with her own life. She might have recognized him. Her friends might."

"I plan to show this picture to her friends and colleagues," Victoria said. "While I'm here, please tell me about Phoebe's disappearance. I'd like to hear it from you."

Sharon leaned back in her chair and twisted a lock of hair around her finger. "This nightmare started when Phoebe didn't show up to teach her athletic conditioning class at Fitness World. A friend and coworker got my number from Phoebe's emergency contact list and called me to find out if I knew where she was. Phoebe was one hundred percent reliable. At the time, we were thinking she'd had a car accident. I was sick with worry. Thought she might be hospitalized somewhere. When she didn't answer my calls, I drove to her apartment. She'd left her car parked outside. She wasn't home, and she hadn't fed Simon."

"Who is Simon?"

"Her cat. He was her baby. The moment I saw him crying and circling his empty food and water bowls, I knew something was very wrong. I called Phoebe's two best friends. They helped check with everyone who knew her. By then, we'd discovered she'd also missed all her private training appointments for the day. The last time anyone saw her was the previous evening. She left Fitness World after teaching a group class. She must have driven back to her apartment. Where she went from there, we still don't know. Her phone and purse were also missing. I called the police."

"Good," Victoria said, thinking Phoebe was lucky to have people who cared about her and noticed she was missing right away.

"From the time she disappeared, there was never another purchase on her credit cards. No withdrawals from her bank accounts. She didn't post anything online related to her business or her life, and she was diligent about posting every day, usually around the same time. Said she needed to train the algorithms and couldn't mess up the scheduling. She worked so hard to build her business and her online platform. I knew she would never walk away from any of it."

A smoky gray cat sauntered into the room with its tail in the air.

"That's Simon," Sharon said, her voice noticeably softer. "He lives with me now."

"I'm sure your daughter would be very grateful you have him," Victoria said.

Sharon nodded and turned toward the long-haired cat, who pressed his body against a chair's fabric. His presence seemed to have a soothing effect on Sharon.

"Before Phoebe disappeared, was she having trouble with anyone? Relationship? Clients? Roommates? Neighbors?" Victoria asked.

"She'd recently broken up with a boyfriend, David. They weren't together long. She hadn't wanted to see him anymore. He wasn't happy about her decision. David was the primary suspect, so the police grilled him. The poor guy. Even held him in custody. He was with his roommates when she went missing. He had several alibis. I don't think he ever hurt her."

"Was she seeing anyone new?"

"Not that any of us were aware of."

"Had anyone threatened her?" Victoria asked.

Sharon shook her head.

Victoria let out a quick gasp, startled by Simon rubbing against her ankle under the table. She leaned down to pet the cat before asking, "Phoebe never mentioned anyone stalking or following her?"

"She had a lot of fans, located all around the world. She never complained or mentioned anyone causing her trouble. The news of her murder rocketed the views on her videos into the mega millions, you know."

"I know," Victoria answered.

"I really wish she could see that. She'd be thrilled. It's what she'd been working toward all along. Why did it take her death to make it happen?" Sharon swiped a finger under her eyes, pulled a tissue from the pocket of her jeans, and stood from the table. She scooped the cat up and hugged him against her chest. "Excuse me, please. I need a few minutes."

"That's okay. I'm going to let myself out," Victoria said. "Thank you for your time. I promise I'll be in touch."

Victoria left Sharon's house and headed straight to Fitness World, the gym where Phoebe had once worked.

When Victoria got home that evening, her fiancé had already fed the dogs, so she didn't have to worry about them. She kicked off her shoes, lined them up in the shoe closet, and sank down into the couch. The day's interviews had drained her, and she was grateful to be home with Ned.

"Did you eat yet?" she asked him.

"I was waiting for you. We got a meal delivery we can pop into the microwave and reheat. There are leftovers, too."

"Sounds good," Victoria replied. "Anything exciting happen at your clinic today?"

Ned grinned. "I had a surprise. You won't believe it. A new client made an appointment for a dog named Lancelot. Guess what showed up instead? A baby goat!"

Victoria's face lit up. "You're kidding? No pun intended," she said, laughing. "Goats are adorable! I can imagine the look on everyone's face when he came in. Or she? Did you take a picture?"

Ned chuckled, reaching for his phone. "Of course. I thought about sending it to you during the day, just in case you needed a little cheering up."

"You should have. Let me see it," she said, extending her hand. "I can always count on a goat video to brighten my day."

Ned unlocked his phone and presented the photo. The goat's mischievous expression resonated from the image as he perched with his front legs on the vet tech's knee.

Victoria laughed. "Looks like you had a lot of fun with your unexpected visitor."

Ned nodded. "We all did. Now, tell me about your day."

There was a distinct, somber shift in their tones as the conversation changed from his work to hers. Everyone had heard about Phoebe Watson from the news, and Ned knew Victoria was working part of the investigation.

"Rivera and I spent the day doing interviews, showing Sullivan's picture around, trying to find a connection."

"Any progress?"

"Not really," Victoria admitted. "I hope the evidence team has better luck. We're still early in the investigation, but we haven't found any direct links between Phoebe and Sullivan. They lived on opposite sides of the city, and there's no record of them crossing paths."

Ned leaned forward, his blue eyes bright with interest. "Couldn't it have been a random crime of opportunity?"

"It's a plausible theory. Here's the catch—Sullivan's past behavior, as documented in his arrest files, doesn't align with impulsive acts. Yet we can't find any evidence he was stalking Phoebe. No one who knew her recognized him. That's why I can't shake the feeling there's more to this."

"Maybe he did all his stalking online?" Ned suggested. "She has a lot of material on the internet."

"I thought that, too. Oddly enough, he never mentioned it, though. Almost as if he doesn't know she has such a big online presence."

"Does it really matter how he found her, Victoria? Ultimately, if the evidence team uncovers something to pin him to the crime, that should be enough, right?"

"You're right. In my mind, the end goal is justice for Phoebe. We just need to find something to get us to that point."

"I don't doubt you will," Ned said.

CHAPTER 12
One Year Ago - Catherine

Catherine crossed the living room, walking past the most recent family portrait hanging over the fireplace. She glared up at John.

It was only last summer when they had the portrait made, though it seemed ages ago now. They had rented a beautiful three-story home on the beach. The weather was perfect. Will was a delight, as always, and even Taylor had suppressed her animosity toward John long enough for the photographer to capture some wonderful shots. Catherine looked gorgeous, which was no accident. From the dozens of images the photographer provided, she chose the one where she looked her best. Last summer…if only she could transport herself back in time and remain there, in control of every facet of her life. Catherine from a year ago would not have tolerated a cheating spouse. Though little did she know what lurked around the corner, just waiting to completely disrupt her life.

Now, before making any decisions about her marriage, Catherine needed to put her emotions aside and think through the entire situation. She needed to consider what would happen to her if she divorced John or taught him a lesson he wouldn't soon forget.

She retrieved her journal from the bedside table and took it outside, where she sat on a chaise lounge in the shade.

Despite her disease, her memory seemed solid, as far as she could tell, aside from the minor glitches with language and names. She'd done a lot of research on Alzheimer's. She also remembered what her own mother went through, suffering from the same condition. As the disease progressed, gaps would appear in her memory from day to day. Chunks of those memories would disappear forever, while some would waver in and out of her brain. Hence the importance of journaling significant events. What she'd seen between John and Phoebe seemed significant.

As if she were writing a novel, Catherine described the intimate interaction she'd witnessed between John and Phoebe. Catherine did not include her suspicions. No need to confuse those with the facts, which would speak for themselves.

As Catherine slid the white-bean cassoulet from the oven, the soft whirring of a garage door signaled someone's arrival. Soon after, John's footsteps traveled through the living room and down the hall leading to their bedroom. He didn't call out a hello. Neither did Catherine. He'd come into the kitchen, eventually. She'd speak to him then.

She set her oven mitts down, picked up her wineglass, and took a generous gulp of merlot. Wine was one of the few things she wasn't going to give up. Not when red wine had antioxidant and anti-inflammatory benefits.

When John emerged from their bedroom, Catherine was chopping carrots with the sharpest knife they owned. With each rhythmic slice, the steel blade knocked against the marble counter. Now that he was home, and she was about to face him, a cloud of anger surged inside her.

"Hey. Making dinner?" John asked. Touching her shoulder, he leaned in from behind and kissed her cheek. He had showered and changed from golf clothes into athletic shorts and a T-shirt. He smelled like fresh soap.

"It's almost ready. Wasn't sure if I would have to eat alone," she said, still chopping, though there were three times as many carrot coins on the cutting board as she needed.

"Count me in. Smells delicious." John's smile was relaxed as he opened the cabinets and grabbed a wineglass. "How are you feeling?"

"Fine," she said.

"No new developments today?"

"No. Health wise, I'm fine." Using the knife's blade, she pushed the vegetables to the side of the chopping board and turned to face John. "I saw you come back to the house earlier. Did you forget something?"

"When was this?" John asked as he poured the rest of the bottle for himself, resulting in less than half a glass.

"Before noon. You talked to Phoebe for a while, and then you left again."

"Oh, that. Yeah, I came back to grab my new driver."

"I saw you touch her," Catherine said in a flat tone. She'd intended to broach the subject with more skill and feel out the situation, but her emotions took over, rocketing her straight to the point.

John stopped moving and stared back at Catherine. He tilted his head to the side and pursed his lips. "I don't remember that. If I did, it must have been…I don't know… automatic? Subconscious?" He narrowed his eyes. "You were spying on me?"

Catherine scoffed. "I wasn't spying on you. I happened to look out the window, and I saw you. She's my trainer. You can't just touch her." Still holding the knife, Catherine raised her hands, emphasizing the stupidity of his earlier gesture.

John backed away, keeping his gaze on the knife. "Okay, Catherine. I shouldn't have touched her." His words dripped with condescension. "However, it wasn't a big deal."

"Maybe not to you. But she might have perceived it as unwelcome contact from the husband of her employer."

John set his drink down and frowned. "Is this about Phoebe's feelings? Or your own?"

"It's about how I expect my husband to act so people don't misinterpret things."

"People who? You know of other people who are spying on me?"

"Phoebe, for one, knows what happened, and George and Christian were around." Catherine squeezed the knife's handle so tightly her knuckles turned a bloodless white. It wasn't like her to lash out like this. For most of her life, she'd kept her feelings inside and hid them well. She was decisive. Not argumentative.

"I'm bringing this up because you should think first before you act so familiar with a girl half your age," she said.

"She might be half *your* age. I'm not that old," John shot back. "Your eyes are glassy. How much have you had to drink?"

For the last few months of their marriage, this behavior had become their norm. Not every night or every week, though often enough. She'd start something—usually related to his frequent golf trips. Later, she'd blame the outbursts on her disease. But what was his excuse when he stabbed back that she was a control freak who wanted to micromanage everyone's lives? Each of them acted eager to win the game of who could insult each other more.

This time, Catherine had nothing. No mean but clever quip. No spiteful yet well-timed response. She only had red-hot anger and surging frustration. She was just as shocked as John when she hurled her wineglass against the wall. The delicate goblet smashed on impact. The remaining droplets of dark red liquid dotted the white paint. Broken pieces of glass littered the floor.

"Really, Catherine?" John said, as if he was speaking to a toddler. "What is going on with you? You're out of your mind."

As soon as the words left his mouth, there was silence. The softening of his face told her he hadn't intended to use that expression. He'd crossed a line, an unwritten rule, by hitting on something she couldn't change. Something beyond her control.

"I apologize," he said, coming toward her. "I know those are early symptoms. Paranoia. Emotional outbursts. I shouldn't have...I'm sorry."

Catherine wasn't finished and intended to have the last word. "I am not paranoid. I am fine. This is your doing. Not mine. Let me remind you that you signed a pre-nup. If we divorce, you get nothing. That's the end of hanging out with your golfing buddies all day. If that's even what you're really doing."

Footsteps pounded down the stairs and toward the kitchen.

Catherine spun around as her son came toward the kitchen. She'd forgotten Will was home for a few days and that she and John weren't alone as usual. She should have kept her voice down.

"Hey!" Will said. "What's going on?" He stood on the opposite side of the kitchen, barefoot and shirtless, running one hand through his tousled hair. He looked at his mother first. "You okay?"

"Yes, I'm fine," Catherine said, trying to sound convincing.

Will settled a steely glare on his stepfather.

"Your mother is having trust issues," John said, stomping out of the kitchen.

"Then you need to watch yourself," Will said, scowling at John's retreating figure.

Will wrapped his arms around his mother. Though he would always be Catherine's baby, he stood six inches taller than her.

"I'm sorry you heard that," she told him. "I don't know what that was."

"It's going to be all right, Mom. You're going to have bad days, but you'll get through them. I know you will. I'll always be here for you. Whatever you need. I promise. I can move back home if you want me to. Law school can wait."

Will had always acted wise beyond his years, and his kindness broke through the internal barrier wall she'd erected. More than anyone in her family, he understood what she was going through. He understood deep-seated worries about her uncertain future were taking their toll on everything she said and did these days. The disease was changing her.

He was so kind to consider her needs above his own. Offering to put off law school! More than ever, she needed someone like her son. Someone dependable to lean on for emotional support. Yet burdening Will wasn't fair. He'd worked so hard at Duke. He'd impressed his professors the same way he did everyone he met. He was currently waiting to hear back from some of the best law schools in the country. In three more years, with his law degree in hand, he'd start an incredible career and perhaps a family of his own. That couldn't happen if he was stuck taking care of an invalid mother. She wouldn't dream of allowing him to give up his life for hers.

Catherine pulled back from Will to take a good look at him. With his dark hair and heavy lashes, he resembled her much more than his father. Thank goodness. She didn't want any memories of her first husband lingering around their lives.

"You're right. I'm just having a bad day," she told Will. "I'm going to be okay, and I'm going to fight this. Because do you know what I look forward to most? Seeing all the wonderful things you do with your life. The places you go. The lives you change. But thank you for even considering putting some of those amazing things aside for me. It's not going to happen, although I can't thank you enough for offering. I love you, honey."

"I love you, too," he said, squeezing her shoulders before turning toward the mess she'd made. "Let me help you clean this up."

"Thank you, but I don't want you to have to do that. I'll deal with it."

"All right. If you're okay, I'm going to head back to my room. I'm going to meet up with Connor and Scott later tonight. Maybe a few other guys who came home for Connor's party."

"Have fun," she told him. "I think it's wonderful you're staying in touch with your high school friends."

As Will's soft footsteps headed up the stairs, Catherine stood alone in the kitchen, staring at the array of red, orange, and green vegetables on the cutting board. She couldn't remember her plan for using them. That's what the argument with John had done to her. That wasn't good. She had to control her emotions, get her life in order, and focus on her health battle. She couldn't waste precious energy on anything else.

A few moments with Will had reminded her of what was important and what she needed.

No matter what John did, no matter how he made her feel, she couldn't push him away. Ridding her life of him as she did with her first husband was not an option. Catherine planned to put her all into fighting Alzheimer's disease. But the odds weren't in her favor. She probably wouldn't win. When the tide turned for the worse, she couldn't face her condition alone.

She looked up as John strode from the bedroom through the center of the house without glancing toward the kitchen. She heard the garage door open and then close.

He needed time to cool off. When he got back, she would apologize. Her attitude change wouldn't stop there. From now on, she would overlook his indiscretions. They were temporary. They had to be. John would never leave her. Of that she was certain. More than anything, he enjoyed the comforts of the life she provided him. Without her, as she had reminded him, his life of luxury would go away.

She would forgive John's mistakes. She had to. Any alternative meant dealing with her greatest challenges all alone. Knowing what lay ahead, that was not the future she wanted for herself.

Her future would be difficult. Her past, specifically her mother's sickness, had shown her what she needed to get through it. Unfortunately, it was her husband.

Catherine's tears had dried when she put the uneaten cassoulet and the chopped vegetables into the fridge and got her journal. Seated in her office, she filled an entire page describing the incident with John, including shattering her wineglass. She finished the journal entry by documenting her decision, lest she forget it.

You will overlook the indiscretions and wait for them to pass. It is in your best interest.

Then she attempted to scrub the ruby wine stains off the white walls.

CHAPTER 13

Present Day - Deja

After learning the murder victim's name, Deja spent hours on social media poring over Phoebe Watson's posts and videos. Deja was approaching obsessive territory in her quest to learn everything about the former fitness trainer. She hadn't known Phoebe, though by morning, it felt like she had. Phoebe was so energetic and full of life. Deja could hardly believe Phoebe was gone because someone had killed her.

Did Catherine know something about Phoebe's death?

On the way to Atrium Gardens, Deja drove past Fitness World, the gym where Phoebe had taught classes. At work, Deja walked slowly down the hallway, eyes glued to her phone. Articles about Phoebe's disappearance kept popping up. They contained the same old information repackaged with a new sentence or two. The police had yet to arrest anyone for the murder. If there were suspects, the articles didn't mention them.

Deja wasn't sure what to say to Catherine, but she had to tell her.

"I'm sorry to say I have some upsetting news," Deja began, as she got Catherine out of bed. "Your fitness trainer, Phoebe, she was the person the police found in the woods a few weeks ago. So, when you said her name, you were right. It's just...how did you know that was Phoebe in the news program?"

Deja didn't expect an answer, yet in response to the question, Catherine's body grew rigid.

"Do you have information that could lead to Phoebe's killer? Is that why you got so upset when you saw the news program?" Deja asked.

Catherine remained silent.

Deja wanted to call the police, but when they couldn't get answers from Catherine, would they question her family next? Deja looked up at the portrait above the bed and shuddered. Catherine's family would not appreciate getting involved in a homicide investigation. Taylor especially. Despite being a grown woman, she gave off the strongest mean-rich-girl vibes Deja had ever experienced. Not to mention that none of Catherine's family members seemed particularly concerned about Phoebe when her name came up at Catherine's birthday party.

Deja imagined the police showing up at Catherine's mansion and knocking on those giant glass doors. They'd say, "Deja Torres thinks Catherine knows something about Phoebe Watson's murder. We're here to interview you." That could be an issue because of the nondisclosure agreement Deja signed. What transpired between client and caregiver was confidential. If Deja called the police, it might constitute a major breach of her agreement. Or would it? A situation such as murder might override the contract she'd signed. Though probably not. More likely, it was exactly the type of reason the agency required her to sign one.

She'd have to dig up the paperwork and read each sentence of the contract carefully, unlike when she signed the documents. There were pages and pages of legal jargon, reminding her of the lengthy terms of agreements for her iPhone. Did anyone actually read stuff like that? She'd barely skimmed over most of it.

Deja didn't want to lose her job. She enjoyed taking care of Catherine. In a short time, she'd grown attached to her client. Catherine was so helpless, and despite having family, she seemed alone in the world.

The longer Deja debated the situation—should she say something or keep quiet—the more confused she became. She couldn't shake the feeling Catherine wanted to help. That's why she'd managed to speak at just the right moment. Yet Catherine couldn't help without Deja's assistance.

After getting Catherine dressed, Deja reached a decision. If the police didn't find the killer by the end of the day, she would contact them. It was her civic duty. Until then, she would keep quiet, try to put it out of her mind.

Catherine ate nothing of her egg salad sandwich at lunch. Deja asked Milton, one of the kitchen workers, for something else. He brought minestrone soup. Catherine wouldn't eat the soup either.

Back in Catherine's room, Deja said, "I don't know about you, but I don't like eggs. Never have. Never will. Something about the smell and the texture. Do you feel the same?"

Catherine didn't answer.

"I wish I knew your favorite foods, so I could request them for you."

The Atrium Gardens kitchen staff whipped up a variety of meals. Most consisted of meat with a green, yellow, or orange vegetable, and mashed potatoes or rice. Intentionally bland and mushy. Everyone had likes and dislikes. Some were pickier eaters than others. Wouldn't it be terrible if, day after day, someone kept offering foods you didn't like?

"I prefer to eat cold foods, myself," Deja told Catherine. "Mixtures with couscous and veggies, and flavorful spices. My grandmother has some amazing recipes. She makes this excellent mixture of grains and carrots and raisins. I'm not sure what spices are in it. There's actually something similar at Trader Joes. I love the texture."

Deja might have imagined it, but Catherine moved her head in such a way and at just the right time that it sure seemed like a nod.

"I'll ask if the chef can make something similar for you, and I'll make sure you don't get egg salad anymore," Deja said.

She wrapped a cardigan around Catherine's shoulders and said, "Do you feel like taking a nap? Or we could—"

A man's voice interrupted her. "Good morning."

Caught by surprise, Deja gasped and jerked her head up.

Will stood in the doorway, a big smile on his face. "Hi. Guess it's not morning anymore, is it? Sorry about startling you. I told you I was coming, didn't I?"

He had. Yesterday, just before Deja and Catherine left the party. With Phoebe Watson consuming Deja's thoughts, she'd forgotten Will was coming.

Will entered Catherine's room carrying an armful of items—a flower bouquet and the iPad he'd given as a birthday gift. He smiled at his mother and said, "I stopped in to say goodbye on my way back to school." His smile didn't change when he turned to face Deja.

She subconsciously tucked her long hair behind her ear and stepped away from Catherine to allow Will more room. "Would you like me to give you some privacy?" she asked him.

"No. You can stay. But thank you for the offer." Will set the bouquet on a table and looked around the room. "Actually, can you get a vase for these flowers?"

"Sure," she said.

"Then come back. I want to show you some things with the iPad. I'm going to call her on it when I'm abroad."

That's right. He was going to Europe as soon as he finished his exams.

Just the mention of going abroad clouded Deja's mood. She'd lost her mother forever because of their trip to London. It was hard for Deja to think about Europe without feeling bitter.

Deja tracked down a vase and returned to room 104. As she filled the vase with water, she listened to Will speaking softly to his mother. Deja couldn't decipher his words, only his gentle tone. Not wanting to interrupt them, she stayed out of the way, taking her time to arrange the flowers.

"Ready for a quick tutorial?" Will asked.

Deja nodded.

"The new audiobooks are on here. Let me show you where to find them," Will said. "She used to enjoy falling asleep while reading."

Deja glanced down at the audiobook he'd chosen. Legal thrillers. Two had the word killing in the title. Though Deja would have picked something more uplifting for Catherine, Will must know his mother's taste in books.

He gave Deja a quick overview of the iPad functions, then focused on his mother. "I've got two more days of exams and then I'm leaving for the Netherlands. I'll call every day, if possible, and share the sights. I hope that gives you something to look forward to." He looked up at Deja. "I'll try to call at the same time every day. I'll aim for three p.m. your time. Can you try to have my mother available then, and put the iPad in her lap so she can see it?"

"Yes. No problem. She'll love that," Deja said.

"Okay. Sorry I have to run, Mom. Gotta get back to Durham." He kissed her on the cheek, straightened, then seemed to change his mind. He bent over again to hug her and whisper something into her ear.

Deja turned away. She didn't want to intrude on their sweet, private moment.

"Gotta go," Will told Deja. "I taped my phone number to the back of the iPad. I'll be in touch soon." He held her gaze, but he was already moving backward toward the door. "Call me if you have trouble figuring out the audiobooks or for anything else."

Deja already had something else. She wanted to ask Will about Phoebe Watson. The questions were right there on her tongue. Should she call the police? Did Will think his mother might know something?

Will was in a big rush.

"Safe travels," Deja said instead.

He tossed his hand in a half wave, and then he was out the door and gone.

At home, Deja checked again for updates on the murder investigation. The police still hadn't named a suspect. As her family gathered in the kitchen to share a meal, Deja imagined what Phoebe's family was going through at that moment. The heartbreak and horror. Someone had taken Phoebe's life way before her time. Her death was incredibly unfair, just like what happened to Deja's mother. Maybe in this case, thanks to Catherine, the perpetrator wouldn't get away with it. But only if Deja did something to help make that happen.

Still confused about the situation, Deja couldn't hold back any longer. "Do you know about Phoebe Watson?" she finally asked once she'd helped her father get the food on the table and they'd all sat down.

"Is she the young woman they found in the woods?" Gran asked, lifting the cover off the casserole dish.

"Yes," Deja said. She took several swallows of water, then told her family everything.

They were all silent for a bit, thinking. Then Gran said, "Sounds like Catherine had a moment of lucidity and was trying to communicate with you. You have to call the police, honey. The sooner the better."

"Should I talk to her family first? Or the agency? Because of the confidentiality agreement."

"No," her father said. "You let the police handle that. You just tell them what you told us. That's all you have to do. They'll take care of the rest. Confidentiality agreements don't exist to protect murderers."

Gran tilted her head and frowned at her son.

"Catherine didn't kill anyone, Dad," Deja told him.

Her father's brows knitted together. "Then maybe she knows who did."

Deja took a moment to gather her thoughts, her fingers tapping lightly on the edge of the table. "I thought maybe Phoebe told her something. Maybe Phoebe confided that she was afraid of someone or she thought she might be in danger. Except, Catherine can't answer questions, so even if she knows something, reporting this might just waste everyone's time."

"She might find a way to communicate again," Gran said. "Don't let her down. You need to call the police on her behalf."

"Okay," Deja agreed. "Who do I call?"

"Nine-one-one," her father answered. He dropped his gaze to her phone resting beside her plate. He meant now.

Deja picked up her phone and dialed the number.

The call connected, and a dispatcher answered, "You've reached nine-one-one. What is your emergency?"

"Hi. Um." Deja stumbled over her words. She looked up and locked eyes with her father. He nodded in encouragement, prompting Deja to follow through.

"Can I speak to someone involved in the Phoebe Watson murder investigation? I have some information. It might be important."

CHAPTER 14
One Year Ago - Catherine

Emotionally drained, Catherine set a fresh wineglass on her bedside table and went into her bathroom. She wanted to wash her face, slather it with each layer of her night-time serums, creams, and lotions, get under the covers, and fall asleep. Yet she knew she shouldn't go to bed before making up with John.

Instead, Catherine brushed her teeth, freshened her makeup, and slipped into a silky, black nightgown, a Christmas gift from John. It looked great though it didn't feel that way. The material wedged up under her body when she slept.

After moving each decorative pillow off her bed and onto the love seat, she sat down on top of the duvet and reclined against the king-sized pillows. Two bestselling legal thriller novels sat on her bedside table beneath her journal and datebook. Lately, she'd tried to read as often as she could, and not just the latest Alzheimer's research. If her treatments failed, the act of reading might soon become a futile task, unless she could finish an entire book in one sitting.

She slid the top novel from the stack. With her long, bare legs stretched out on the bed, she read, sipped her wine, and waited. She completed five chapters before John came home.

He gave her a curt *hello* before entering their bathroom and closing the door behind him. The toilet flushed. Water ran in the sink. Then the shower, which seemed unnecessary because he'd showered a few hours ago when he came home from playing golf. He was drawing out his time in the bathroom to avoid dealing with her.

Catherine read another ten pages before John emerged wearing boxers and a T-shirt. With the overhead lights still on, he pulled back the covers on his side of the bed and slid under the sheets, his back to her.

She set her book aside and turned off the lights. She scooted close to her husband and put her hand on his shoulder, just listening to the sound of his breathing. When he didn't respond, she caressed his body with a slow and gentle touch. Finally, he flipped over to face her.

With her hip touching his, she looked deep into his eyes and said, "I'm sorry about earlier."

John sighed. "You don't have to apologize. I should have been more sensitive. The thing with Phoebe didn't seem like a big deal, and I resented the implied accusation. But you were right. I shouldn't have done it. I don't want Phoebe to think I'm a creepy old man."

At forty-five years old, John was handsome and fit. Nothing about him said creepy old man. Phoebe once mentioned that both Catherine and John were in great shape, though Catherine wasn't about to share that information with him.

"And most important, you don't have anything to worry about," he said, his fingers stroking the dip between her ribs and hip.

She knew John was referring to his loyalty. As much as she wanted to believe him, his words were just that. Words. He wouldn't be the first husband of hers to profess his innocence with lies.

"I was thinking of switching trainers," Catherine said.

His hand had moved to her thigh, and she willingly softened under his touch.

"You've been exercising with Phoebe for over a year, haven't you? I thought you really liked her."

"I do. However, it's important to switch things up. We can't keep doing the same things and expect different results." And while that made sense, it didn't apply to Catherine. Her results were excellent. Her reasons for switching had nothing to do with fitness gains. She no longer wanted to tempt misfortune by bringing a beautiful young woman into her house several times a week. For her next trainer, she would choose a man.

"What you're doing works so well," John whispered. He stroked her skin in small circles, pausing for a second only to slap her butt. He sounded so sincere, reminding her why she fell hard for him. John could be so charming. He could make her feel like she was the most beautiful and intelligent woman in the world. He was also right. Every bit of her was toned and firm.

Unlike my mind, which is decaying long before it's time.

That negative thought almost pulled her right out of the moment, and she couldn't let that happen. She needed to lose herself with John, to block out all else except reconnecting with him. Concentrating on the feel of him against her, she let herself succumb to his hands touching her in all the right places. Soon, she could think of nothing except their bodies moving in sync and causing a growing warmth inside her.

After they made love, John held her in his arms and kissed her gently. She nuzzled his neck and snuggled against him. By the time he rolled over on his side, she felt more relaxed than she'd expected to feel considering their interactions earlier that evening.

Smiling, she got out of bed, grabbed a soft sleep shirt from her dresser, and went into the bathroom. She cleaned herself up and opened the hamper. Before she dropped her nightgown on top of John's dirty clothes, she lifted his shirt out, brought it to her nose, and inhaled John's scent. That wasn't all she smelled. Another odor had mixed with the cologne he always wore. A light floral fragrance. Perfume.

And Catherine didn't wear perfume.

A wave of nausea came over her. Every languid muscle tensed. But instead of wallowing in pain or letting her anger take over, she took deep breaths. She reminded herself that John couldn't afford to leave her. The affair would pass. Catherine needed to forgive him now. No more arguments.

She'd maintain her dignity while looking away. Women had done it since the beginning of time. Jackie Onassis Kennedy, for example, on the world's stage. It wasn't Catherine's style, yet it was in her best interest, though doing so would pose a challenge. She couldn't stop herself from thinking about another woman's scent on her husband's clothes. She couldn't help wondering who the other woman was.

One small detail provided some reassurance. Phoebe didn't wear perfume. At least not during their training sessions.

Catherine returned to the bedroom where John snored with rhythmic snuffling sounds. She grabbed her journal, took it into her office, and wrote what she'd discovered.

CHAPTER 15

Present Day - Victoria

In the parking lot of the Atrium Gardens Assisted Living Facility, Victoria sat in her customized Suburban and finished the last few sips of her latte. With her window down, she enjoyed the fresh air, knowing the cool temperatures would soon turn warm and muggy and stay that way for most of the day.

A tip from Deja Torres had traveled from the police to the FBI and made its way to Victoria. She cross-referenced Catherine Bower's name with Dan Sullivan's, checking for connections between them. She'd found none. No family or friends. No hobbies or geographical proximities. Catherine Bower and Dan Sullivan had existed in completely different social circles. That's why this tip, like so many of the others that came after Phoebe's missing persons show, would most likely lead nowhere. Yet, perhaps because it was so unusual, and nothing in the investigation had proven significant so far, Victoria had pursued the lead herself.

Last year, a detective named Brady had interviewed Phoebe's private training clients, including Catherine. Brady hadn't uncovered any relevant insight. Perhaps circumstances had changed since then.

Victoria had gathered her own information on Catherine Bower. At fifty years old, she was the sole heir of the Smartbox fortune. Catherine's father had founded the company. He'd served as its CEO and Chair of the Board for over thirty years. He sold it in a large eight-figure deal shortly before his death. Catherine had remained a board member until recently. She'd attended Vanderbilt University, where she studied performing arts, specifically concert piano. She'd also received an MBA from Northwestern. Everything in her background pointed to an accomplished, extremely privileged woman. Though not without some hardships.

Catherine's first husband, Charles Montgomery, had died in a boating accident. He'd taken his boat out and never returned. And fifty-year-old women did not live in assisted living facilities by choice, so something unusual must have happened to her. Perhaps a stroke.

Victoria got out of the car, tossed her empty cardboard cup in a nearby recycling bin, and entered the facility. It wasn't her first visit to Atrium Gardens. Some of her grandparents' friends had lived there. A few of them probably still did. She signed in at the front desk. The receptionist provided directions to room 104. When Victoria got there, the door was partway closed. She knocked.

"Hello?" a muffled voice answered.

"Hi. I'm Victoria Heslin, with the FBI," she said from the hallway. "I'm looking for Deja Torres."

"FBI? Oh. Sorry," the distant voice answered. "Can you hold on a minute? Be right there. I'm Deja. I just need a few minutes."

Victoria peered through the door's opening. She didn't see anyone inside the room.

"You can come in," Deja answered. "We'll be right out."

As Victoria entered, an interior door to her left shut with a sharp click.

Alone, she surveyed the open space. A sitting room with modern furnishings on one side, and a hospital bed on the other. A family portrait above the bed immediately grabbed her attention. The central figure, a woman, looked satisfied and in control, like a regal queen. The photograph perfectly captured the beautiful family and the moment. Yet the frame surrounding the portrait didn't seem like the best choice.

A toilet flushed from behind the other door.

Victoria moved toward the portrait. She tilted forward to get a closer view and studied the frame. The sun streaming through the window glinted off a tiny speck of the frame's surface. She ran her finger over the top wood panel.

When the bathroom door opened with a click, Victoria moved away from the frame.

A lovely Hispanic female came out, pushing a middle-aged woman in a wheelchair.

"I'm Deja," the younger woman said, her voice low, her expression serious. "You're from the FBI? Is this about..."

"You called a tip line. Your call found its way to me," Victoria said.

"Oh. Okay. Thank you for coming. This is Catherine." Deja placed her hand protectively on the woman's shoulder. "I'm sorry to keep you waiting. It's just bad timing. Catherine isn't feeling well. She's been sick all day. Maybe something she ate. The nurse thinks it's food poisoning, but no one else here seems to have it. We might have to hurry back into the bathroom."

Deja had done all the talking so far. Catherine had yet to say a word and seemed to look straight through Victoria. The smooth skin on her face was void of any expression, as if every muscle had its share of Botox. She was obviously the woman in the center of the portrait above the bed. Except her face was no longer tan and glowing. Her skin was now an ashen shade that almost matched her soft gray cardigan. A blanket covered her body, draping from her waist to her ankles.

Victoria faced Catherine and said, "I read over the information Deja gave the police. It was you who identified Phoebe?"

"She did," Deja answered. "The thing is, Catherine almost drowned and now she can't really speak because her brain got injured. But I know she was trying to when she said Phoebe's name. I'm sure of it. Look, I found the exact news program she was watching. I recorded it on my phone.

Here. You can see it." Deja scrolled through her phone, found the clip, and handed her device to Victoria.

The video clip showed glimpses of the woods from different angles, the crime scene cordoned off with yellow tape and news vans outside it. There wasn't much in the footage to differentiate the wooded area from any other, until the reporter announced the location as Madison Creek Woods.

"Catherine saw that clip and said *Phoebe Watson*. I even wrote the name down in the notes I keep for each day. Catherine was one of Phoebe's exercise clients." Deja motioned with her hands as she explained. "I think she wanted the right people to know so she could help you somehow."

Catherine still hadn't spoken or given any sign she was following the conversation.

"How did you know the body discovered in those woods was Phoebe Watson?" Victoria asked her.

Catherine closed her eyes. A loud gurgling sound came from her stomach or bowels. Her jaw moved slightly, teeth grinding. The corner of her eye twitched. In an otherwise healthy person, those tiny tells were significant signs of stress. With Catherine's health conditions and possible food poisoning, Victoria couldn't be sure what they meant.

"How long have you cared for her?" Victoria asked Deja.

"It's only my second week."

Not long enough to know much about Catherine's life at the time of Phoebe's disappearance. If Catherine couldn't communicate, Victoria would have to follow up with her family.

Catherine moaned. Her skin looked sickly pale.

"Who visits Catherine regularly?" Victoria asked, planning to speak to the people who knew Catherine best.

Deja lowered her voice to a whisper. "Uh, well, she hasn't had many visitors since I started working here. Only her son, who just left for Europe, and a man named George Martin. He came after my shift."

Victoria made a mental note to find out if George Martin was the same George the police interviewed a year ago, the man Phoebe had spoken with at the gym before her mysterious disappearance.

Another gurgle.

"I'm sorry, we'll be right back." Deja said, whisking Catherine and the wheelchair toward the bathroom.

"It's okay," Victoria said. "I have to head out. I'll be in touch."

Before leaving, she stopped at the registration desk and asked for information on who visited Catherine, just in case there were other visitors Deja wasn't aware of. The woman working the desk politely denied the information because it was private.

As Victoria left the facility, she called Agent Rivera and went over what Deja had told her.

"You think it's more than a coincidence that Mrs. Bower said Phoebe's name?" Rivera asked. "Maybe Phoebe was the only missing person Mrs. Bower knew, and that's what prompted her response."

"Maybe, but I'm not going to drop this until I find out more."

"Okay. Keep me posted. Let me know how I can help," he said.

"I will. I just have to get some questions answered first."

To begin with, who else knew there was a hidden camera within the frame of Catherine's family portrait?

CHAPTER 16

One Year Ago - Catherine

Heat coursed through Catherine's body. Sweat gathered across her forehead, between her breasts, and behind her knees. Her hot flashes made her feel like she'd woken up in a sauna. Instinctively, she reached for John. Her hand felt only the tangle of blankets she'd kicked to his side of the bed. She hadn't heard him get up.

Yesterday's discovery hit her then, bringing with it a discomfort more powerful than the hot flash. John was cheating on her. Not possibly. Definitely.

She curled into a ball and pulled just the top sheet over her shoulders. On the plus side, she clearly remembered smelling perfume on her husband's shirt, which meant her short-term memory was operating in fine form.

Still in bed, she grabbed her datebook off the side table and read over her schedule for the day.

7 - swim

10 - deep tissue massage at Scenic Spa

12 - consult with Healing Acupuncture

Automate online payments and check SmartBox Financial Report.

Confirm Duke presentation for Thursday.

John - golf trip in Kiawah through Sunday.

So that's why he got out of bed so early. He must have a tee time that afternoon. Wanting to say goodbye before he left, she made a quick trip to the bathroom, then went to find him. The kitchen was empty. So was his office. She peered into the garage. His SUV was gone.

When she tapped his name on her phone, he answered on the first ring.

"Good morning, Babe. I was just thinking of you. Didn't want to wake you before I left."

"Hmm," she said, channeling a peaceful vibe she wasn't feeling. "You should have."

"I hope you remembered my trip. I planned to talk to you about it yesterday, you know, before things got a little out of control."

"I saw it on my calendar," she said. "So, I take it you're already on the road?"

"Yes, we're playing at two. It was hard to pull myself out of bed. Last night was great. Let's have a repeat as soon as I get back, okay?"

"Something to look forward to," she answered, trying to sound convincing. Their makeup sex was great. But having her suspicions confirmed right after that had ruined any lingering gratification. Her jaw clenched into a grimace as she wondered again if he'd had sex with his mistress yesterday and if that sex was equally nice, not as good, or better. Catherine's angry side wanted to pose the question and demand an answer. Her rational side prevailed, telling her not to go there.

Fuming over her situation, Catherine went through her morning routine of swimming, showering, and eating a healthy breakfast—avocado toast and a green smoothie—before heading to her first appointment.

When she got home in the afternoon, the cleaning crew was leaving the pool house with their cart of vacuums, dusters, and cleaning solutions. Perfect timing. They always cleaned the main house first, so now they were on their way out.

With a glass of iced tea, Catherine went into her office and logged into her online banking account. A financial adviser managed her investments and handled other financial matters, but ever since her first husband's death, she'd taken care of the bills. Automating them would help, though eventually, John would have to step in. They weren't at that point yet.

She logged into her online banking portal and stared at her accounts. She furrowed her brow and blinked, then stared at her screen again. The account she'd labeled *Disbursement* blurred with the one she'd labeled *John* and the one below that labeled *Taylor*. The screen was unreadable.

Catherine moved closer and squinted at her laptop, waiting for her vision to correct itself. She rubbed her eyes, though she knew the problem was inside her brain, not her eyeballs. A symptom of her disease. The blurriness only got worse. She slumped in her chair and closed her eyes. This wasn't going to work. Not today.

Abandoning her task and her iced tea, she strode to the kitchen and poured a glass of wine from an already opened bottle. She took it onto the patio. With her legs stretched out on a chaise lounge, she sipped her wine overlooking the pool, and reflected on her life until she dozed off.

Alone in the bed with her vision restored, Catherine read until her eyes burned before putting her book aside. Thanks to a three-hour nap earlier, she couldn't fall asleep.

Late night turned into early morning. Her mind stubbornly refused to shut down and recharge. She inhaled for four counts, held her breath, and exhaled slowly for another four counts. She repeated the exercise multiple times. It didn't work.

Admitting defeat for now, she got out of bed and draped a knit blanket over her shoulders. She padded into the butler's pantry and selected a Barbaresco, one of her favorite Italian wines. Carrying the bottle in one hand and a goblet in the other, she went out to the back patio and sat down in the same chaise lounge where she'd slept earlier in the day.

Pool lights illuminated the water in calming shades of lavender, blue, and gray. She thought about stripping her clothes and swimming laps in her underwear. The warm water would soothe her mind, and the exertion might be what she needed to sleep. But she wasn't motivated enough to remove her sleep shirt and get wet.

She pulled the blanket tighter, covering her feet from the cool night air, and stared up at stars dotting the sky. She wondered what John was doing.

When she finished the wine bottle, she went inside for another. The cork resisted. She pulled harder. Her hand flew back as the cork released with a squelch, and her knuckles whacked her nose.

"Damn it," she muttered, wincing at the pain that made her eyes water.

Ignoring her glass, she drank straight from the bottle. She chugged as if she were back in high school drinking in the woods with the sole intent of getting fall-over wasted. She took the bottle outside with her and let her frustrations take over as she wandered around drinking.

Landscape lighting cast a glow on the meticulously maintained gardens. As she strayed from the stone path, dark shadows concealed her surroundings. The ground beneath her bare feet felt cold and damp. Soft dirt slid between her toes. A sudden collision with an unseen obstacle sent a jolt of pain through her foot. She screamed, releasing a mixture of cries that turned into laughter. She staggered aimlessly. Amidst her wandering and more drinking, tears streamed down her face, their origin a mystery even to herself.

She couldn't recall the exact moment she lost consciousness, suffering a temporary blackout. All she knew was that she found herself sprawled on the ground. Summoning her strength, she struggled to rise and stumble into the pool house.

Catherine collapsed onto a bed in one of the guest rooms and passed out again. Eerie noises disrupted her stupor, tugging her consciousness from the depths.

A shadowy figure loomed above her. The intruder's soft voice found its way through the fog. "What are you doing here?"

Catherine mumbled incoherently, lost within the realms of her strange dream. "I couldn't sleep…"

"It's okay. I have to leave you now," the stranger whispered, letting her drift back into a restless slumber.

CHAPTER 17

Present Day - Victoria

Catherine's second husband, John Murdock, lived in a house Catherine owned before they got married. He answered his door wearing slacks, a golf shirt, and a vest. He was in his mid-forties and appeared to be in good health, maybe the prime of his life.

Victoria showed her identification and said, "I'm here about Phoebe Watson."

"Oh. I heard they found her. It's terrible what happened. You still don't know who killed her, right?" John asked.

"That's right."

"I don't know how I can help. She was my wife's trainer, and that's about all I know."

"I'd like to come in and ask you some questions. Maybe something you remember can help steer me in the right direction," Victoria said.

"That seems like a waste of our time," John said, "But come in." He opened the door wider and stepped aside, then led her through the house and into a butler's pantry with wine racks and glass cabinets. He took a bottle of Fiji water from a beverage refrigerator. "Would you like one?" he asked.

"Sure. Thank you," Victoria said, accepting the bottle he handed her. John reminded her of a charming southern host who appeared to be in no hurry. "What sort of work do you do?" she asked.

He tilted his head and smirked. "Not everyone has to work for a living, Ms. Heslin."

Victoria understood the concept well. Thanks to her grandfather, she fit into that small group of fortunate individuals. Yet here she was trying to figure out why John's wife, who couldn't communicate because of an accident—which was suspicious in itself—might have inside information on the mysterious death of her fitness trainer.

John apparently didn't know anything about Victoria. That was a good thing. Less distraction. The focus would stay on the current investigation. A quick Google search would change that. He'd find out about her mother's untimely death, a direct result of her family's wealth. He'd see numerous articles describing Victoria's critical involvement in several high-profile criminal cases, from murders to abductions, and countless news clips listing Victoria as a survivor of Flight 745.

She twisted the top off her water bottle and took a sip as she followed him to a kitchen flooded with sunlight. Tall iron-framed windows and glass doors overlooked the backyard. It held a tarp-covered pool and a white brick building, a small version of the main house.

John gestured to the kitchen table. He took a seat and settled back against his chair. He still appeared relaxed, though maybe cocky was the best word to describe him.

Victoria's position gave her a view of the living room and the bare space above the fireplace mantel.

"Catherine has a family portrait over her bed," Victoria said. "Did it come from the mantel over there?"

John swiveled in his chair and peered into the living room for a second or two. "Yes. Her children thought she would want it with her."

Other pictures graced the mansion's white walls. All had smooth, modern frames. The frame in Catherine's room was thicker and more ornate. Better for hiding a camera.

"You had the portrait reframed for her?" Victoria asked.

"What?" John's brows pulled together. "I don't know what you're asking."

"I was curious about the camera in Catherine's room."

"You were in her room?"

"At Atrium Gardens."

"Oh. What camera?"

"The video camera in a picture frame there."

"I don't know what you're talking about," John said, looking at her strangely. "What can I help you with, Ms. Heslin? What is it you came here to discuss?"

"Your wife mentioned Phoebe's name before the authorities identified her," Victoria said.

Tiny wrinkles appeared across John's forehead as he scrunched it further. "Again, I'm not following you."

Victoria explained the circumstances.

"Hmm, I'm afraid my wife's caregiver imagined that, or it's just a coincidence. With Catherine's condition, it's probably not possible."

"Probably?"

"Most likely it didn't happen."

"Where were you the night Phoebe disappeared?" Victoria asked.

John tilted his head as he'd done earlier and gave her a *you-can't-be-serious* look. "You expect people to know where they were a year ago? You think I can answer that question now?"

"She was last seen on May fourth."

"You know, if I was responsible for what happened to her, I'd have an answer ready for you. I don't. That should tell you it doesn't matter where I was, because I had nothing to do with Phoebe's death." John's expression suddenly changed. Victoria could see the gears turning in his brain.

"Actually, hold on," he said. He got up and went to the kitchen island, where he picked up an iPhone in a black case. "I don't keep a calendar, per se. However, I do track my golf stats."

Victoria waited while he swiped at his phone.

"This is a stroke of luck. Fortunately, I *can* tell you where I was then. Golfing with friends in Kiawah the entire week. The trip got extended because of heavy rains. I went with three other guys. They can confirm that for you. We stayed at the Winston Retreat. I've got credit card charges. Pictures."

"Thank you for providing the information. It will help us rule you out and move on," Victoria said, writing the hotel's name in her notebook.

"I probably should have an attorney present. Seeing I haven't done anything wrong, I'm trusting you to do your job properly." John smiled as he spoke, though his words weren't friendly. "Please do make it known that I fully cooperated with your investigation," he added, returning to his seat.

"Noted," Victoria told him. "And Catherine? Where was she when you were on your golf trip?"

"She was here, I imagine. Well, now that I think about it. The Kiawah golf trip occurred during my wife's first visit to Duke Medical. I wasn't able to go with her. We were in touch often."

Victoria took another sip of her water, then said, "If you don't mind, I'd like to understand more about the incident that led to her brain injury."

"Okay. Not that it's even a small bit relevant, and the visit to Duke had nothing to do with that." John shifted his unopened bottle from one hand to the other. "Her brain injury was the result of Catherine almost drowning. Not quite a year ago. In our own backyard."

Victoria looked toward the covered pool and asked, "Did she know how to swim?"

"She was a strong swimmer. She swam laps several days a week, year-round. She also jogged and worked out with a private trainer regularly." John winced as if he'd just remembered the private trainer's demise was the very reason Victoria sat across from him asking questions. He opened his bottle, raised it to his lips, and drank.

"Was she wearing her bathing suit at the time of the incident?"

"She was wearing her workout clothes."

"Was there any indication she'd perhaps slipped, hit her head, and fallen in?" Victoria asked. She couldn't access Catherine's medical records, so she was depending on John to tell her the truth about what happened.

"No," he answered.

"Who found her?"

"George. Her yard guy."

Victoria noted John's use of *her* rather than *our*. And there was George's name again. Was he the George who visited Catherine at Atrium Gardens? Victoria wondered if his landscaping business used the same organic pesticides found in Phoebe's hair.

"What is George's last name?" Victoria asked.

"It's...it's...I'm drawing a blank right now. I'm not sure."

"Was anyone else with George at the time of the incident? A landscaping crew?" she asked.

"Not a crew. I'm pretty sure he only had one other worker. His brother, I believe. That guy was also here when it happened."

"Any reason George or his brother had to harm her?"

John shook his head as if the question was ridiculous. "No. Never even considered that. Catherine had employed George for over a decade. He'd taken care of another property before this one. Not just yard work. Maintenance work, too. They were friends."

"What sort of friends?"

John laughed. "I don't mean he came for dinner, or they went shopping together. Just that Catherine spoke highly of him. I assume she paid him well. She seemed to care about what was going on with him and his family. She was good to him. They were friendly, that's what I should have said."

"And George is the one who pulled her out of the water?"

"Yes. I got home a few seconds after he found her. He got to her first. He's the reason she's still alive."

"You were here?"

"Like I just said, I got home after he found her." Irritation laced John's words. Then his voice changed, getting low and thick with what she could only imagine was regret. Or what he wanted to pass off as regret. "If only I'd gotten here earlier. I had just gotten home from our club. Quail View. I came into the kitchen and heard someone shouting. That was George. He sounded desperate. Frantic. I thought maybe he'd had a fall and cut off an arm or leg with one of his machines. I looked out the window here, and that's when I saw Catherine lying beside the pool. At first, I had no idea what was going on. Seeing her like that, George was on top of her. Their clothes and hair were all wet. I was baffled. It looked like...." John shook his head. "It took a second for all of it to sink in. He was resuscitating her. I grabbed my phone and called 9-1-1 as I ran outside. Later I learned George's brother had already called them."

Victoria turned to the window, trying to imagine the scene as John witnessed it. "How did George know Catherine was in the pool?"

"I can't answer that. You'll have to ask him."

"Do you have any evidence to suggest it really wasn't an accident?"

John took a long inhale and let it out slowly. He looked down at his hands. "For obvious reasons, the incident is not something our family ever talks about. We'll never know for certain what happened. As I'm sure you can understand, her children and I prefer to believe it was an accident.

That's how we've always referred to it. It's what we've told everyone. A terrible, unfortunate accident."

"But you don't think it was?"

"Catherine wasn't herself when it happened. About three months before, she learned she had early-onset Alzheimer's."

"Was she experiencing symptoms?" Victoria asked.

John nodded. "She experienced mental lapses. Her whole personality seemed to change. She became paranoid."

"Paranoid about what?"

"Different things. She accused me of cheating on her when I wasn't. She knew her challenges would only grow as her condition progressed. Her mother suffered from the same disease. It was difficult for any of us to imagine Catherine losing control. If you knew her, she was always working. She constantly had projects underway with one of the houses, or a charity, or with her children. Smartbox board meetings. She was incredibly focused and full of energy. Even though she was older than I, it never seemed that way. But Catherine had witnessed her mother's decline firsthand. She knew how the disease would progress. The toll it would take."

"And you think she wasn't handling that well?"

"Well, to be honest, she was drinking. A lot. She'd also started a clinical trial at Duke Medical. That's the visit I mentioned earlier. The one that occurred during my Kiawah outing. She only had one or two treatments. Then...I don't know how to explain what happened, but something changed. She got even more paranoid. Depressed. Withdrawn. Those are all early symptoms of dementia. It's almost as if the treatment accelerated her condition and made it worse. At the time of her accident, she really wasn't herself at all. An ambulance took her right to the hospital after the pool incident. The tests there showed her blood-alcohol level was sky high. She'd also taken sleeping pills."

Victoria stared at John, studying him. He seemed convinced Catherine's medical condition and alcohol consumption had contributed to a suicidal act.

John straightened in his chair. He crossed his arms on the table and sharpened his focus on Victoria. "I don't understand why you're asking so many questions about Catherine? What does her accident have to do with Phoebe Watson's murder?"

"I don't know yet. Maybe nothing," Victoria answered. "Thank you for the explanation and your time. Before I leave, would you help me with something?"

"That depends," he answered.

"Fair enough. I'd appreciate it if you could show me where George was working before you got home. If you know, that is."

With Victoria following, John went out the back door and walked around the side of the house on a pebbled garden path. They passed layered rows of viburnums, azaleas, and hydrangeas, all overgrown. Random offshoots stuck out across the path. John pushed aside a branch.

"The replacement service doesn't do as good a job as George used to do," John said as the branch snapped back against Victoria's chest.

"George doesn't work for you anymore?" she asked.

"No. He quit after the incident. Said finding Catherine traumatized him and he didn't want to keep reliving what had happened. Guess he didn't need the money."

They stopped walking.

"Here's where George said he was when he heard something," John said.

From where they stood on the side of the house, the driveway wasn't visible.

What if George hadn't heard a sound at the pool? Perhaps instead, he had heard John's car approaching or the garage door opening and only rescued her then. "Saving" her was the best way to look innocent. If he believed it was already too late for her survival, he had nothing to lose.

Victoria was only speculating. Thinking through all the possibilities. She had no reason to believe the man who took care of Catherine's yard wanted to hurt her. John was likely the one who had the most to gain from his wife's demise.

The accident's relevance hinged on its connection to Phoebe's death.

Victoria's experience and instincts told her the two incidents were linked.

CHAPTER 18

Present Day - Victoria

Taylor's condominium looked clean, but messy. Clothes dangled over chair backs. An expensive purse and tall suede boots were piled together near the door. Dishes, unopened envelopes, and scattered papers cluttered the white marble countertop. An ashtray rested on the kitchen island and another on the coffee table. Both contained barely smoked cigarettes.

Seated in a wide, cream-colored chair across from Victoria, Taylor tucked her thin legs underneath her. She tilted forward, as if she was having a conversation with a close girlfriend. Tiny blue veins lined the underside of her pale arms. They reminded Victoria of the way she'd looked right after her plane crash rescue. Much too thin.

"When they found Phoebe, was she in one piece? Or, you know, did the killer dismember her?" Taylor asked.

"She was in one piece," Victoria answered, surprised by Taylor's callous bluntness.

"Oh. I was just curious. I never met her, you know, Phoebe Weston."

"Watson," Victoria corrected.

"Right. I know my mother adored her. However, the helper is wrong if she thinks my mother can shed light on your murder case. She doesn't know what's what these days. Her brain is essentially screwed. It's so unfair." Taylor shook her head. "So totally unfair."

"That was your stepfather's opinion, also," Victoria said. "I spoke with him yesterday."

Taylor huffed as she grabbed a pack of cigarettes and a lighter from the coffee table. "He and I don't share many opinions. Whatever John told you, it's probably a lie."

"We mostly discussed your mother's accident."

"He told you my mother tried to commit suicide because of her Alzheimer's, didn't he?" Taylor asked, crossing her legs as she lit a cigarette.

"He didn't actually say those words, but yes, that was my takeaway from our conversation."

Taylor scowled. "It's what he believes. And it's total BS. The Alzheimer's was affecting her already, I won't deny that. She was writing everything important down in a journal, worried she might forget something. She'd get confused, which made her super frustrated. But she could still do everything she'd always done. Drive. Work out. Smartbox stuff. If it weren't for my grandmother, my mother wouldn't have even known she had Alzheimer's until a lot later. She visited specialists who confirmed the diagnosis with MRIs and CT scans. She told me everything she was doing because I could have it, too, someday. By the time it affects me, if it does, there should be a cure. I'm supposed to get tested for a genetic mutation, but it's like, do I even want to know that's coming?" Taylor sucked from the end of her cigarette and turned her head to the side to blow out a line of smoke. "I've got enough on my plate already. I've decided I'd rather wait until the cure comes and deal with it then."

"I certainly hope there will be a cure soon," Victoria said.

"Me, too. So did my mother. Meanwhile, she didn't just sit back and feel sorry for herself. She sought the best early intervention treatments. She was already in a study for some new treatment at Duke."

"Your stepfather mentioned the treatment protocol. He said her condition worsened after starting it."

Taylor shrugged. "Maybe. Not like there's anything she could do about that except stop it. She signed things saying she couldn't sue if the drugs did something weird to her. She's not a candidate now. When she almost drowned, it killed so many brain cells, it destroyed her mind in an instant, beat the Alzheimer's to it. There's no chance of her ever getting better now."

"I'm sorry to hear that," Victoria said.

"She still gets brain scans every so often. Only because Will keeps insisting on them. In reality, between the accident that cut off her oxygen and the Alzheimer's advancing—she can't recover no matter what. Like I said, totally unfair." Taylor straightened one slender finger and shook it. "Before the drowning incident, all I can say is my mother was a fighter, not a quitter. She didn't give up, and she didn't let anyone push her around. No one and nothing could intimidate her. Including a disease."

"If it wasn't a suicide attempt...?" Victoria asked, intentionally leaving her question unfinished.

"I never said it wasn't, I just can't believe it was. You know?"

Victoria nodded, though she wasn't entirely sure.

"My mother was an incredible swimmer. She worked out constantly, trying not to get old and all that. That's what happens when you marry an untrustworthy guy so much younger than you."

"Untrustworthy?"

Taylor held her cigarette off to the side. Smoke swirled from the tip. "He was cheating on her, and she knew it."

"Did you have proof of that?" Victoria asked. "John mentioned she was paranoid."

Taylor huffed again. "Of course he would. If your husband was cheating on you, wouldn't it drive you extra wacko if he claimed you were paranoid? Look, I know my mother. I can't believe she would try to end her life. She had too much to live for. She was crazy about Will and me. Oops. I shouldn't have said crazy. What I mean is that she adored us."

"Then tell me what happened to your mother."

Taylor uncrossed her legs. Though she'd only taken one puff, she ground her cigarette into the nearest ashtray. "I can't prove what happened, or how he did it. But think about it. Now John doesn't have to see her condition worsening. He doesn't have to deal with nursing staff turning the house into a hospital ward. Her almost-drowning worked out nicely for him. Better than if she actually died, in which case most of what she has goes to Will and me. You get what I'm saying? Maybe while you're investigating Phoebe, someone should finally take a closer look at John. I don't trust him. Never have. He's nothing like my real father."

"I saw your father passed away. I'm sorry for your loss."

"Yeah. Boating accident. It was a long time ago. I was only seven. You never really get over something like that, you know? Probably screwed me up and I just don't know it yet. First my father's accident, and then my mother's."

Victoria had also experienced a profound loss. Her mother's death was sudden and unexpected, after her abduction took a devastating turn. That loss had forever altered the course of Victoria's future, becoming the primary factor driving her decision to pursue a law enforcement career. Did that mean the incident had screwed her up? Some might think so. Her role as a field agent meant sacrificing her own comfort and safety, rather than relying on the safety net of her inheritance. For Victoria, it was a way to confront her demons head-on, to make a difference in a world that desperately needed it. Her work would never bring back her mother, but it gave her purpose and the opportunity to prevent others from enduring a similar tragedy.

Taylor leaned back and stared at Victoria, then asked the same question her stepfather had. "How did we end up talking about my mother's accident? What does it have to do with Phoebe?"

"I don't know yet," Victoria answered. "What was your mother's relationship with George Martin like?"

After visiting John, Victoria had confirmed the landscaper's last name was Martin. The same George listed in Phoebe's missing person file. The same man who visited Catherine at Atrium Gardens.

Taylor frowned. "Who?"

"Your mother's landscaper and maintenance worker. John said he worked for your family for over ten years."

"Oh. That George. Not the good-looking one. The other guy. The one who got my mother's heart pumping again. Not sure if she would thank him for that or not, considering how she ended up. He cracked four of her ribs. Apparently, that's a thing with CPR. In any case, there's no way my mother was having an affair with him, if that's what you're getting at," Taylor said with a scoff.

"Did you ever see them arguing?"

"Even when I lived in her house, I didn't pay much attention to what was going on outside. I'm more of an indoor enthusiast, if you couldn't tell." Taylor slid her fingertips over the pale skin on her arm. "However, I assure you, my mother would not *argue* with the yard guy. I mean, obviously my mother trusted the guy. He had keys to our house and the pool house. He came and went as he pleased." Taylor's expression grew more skeptical as she raised one of her thick, sculpted eyebrows. "Why are you asking about him? You think he knows something about Phoebe?"

CHAPTER 19

One Year Ago - Catherine

Catherine opened her eyes and blinked, turning away from the glaring light coming in through an immense window. Her head pounded. The skin surrounding her left eye felt tender. Her mouth was so dry she couldn't swallow. Her tongue felt swollen. The water bottle she always brought to bed wasn't there. She wasn't in her bedroom. It took several more breaths to get her bearings. She'd awakened in the pool house.

When she was younger, waking up with a hangover in a strange location meant she'd had a great time. She didn't think that was the case now, though she remembered nothing of the previous night. She waited for the memories to return and form a picture of her activities. They didn't come. She drew only blankness.

Alarm bells went off, screeching inside her.

Was this how it began? She didn't know if she'd lost a chunk of her memory to the plaque crippling her brain, or if she'd gotten so drunk she'd blacked out.

With shaky legs, she pushed herself up from the bed and staggered toward the bathroom. Her usually superb balance was off. She hoped the lack of stability was her hangover talking, not the disease.

As she passed the mirror, she did a double take. A purplish bruise had formed around her left eye.

On the toilet, Catherine glanced down at her feet. Dirt coated their sides, with a thicker layer beneath her soles. Baffled, she turned on the sprayer in the shower and washed them clean.

Though there was no one around, she did a walk of shame across the patio and toward the house, hurrying with her head down. Halfway around the pool, she stopped in her tracks. A heaped towel lay on the stones. The once pristine white stripes were streaked with a crimson liquid resembling blood. Panic welled inside her.

She moved closer to the towel. The red stain wasn't thick, like she expected. It wasn't blood. It was red wine. Relieved, she picked up the towel and brought it inside. Her phone rang, shattering the silence in her home. She hurried to snatch the device from her bedroom before the ringing stopped. It was John.

"Just calling to say good morning. How are you?" he asked.

"I'm fine," she lied, as she reached for her datebook. "Where are you?"

He hesitated before answering, "Golf trip. Did you forget?"

She looked down at the open page of her calendar.

10—Phoebe training.

John in Kiawah Day 2 of 4.

"I didn't forget," she said. "I just woke up and I'm still a little out of it. Barely got any sleep last night."

"I thought you sounded tired. Take a nap if you need one."

"I took a nap yesterday. That's why I couldn't fall asleep. Not doing that again."

"Okay. Well, do whatever you need. Take it easy and take care of yourself. I'll check in with you later. Love you."

"I love you, too. Enjoy your trip."

Still woozy, Catherine got dressed and went to the kitchen. Priority one—make her head stop pounding. She swallowed three pain pills, chasing them with an entire bottle of electrolyte-laden water.

Leaning on the counter, she massaged her temples while the espresso maker heated water for her tea. Her gaze moved to the cabinet doors hiding the trash and recycling bins. She was curious to know just how much alcohol it had taken to leave her feeling so awful. It hardly mattered now. The damage was done. She was better off not knowing. Yet she opened the doors anyway and peered into the containers. The trash and recycling bins were empty. They weren't even lined with plastic bags.

She didn't know what had happened to the empty bottles. The cleaning crew would have removed the trash and recycling items when they were working yesterday morning. They always replaced the bags. Half a day had passed since they left. Catherine might have left the empties elsewhere. Yet the bins should have held some evidence of her presence from yesterday. Food wrappers. Tea bags. A few used paper towels. The completely empty bins puzzled her.

By ten o'clock, Catherine had drunk two cups of green tea, showered, and changed into workout clothes. A dull pang had replaced her headache. She was ready for her training session.

As always, when she approached the front door, she caught her reflection in the large mirror. Fortunately, she looked much better than she felt. Flat abs. Lean, muscular legs. Nothing sagging or jiggling. Maybe she wouldn't fire Phoebe after all.

Because Phoebe didn't wear perfume.

With her feet on an ottoman, Catherine waited in a chair with a view of the driveway, sipping water from her sports bottle. Ten o'clock came and went. That was unusual. Phoebe always arrived on time. Except for one recent occasion where she had to stop for gas and apologized for being a minute late. She had a routine of showing up early, waiting in her car until 9:55, then getting out and ringing the doorbell.

Catherine checked her phone messages. She expected to see a message like, *Sorry, running late. I'm on my way.*

The only message came from Taylor, along with a link to an art gallery. *Check out this painting. Wouldn't it look amazing in my bedroom? Birthday idea, hint, hint.*

Five more minutes passed. Catherine texted Phoebe. *We had a session scheduled for 10. Are you coming?*

Another fifteen minutes went by. No Phoebe. No response to Catherine's text.

Catherine paced a circle through the first floor and straightened a pillow on the couch. She tossed two wilting flowers from the bouquet in the foyer and moved her sunglasses from one end of the counter to the other end, where she preferred them. With mounting irritation, she pondered what had happened to Phoebe. She was thirty minutes late.

Catherine called John, though she expected he was on the golf course. He didn't answer, and she didn't leave a message. She walked outside and called him again. After that, she sent a text. *Call me.*

Catherine rested her hands on the back of the chaise lounge, the same one where just last night she'd had too much to drink.

John was out of town, and Phoebe hadn't shown up for the workout. Coincidence?

Phoebe doesn't wear perfume. Or maybe she does when she isn't exercising.

Catherine wanted a drink. At ten thirty in the morning and still hungover from earlier, it felt too much like giving up.

Her phone vibrated on the side table. Her husband's name lit up at the top of the screen. She let the device ring two more times, considering what she would say, before she slid the answer button to the right.

"I saw some missed calls and your text," John said, sounding worried. "What's wrong?"

"Where are you?"

"On the course. I shouldn't be on the phone, but I was worried about you. Is everything all right?"

"Who are you with?" she asked, her voice deepening with each question.

"Dean. Todd. Jeff. I'm sure I told you. What's going on?"

Catherine didn't miss the way John's concern was turning into impatience. "Phoebe never showed up for my training session," she said.

Silence followed. Enough time for Catherine to get up from the chaise and start walking back to the house. Enough time for John to come up with an excuse.

"Didn't you fire her?" he finally asked.

Catherine's response was sharp. "No, I didn't fire her."

"You were talking about it the other night. Sounded like you were going to do it. Is it possible you forgot?"

Catherine's first instinct was to snap at her husband. But what if she *had* forgotten? The not knowing, not being certain about what she had or hadn't done, made her stomach clench with dread. She was only ninety-something percent positive she hadn't fired Phoebe.

Someone in the background—Dean, Todd, or Jeff—called John's name.

Hearing another man's voice nearby provided some reassurance. Whoever was talking to him, it wasn't Phoebe.

"Catherine, I have to go. Are you going to be all right?"

"Yes. I'm fine. Goodbye," she said and hung up first.

She checked her phone messages again and selected Phoebe's name. The most recent message exchange before today occurred last Sunday. Phoebe had asked if she could record a video by the pool. Catherine had sent back a thumbs-up emoji.

She glanced toward the butler's pantry again. *Still too early*. She stomped across the floor to her datebook. In large print, she scrawled, *get a new trainer*. If she went to the club, she could exercise and perhaps ask if anyone in the gym had recommendations.

She grabbed her belongings and got into her Mercedes. On autopilot, she tossed her purse on the passenger seat, strapped on her seatbelt, then pushed the button to start the SUV.

It didn't start. A message lit up on the console in front of her. *No Key Found in the Vehicle.*

She slid her hand into the inner pocket of her purse. The key wasn't there. After rummaging through her entire bag, she still hadn't found the key. This sort of thing never happened to her, though it was happening now. As if she wasn't already frustrated enough.

She never misplaced items. Not sunglasses or phones or earbuds, and especially not keys. She had a system that worked for her. A place for everything and everything in its place. Her keys belonged in the inner pocket of her purse. If they weren't there, someone had moved them.

As Catherine got out of the car, something small ground against the all-weather floor mat beneath her foot. She bent over for a closer look.

A gold necklace with a barbell pendant lay half on the floor mat and half on the carpet behind it. A necklace just like the one she gave Phoebe. The one Phoebe seemed to always wear. Its presence was enough to convince Catherine that John and Phoebe *were* having an affair. No question about it. If it looks like a duck and quacks like a duck. She had no problem remembering that specific phrase. Many things were exactly what they appeared to be.

She could hardly believe it, after all Catherine had done for Phoebe! Gifts, bonuses, glowing recommendations to friends, letting Phoebe record her videos at the pool. Just how awful and ungrateful could someone be?

Catherine stormed inside and spotted her keys on the foyer table next to the floral arrangement. That wasn't where she usually kept them. She was too angry with John and Phoebe to think about how they got there.

She mashed her finger onto her phone and snarled, "Call Phoebe."

Catherine had to listen to Phoebe's cheerful greeting first. "I'm probably busy with a client. If you're interested in getting in the best shape of your life, leave a message and I'll get back to you soon." Then the leave-a-message beep.

"How dare you?" Catherine said. "How dare you?"

CHAPTER 20
Present Day - Victoria

Victoria stopped outside Murphy's open doorway, where the smell of takeout food wafted from the room. An empty container smudged with red sauce rested on top of the recycling bin by his desk.

"Good timing," he said, holding a thick stack of folders against his chest. "The DA just left me a message. What can I tell him?"

"Tell him we need additional time."

"You still haven't found anything linking Sullivan?"

"Not at the moment. Rivera is collaborating with the police, and I believe I'm onto something promising."

Murphy nudged aside folders on his desk, making room for the new ones. "What have you found?"

"It started with a tip from one of Phoebe's private training clients. Catherine Bower. She knew that was Phoebe in those woods before anyone else did, despite Sullivan never explicitly naming her."

"How did she come across the information?"

"That's what I'm trying to find out. Catherine almost drowned shortly after Phoebe's disappearance. I think what happened to her might be relevant. I'm thinking Catherine knew something, so someone tried to silence her."

"Well, what does she say about it?"

"Given what happened with the accident—," Victoria said, making air quotes. "—communication is a challenge. She can't tell me."

Murphy opened his mouth to say something else, then changed his mind. He ran his hand over his bald head. "Do you have potential suspects? Ones who might have hurt Catherine and Phoebe?"

"Yes. Catherine's husband and her landscaper. And, get this, the landscaper was a person of interest when Phoebe disappeared."

"Was he cleared?"

"Yes. He had an alibi for the time of Phoebe's disappearance. The detective moved on to other leads. Back then, the police didn't have Phoebe's body. Now we do. Forensics told us someone struck Phoebe with a shovel, or a similar tool, and her hair contained traces of organic pesticides. If we could test George's landscaping tools…"

Murphy shook his head. "Most people own shovels. No judge will grant you a warrant based on that, especially if the investigation already cleared him. Besides, if he killed Phoebe, surely he disposed of the murder weapon by now. You're going to need more than that."

"I know. That's why I need more time," she said, just as his phone rang.

"Wait, don't leave yet," Murphy said, lifting his finger in the air before answering his phone.

Victoria leaned against the wall outside his office, mentally reviewing her list of persons of interest. Dan Sullivan, John Murdock, George Martin, and Catherine Bower. Victoria had bits of circumstantial evidence to cast suspicion on each of them. The only one with a solid motive—financial gain and freedom—was Catherine's husband, John.

John made good on his word. He'd already sent supporting documents, photos, and names of people who could back up his claim of golfing in Kiawah. But he and his golf buddies all had separate rooms. They couldn't know if he was in the hotel all night. He could have driven back to Virginia, killed Phoebe, and shown up for his golf round the next day. Victoria needed to see video footage from his hotel before she could rule him out.

And then there was the hidden camera in Catherine's room. The device could simply be a nanny cam to spy on the caregivers and prevent mistreatment. Victoria had to find out who put it there, and who was watching the footage.

Murphy finished his call and nodded to Victoria. "Where were we? Your suspects, right? Is there any connection between them and Sullivan?"

"No. Not yet," she said, the repetition of her words bothering her. She'd said, "not yet," too many times recently. "There may not be one...if Sullivan didn't kill Phoebe, and someone from Catherine Bower's circle did."

CHAPTER 21

Present Day - Deja

Knowing it was Will's first day in the Netherlands, Deja was ready and waiting for his call at three p.m. She didn't know him well enough to be certain he'd follow through. When he did, just a few minutes after the agreed-upon time, she was grateful for Catherine's sake.

Deja answered the video call and propped the iPad in front of Catherine, facing it away from the window and the sun's glare.

Will explained he'd taken an overnight flight and hadn't slept. He looked tired.

Once she was sure the iPad was situated correctly so Catherine and Will could see each other, Deja moved to the other side of the room. She busied herself by straightening the scented candles and décor items on Catherine's dresser. An unnecessary task.

Will talked about a delay with the already long flight. The airline lost his suitcase and would bring it to his rental home once they found it. Despite those events, and his lack of sleep, he seemed in pretty good spirits, describing the "sweet" cottage he'd reserved for the next two days. He gave his mother a room-by-room tour.

"This is the balcony off the second-story bedroom," he said. "Check out the canals."

Deja pictured scenes from a Hallmark romance movie she'd recently seen. When the couple realized their destiny, they sipped wine at sunset, looking out over canals.

"Deja, are you there?" Will asked. "I've got a question for you."

She pretended she didn't hear him at first. A silly thing to do, but she didn't want him to know she'd heard every word he'd said so far. After he called her name a second time, she responded with, "Yes? Coming."

"Do you know who Phoebe Watson is?" he asked.

She wasn't expecting that. A smatter of nervous energy hit her. "Yes," she said, unsure of what would come next. Did he know she had contacted the police and already spoken with an FBI agent?

"Someone from the FBI left me a message. Something about you contacting them regarding Phoebe Watson and my mother. What's that about?"

Deja swallowed. "I called the police to see if your mother could help them." Deja explained what had happened and why she alerted law enforcement.

"My mother said Phoebe's name?" Will asked.

He sounded as if he didn't believe it actually happened. Which made Deja question everything she'd seen. But no...it had definitely happened. "Your mother was very upset about it."

"Do you really think she knew what she was saying?"

"Maybe...or maybe not. She has moments where she communicates with me."

"She does?"

"Yes. After that happened, it was all I could think about until I called the police. I was sure that's what your mother wanted. Then I figure the police had other leads because they never followed up with me."

"Well, it seems they took your tip seriously. The same agent who called me also visited my stepfather and my sister. I still have to call her back. Not that I can help. I'm just genuinely interested in learning what she's discovered. Phoebe was my mother's trainer, you know."

"I know. I apologize for not telling you when you stopped by to visit. I should have and I guess I forgot. You were in a rush."

"No need to worry about it. Get this—my sister said they're focusing their suspicions on our family's landscaper. Maybe my mother knew what she was talking about when she mentioned Phoebe's name. Maybe my mother witnessed George do something."

CHAPTER 22

Present Day - Victoria

In the fading twilight, Victoria reached George Martin's address. She was eager to speak with the former landscaper, handyperson, and so-called friend to Catherine Bower.

A *George's Landscaping* sign was prominently displayed on a truck parked in front of his house. The truck had an open trailer attached to the back. The trailer contained a wide lawnmower plus an array of large tools hanging from side hooks.

Victoria's senses heightened at the prospect of questioning George. His name had come up again and again.

She parked and sent a note to Rivera. *I'm at George Martin's place. 541 Sugar Grove Lane.*

George didn't have an arrest record. Not even a traffic violation to his name. His first encounter with law enforcement came when they questioned him about Phoebe's disappearance. A gym employee had seen him in the parking lot talking to Phoebe the night she disappeared. George was a first-time gym visitor, rather than a member. No one knew him, which made him seem suspicious. When the police learned George and Phoebe worked for the same person, he became a potential suspect.

With her gun in a holster at her hip, Victoria walked toward the ranch-style home with gray vinyl siding. A chain-link fence surrounded the property. Someone had recently mowed the yard, and the fragrance of freshly cut grass hung in the air.

She hesitated by the gate, listening and watching for any sign of a guard dog that might charge her, though she didn't expect to see one, despite the fence. Not when the grass was a uniform green. No trace of brown or yellow spots or unsightly holes with mounds of dirt beside them. The freshly mulched, weed-free flower beds were pristine.

She unhooked the gate and swung it inward.

George Martin opened his door before she got to his porch. He wore gray nylon shorts and a navy T-shirt. His legs were several shades lighter than his tanned face and arms. Though his face was round, it appeared gaunt, his eyes hollowed. Nothing about the man's posture or the way he ambled from his house felt threatening. His expression was that of a curious person about to ask a question, rather than someone planning to run Victoria off his property. Since she suspected him of murder, she'd imagined there would be some visible indication of a callous, evil streak lurking just beneath the surface. Standing less than two yards away from him, his hand up in a welcoming wave, she didn't see anything like that.

But looks could deceive.

"Nice yard," she said. In case she was wrong about his involvement in Phoebe's death, there was no reason to be other than civilized. The man was innocent until proven guilty, unless her gut instinct or the evidence screamed he'd done it.

George's eyes went to the badge hanging around her neck. She held it up for him to see.

"I'm Victoria Heslin with the FBI. Not sure if you're aware, authorities found a woman's remains in Madison Creek Woods last week. We recently identified her as Phoebe Watson."

His hand rose to grip his earlobe between his thumb and forefinger, a possible "tell." Before answering, he looked over his shoulder toward his house. "Yes, I heard. Very sad news," he said.

There was still nothing hostile about George's demeanor. Quite the opposite. His shoulders slumped forward, making him seem smaller than his approximate five-feet-ten or eleven inches. He wasn't tough, nor was he smooth or charming, traits many killers hid behind.

"Why are you here?" George asked.

"I have questions. You and Phoebe knew each other because you had the same boss?" Victoria asked.

George lowered his hand and cleared his throat before answering. "We didn't really know each other. I saw Phoebe occasionally at Catherine's house. We never talked. Just said hello."

"You saw her the night she disappeared."

"Yes. That's just a coincidence. I introduced myself after I took her class. I don't think she recognized me. When I left, I saw her drive away from the gym, alive and well. The police still questioned me. I told them what I did that night. I went home and ate with my mother. A friend came over later. We watched a game. I worked most of the day, starting around eight a.m."

George's story matched what he'd told the police a year ago, as documented in the missing person's file. A surveillance camera captured him driving in the opposite direction of Phoebe after they left the gym. Another video caught him in the drive-through at a Bojangles across town. His friend and his family backed up his alibi. Law enforcement had nothing to link George to Phoebe's disappearance and no reason to question him further.

"What game did you watch?" Victoria asked, not ready to give up.

"Soccer. Real Madrid versus AC Milan," he said. "The police asked me about it more than once. That's why I remember."

"Did you ever see Phoebe arguing with Catherine Bower?" Victoria asked, shifting gears.

"No."

"How about with Catherine's husband? Did you ever see him and Phoebe together?"

George shook his head. His hand went to his earlobe again.

"Do you know Dan Sullivan?" Victoria asked.

"No. Who is he?"

"Someone who claims to have murdered Phoebe. He's the reason authorities found her."

Something flashed behind George's eyes, only for a split second. If Victoria hadn't been watching carefully, she would have missed the change.

"You have proof he killed her?" George asked.

"He confessed, and he gave the police the location where he buried her."

George gulped, his Adam's apple receding and protruding as they stood on the porch in silence.

"We think he might be lying. What do you think?"

A drop of sweat rolled down George's temple.

"Catherine's husband told me you were there when she almost drowned. Do you remember that day?" Victoria finally asked.

George looked away, his gaze settling on the cedar planks beneath his feet. "I remember. It's not something I'll ever forget," he said, his voice just above a whisper, so she couldn't be sure of the last two words.

"Walk me through that morning," she said.

Without meeting Victoria's eyes, he answered, "Catherine and I talked when I got to her house. She'd had too much to drink."

"How could you tell?"

"Just the way she was talking. Her eyes were a little unfocused."

"That was in the morning?"

"Around ten," he answered. "The irrigation system ran at five. I waited a few hours before going over. Until the grass was dry enough to cut."

"Was it unusual that Catherine was drunk at ten in the morning?"

He shrugged. "I don't really know. I can't answer that."

"What were you and Catherine talking about?"

"Maintenance projects." He still had trouble meeting Victoria's gaze. He was hiding something.

"Really? She wanted to talk about maintenance projects even though she was drunk?" Victoria asked.

George gulped again and nodded.

"Were you concerned about her welfare that day?"

"I knew she was struggling with a lot of issues."

"What sort of issues?"

"Her health. She had a disease. It was changing her. I think she was having trouble remembering things."

"What happened next on that morning?"

George took a few steps forward, latched onto the porch railing, and locked eyes with Victoria. "My brother-in-law and I were working together on the side of the house for a few hours. I finished and went around the back. Catherine was lying at the bottom of the pool. She wasn't moving. She wore her normal clothes. Not a bathing suit." George paused then and ran a hand over his chin as if he needed a break before continuing with the story. "I jumped in and got her out. She wasn't breathing. Her heart had stopped. I did CPR."

"How did you know CPR?"

"My mother and sister and I took a course at the YMCA. In case someone ever needed saving, we'd know what to do."

"Was anyone else there besides you and your brother-in-law?" Victoria asked.

"John."

"John told me he arrived at his house just before you pulled Catherine out of the water."

"That's right. That's what he said. I forgot."

"Did you see his car coming down the driveway before you saved Catherine?"

George let go of the railing. He scraped his hand through his thick hair and cleared his throat for the second time. "No, I was working. Then I was with Catherine. I didn't see him come home. He was there before the ambulance came."

"How did Catherine end up at the bottom of the pool?" Victoria asked. She caught George's gaze and held it.

"I...I don't know. She was having a difficult time with some things."

Victoria waited, but that was all George had to say about it. "And you stopped taking care of Catherine's property...when?" she asked.

George stuffed both hands into his pockets and lifted his gaze skyward, as if searching for the answer. "About a month after she almost drowned."

Children's laughter came from somewhere nearby. Victoria turned toward the sound of voices and movement.

A girl with pigtails in pink shorts and a tank top ran toward them from the side of the house. She was probably four or five years old. A slightly older girl ran after her. They spotted Victoria on the porch and stopped a few yards away from her.

"Hi," Victoria said, smiling at the girls.

They stared back with big brown eyes and dark lashes.

"Are these your daughters?" Victoria asked George.

"My nieces," he answered. "My sister's children."

"We're living here while my dad is in prison," the younger one said.

The older girl poked the younger one in the side and said, "Shush up. You don't tell people stuff like that."

"Go play in the backyard so I can have an adult conversation. Or go inside and start getting ready for bed," George told them, not unkindly and without raising his voice.

"Not bedtime. It's nowhere near bedtime," the little one said.

George watched the girls as they raced off. When they disappeared around the side of the house, he faced Victoria again.

"What prison is their father in?" She waited with anticipation for him to answer Rutherford Correctional Center, the same prison holding Dan Sullivan. That would have presented the first connection between Catherine and the man who claimed he'd killed Phoebe.

Instead, George answered, "The Federal Correctional Institution in Petersburg."

"What's your brother-in-law's name?" she asked.

"Christian Davis."

"What is he in for?"

"Counterfeiting. A one-year sentence."

"Do you think Christian knows what happened to Phoebe Watson?" Victoria asked.

"No. He's never hurt anyone," George said with the most passion she'd heard from him since their conversation began.

Victoria handed him her card. "You think of anything else I should know, please call me."

"I will," he said.

Walking down the front path to her car, Victoria turned her head several times, keeping an eye on him as he remained on his porch. His story aligned with everything she knew so far, and yet his behavior signaled there was more he wasn't telling her. Unlike John and Taylor, he hadn't asked a key question. Why had Victoria visited because of Phoebe's death, yet questioned him about Catherine's accident?

CHAPTER 23

Present Day - Victoria

The night sky was pitch black when Victoria settled into her office to continue working, and her dogs arranged themselves in the nearest beds. As she logged into her computer, the tall windows reflected the chandelier lights and her own profile seated behind her desk.

After searching the federal prisons database, she learned Christian's current location wasn't his first. He was held pretrial at the Rutherford Correctional Center. Same location as Dan Sullivan. They weren't cell mates, though they would have had opportunities to speak during meals or in the exercise yard. Only a few degrees of separation existed between Catherine Bower and Dan Sullivan now. The connection convinced Victoria she was on the right track.

She left a message for Christian's case manager, asking to set up a meeting with Christian.

Since counterfeiting is a federal offense, Victoria had access to Christian's arrest files. As she waited for the FBI database to open, she called the federal agent who arrested him. It was almost ten p.m. Victoria didn't expect him to answer, and he didn't. She left a message to call her back. She'd only read the first page of Christian's case files when the agent returned her call. His quick response surprised her.

"Thanks for getting back to me right away," Victoria said. "I really appreciate it."

"Sure. I've got the case files for Christian Davis up on my screen right now."

"So do I. Haven't read through them yet. I didn't expect you to call back so soon. I'm looking at Christian for the murder of Phoebe Watson."

"I know the case."

"What can you tell me about Christian?" Victoria asked.

"His conviction had nothing to do with murder. He got a one-year sentence on a counterfeit charge. He'd tried to buy a new vehicle with cash. The dealership notified the police. We don't know who he was laundering for. He refused to tell us where he got the money. We could only charge him for that one offense. Maybe it was his first one, since he clearly didn't know what he was doing."

"Did the prosecuting attorney subpoena his financial records?" Victoria asked.

"Yes. His only reported income came from George's Landscaping, so that business got pulled into the investigation."

"Oh, good. George Martin is also a suspect. Is that information in the file?" she asked, scrolling through the scanned pages.

"It should all be included. I'm looking at the summary report right now. The bulk of George Martin's income came from the estate of Catherine Bower. He gets paid well, that's for sure. More than I would have thought. That raised concerns. But it all checked out. He gets a weekly automated payment for taking care of the property. Same amount on a schedule right until our investigation ended."

"When did your investigation end?" she asked.

"Four months ago," he told her.

Victoria sat back against her chair and scrunched her forehead. "George was receiving income from Catherine Bower four months ago? That doesn't seem right. I was told he quit working for the family eight months ago."

"Not according to his financial records. He got automatic transfers into his account through our investigation period."

"I wonder if the family forgot to stop the automated payments," Victoria said, thinking aloud.

"Could be. Did you see the payments George received in May?"

"What are you talking about?"

"He received a large sum deposit and a hefty raise for his work last year. Considering the brother-in-law's activity, we had to check it out. The money definitely came from the same account that's been paying him for over a decade. No exchange of cash. All electronic. All legit. But it sure seemed suspicious."

"Hmm. I'm going to read through the files. I might get back to you if I have questions," Victoria said. "Thanks for calling me and for the summary."

"Sure. Anytime, Agent Heslin. Keep me posted. Actually...."

"You thought of something else?"

"Not related to the case. I have a daughter. Kylie. She's twelve, and a big fan of yours. She has a magazine picture of you on her wall from Flight 745. If I was to drop it in the inter-office mail, would you mind signing it for her?"

"Um, sure."

"Great. She's going to love it. Sign it *To Kylie*. I'll put a note in there, so you know how to spell her name and everything. Thanks again."

"Have a good night," Victoria said.

She continued to look through Christian's case files. She stopped scanning at the last large payment George had received. Six-figure large. It was the date of the payment that grabbed her attention. May 19th of last year. One week after Phoebe disappeared.

A large sum. Then payments from the Bower family, which continued after he stopped working for them.

That didn't seem like a strange coincidence. It seemed like extortion.

Was George blackmailing the Bower family?

Even if he was, proving extortion wasn't easy. It required evidence he'd threatened Catherine. George wasn't going to admit to it, and since Catherine couldn't speak on her behalf, the evidence would be hard to come by.

Yet based on Victoria's interactions with George, the blackmail possibility just didn't feel right. He didn't strike her as the type to make demands of anyone, especially someone as powerful as Catherine Bower.

Taylor's words echoed in Victoria's ears. *No one pushed my mother around. No one could intimidate her.*

Yet there was something going on with George. He could barely meet her gaze when they spoke, and there was the nervous habit of grabbing his ear. He acted guilty of something. No...guilty wasn't the right word to describe his behavior. It was more like shame.

Was he ashamed of something his brother-in-law had done? Was Christian the blackmailer? If he was, what did he have on Catherine?

Without a doubt, Catherine and her landscapers harbored secrets. There were too many red flags to ignore.

CHAPTER 24

Present Day - Victoria

The next morning, after an early run with Ned, Victoria showered and headed to the Federal Correctional Institution to meet with Christian Davis. His case manager, Maria Ruiz, hadn't returned Victoria's call yet. Without Maria's involvement, getting into the prison to see Christian might take a few days. Victoria didn't have that time.

Her boss wanted an update on her progress. It felt like every minute counted, and every hour that didn't get her closer to finding the truth was wasted. Because if Sullivan got to claim Phoebe's murder as his own and he was lying, the actual killer remained free.

Victoria knew she'd crossed the line into being annoying, still, she left another message for Maria. Persistence was often the only reason something got done. Then she called Catherine's husband, John Murdock.

"This is Special Agent Victoria Heslin. We met the other day."

"Yes. Did you get the information I sent you?"

"I did. Thank you so much. I really appreciate your cooperation."

"I trust that clears me of any wrongdoing."

"I have a few more questions regarding George Martin, your former landscaper."

"Go ahead," he answered.

"I noticed payments from the Bower estate continued going to George after he stopped working for you."

"I don't know what you're referring to. You're saying we're still paying him?"

"Yes."

"How do you know that?"

"From a related investigation."

"Another investigation? I don't know anything about it. If we're currently paying him, obviously that isn't right. I still have a lot to work out with our finances. Catherine handled everything, much of it automated. I'll let our accountant know there's an issue. How much money are we talking about? Never mind. I don't need to ask you about my expenses. I'll find out. It's clear you suspect George of something. All those questions you asked the other day. I take it he's your prime suspect in Phoebe's death. You also think he might have tried to drown Catherine. Am I right?"

"I didn't say any of those things, Mr. Murdock," Victoria answered, though she had thought them. "Would you mind if I spoke to your accountant?"

Victoria hated asking because she had a feeling the answer would be no.

"That's crossing a line into our personal, private business. I'm going to have to say no."

"If you could find an explanation for the ongoing payments to George and a onetime six-figure payout last May, I'd appreciate knowing."

John didn't respond immediately, giving Victoria the impression he knew nothing about the money. Or, on the flip side, he knew everything about it, didn't want to tell her the truth, and didn't have a good lie ready.

"I'll let you know if I think it's relevant to your investigation. I doubt it will be," he said. "And from now on, you can call our attorney."

"Send me the number, please," she said before he abruptly ended their call.

Victoria was halfway to the prison when Maria Ruiz called back.

"He won't meet with you," Maria said.

"Why not?" Victoria asked.

"He's two months into a year sentence. He'll get out early for good behavior. This is his first offense. Let the man get out in one piece," Maria said, sounding protective of Christian.

"I think he knows something about a woman's murder. I need to speak with him. In person."

"You know how the grapevine works in prison," Maria said. "If the other inmates think he's cooperating with the Feds, he's in trouble. Christian is not a violent man, and he's had a tough enough time already."

"I need to talk to him. Make the appointment for Victoria Heslin. I'll show my driver's license only. No badge. No gun. No one will know who I am."

"Are you kidding me? Everyone knows who you are. The world watched the search for Flight 745. Your name and picture were everywhere. Then after the abduction of the college girl in Mexico…everyone knows who you are."

"Maybe everyone in law enforcement, but certainly not everyone. You can call the meeting whatever you need to call it to protect him. Please. Can you get me an appointment for around noon?"

Maria sighed. "When?"

"Today."

"Today? Are you serious?" Maria scoffed.

Victoria glanced at the ETA on her center console. "Listen, Maria, I wouldn't ask if it wasn't important. Your cooperation could help us get justice for this young woman. Don't you want to be part of that?" Victoria said, forcing herself to sound cheerful though she was practically begging because her GPS had her thirty minutes from the prison.

"Fine. I'll see what I can do. He should have an attorney present."

"My case doesn't have the time for that. Just help me out here. You can sit with us."

"Yeah, thanks. As if I don't have anything else to do today. Listen, even if he agrees and I can set this up, he doesn't have to answer your questions. Oh, and keep your hands in your pockets so your fingers don't give you away."

Despite Maria's protests, the case manager came through with the appointment right before Victoria arrived at the prison.

Honoring her promise, Victoria stopped at a service station to fill her gas tank and change her clothes. In a tiny restroom stall, she exchanged a charcoal business suit for jeans, sneakers, and a gray T-shirt she kept in an overnight bag. With her blonde hair pulled into a ponytail and threaded through the back of her cap, she looked like she usually did on the weekends and anytime she wasn't working.

Inside the prison, she held her hands in loose fists to hide her missing fingers. After showing her license at the check-in area, she spotted a woman with dark-rimmed glasses and black hair staring at her.

The woman nodded to Victoria and said, "I'm Maria Ruiz."

"Hi, Maria. Thank you for setting this up. I really appreciate it."

"I have another appointment here in half an hour. So that's all the time you have," Maria said.

A prison guard called them from one end of the visitor's center. They followed him to a private room with greenish-gray concrete walls and a metal table.

The same guard came back a few minutes later with Christian. In a khaki prison uniform, he was muscular and compact, on the small side for a man. He was handsome, even with a wide, fresh scab on his temple. He had nice straight teeth, deep brown eyes, and enviable, thick lashes. His case manager's words made sense now. Christian's size and his undeniable good looks would create difficulties for him.

Maria made introductions as Christian took a seat. "Obviously there wasn't time for his attorney to be present, but Christian was willing to meet with you," Maria said.

"Thank you," Victoria said.

Christian dipped his head. "You're welcome. What can I help with?" His tone was polite. He sat with his back straight and his chest pushed forward, but Victoria could see the desperation in his eyes and the slight tremor in his hands.

"I spoke with your brother-in-law yesterday," Victoria said.

"George? And?" Christian asked, scrunching his face so that small creases formed around his eyes and forehead.

Victoria got right to the point, taking a chance, hoping to shock him into spilling his secrets. "Dan Sullivan told the police where to find Phoebe Watson's body. He knew where to find her because you told him. We're analyzing evidence from her remains and the crime scene right now. We'll find out who killed her. If it was you, now is the time to get out in front of this."

Christian blinked several times. The left side of his mouth quivered. "What are you talking about?" he asked, though it was too late to pretend he knew nothing, and Maria must have seen that, too.

Maria waved her hand through the air. "Whoa, whoa. You said he might know something that could help your case. You didn't mention you were going to accuse him of murder."

She was right. If Christian confessed, the evidence wasn't admissible. Victoria could question him about the counterfeiting because he'd already been convicted, and about anything he witnessed. If she suspected him of more, she had to tread carefully.

"Sullivan didn't kill Phoebe, I'm sure of it," Victoria continued. "Yet he knew where to find her body. Someone gave him that information. I know it was you. Maybe you didn't kill her. Maybe your brother-in-law did. Or maybe it was someone else. You know who it was."

Glaring at Victoria, Maria said, "You don't have to say anything, Christian."

He shook his head. "You got it all wrong. I'm not a killer. Neither is George. If you met him, that should be obvious to you. We don't know who killed the girl. Honest to God's truth. I swear on the life of my little girls, neither of us killed her."

Christian's conviction was persuasive.

Maria's frown deepened. "I shouldn't have agreed to this. Christian should have a lawyer present."

"If he doesn't help me now, I'm forced to work with what I've got, which could mean adding accessory to murder to your current time," Victoria said.

"Don't do that, please. I have nothing to do with anyone's murder." Christian leaned forward, pleading with her to believe him.

"You knew where to find Phoebe, didn't you? You gave the information to Sullivan. Dan Sullivan is a hulk of a guy, and you aren't. I'm thinking you traded your information for his protection."

Christian's face tightened, telling Victoria she'd guessed correctly. He opened his mouth a few times to say something but stopped.

Victoria shifted gears. "I know Catherine Bower saw something. She can't communicate now. I'm looking into what really happened to her, and I'll find out. For now, I need you to tell me what you know."

Christian bit down on his bottom lip. "I've never hurt anyone. Never."

"Then who did?"

Christian shook his head.

Victoria tried a different angle. "Why does George still get paid from Catherine Bower's estate when he doesn't work there anymore? From my perspective, it looks like you and George were blackmailing her."

There was only the slightest pause before Christian answered. "That's a retirement account. Like a 401(k). I'm sure you have one. Most companies provide them for full-time employees if they can afford them. The Smartbox family can."

Was that the truth? Victoria paid her yard crew well. That didn't include a retirement account. Though she wasn't their full-time employer.

"What about the large payment George received from Catherine Bower last May?" Victoria asked.

"Same. The payment made up for not putting together a retirement plan when he stared working for her. That's what she told him. All businesses have those. It's fair. For once, a little guy got what he deserved in a good way."

The retirement account may have been fair and deserved. It was also unusual. Was Catherine Bower really that wonderful an employer? The timing of the payments implied there was something else at play. Blackmail fit the bill. But George didn't seem to have what it took to intimidate a woman like Catherine Bower. Now that Victoria had met Christian, she didn't think he did either.

So if they weren't blackmailing *her*...was she bribing *them*? Paying them hush money to keep quiet? Suddenly, that explanation seemed more fitting.

"Why did Catherine want to keep George quiet?" Victoria asked. "What do you and George have on her?"

Christian remained tight-lipped. Perspiration glistened across his brow.

Victoria wanted to rattle him to get him to talk. So far, he hadn't offered her nearly enough. She had so many questions and she didn't know how the pieces she'd gathered fit together.

"I know you and George were there when Catherine had her so-called accident," Victoria said. "Were you tired of the control she had over you?"

Christian's eyes grew big. "George is the one who saved her life. I told you, we aren't the killing kind, and we had no reason to harm Mrs. Bower. Just the opposite. She was our boss, and an excellent one. Paid well. Almost never complained about our work. She let George take care of her place as if it was his own. George loved working there. We both did."

"Then why did he quit?" Victoria asked.

Maria's chair scraped the floor as she stood. She stared down at Christian. "You've said more than enough. Time to go." She called for the guard.

"I'm looking for the person who brutally murdered a twenty-six-year-old woman and left her buried in the woods," Victoria said. "That's what I care about right now. I'm sure you know more than you're saying. I will find out what happened to her, and who is involved."

The guard arrived and Maria said, "We're done here. You can let us out."

"Did Catherine kill Phoebe Watson?" Victoria asked.

Before the guard escorted Christian away, there was more than enough time for him to say *no*, or even, *I don't know*.

Christian didn't respond.

CHAPTER 25
One Year Ago - Catherine

Under a cloudless blue sky, with minimal traffic, Catherine stayed in the middle lane, wondering how much longer she could drive.

She was headed to Duke University to meet Dr. Tarro. Her first medical infusion couldn't come fast enough for her. The sooner she started the treatment, the stronger her chances of getting better. Or the slower she would get worse. She preferred the former. The treatment needed to work. It needed to provide some benefit.

Catherine changed the satellite channel. Familiar lyrics filled the car. *Yesterday. All my troubles seemed so far away.* The song had never resonated more with her life than now. The Beatle's song brought to mind Paul McCartney's late wife, Linda. She had succumbed to breast cancer at fifty-six, a mere three years after her diagnosis. That bit of knowledge had always bothered Catherine, serving as a stark reminder of everyone's inescapable mortality. Despite Paul's tremendous fame and resources, a desperate pursuit of the best medical treatments could not save her.

Steve Jobs was another example. The Apple cofounder and chairperson's creativity was abruptly halted by cancer in his fifties. Maybe his diagnosis came late because he neglected regular checkups. Catherine didn't know. The truth remained. Neither wealth, power, nor fame had control over premature deaths and life-altering illnesses. Catherine joined countless others who suffered despite their means. She wasn't the first and she wouldn't be the last. But she would fight back with all she had. She refused to surrender quietly into the darkness. She had too much to live for. Too many things brought her joy. Piano concerts. Vacations at the house in Thailand. Her family, especially Will, the only one who didn't actively try her patience.

With her hands firmly at ten and twelve on the wheel, she adopted a positive attitude and counted her blessings. She'd already hired a concierge physician with expertise in Alzheimer's care. The private arrangement guaranteed her immediate access when she had questions regarding her condition, and she was now headed to one of the best medical research centers in the country.

She'd commissioned people in the Alzheimer's field to find the most promising new treatment protocols. Based on those findings, she'd considered The Mayo Clinic. A team there recently had some exciting, preliminary results. Fortunately for her, Dr. Tarro's team at Duke Medical was also experiencing success. Their medical campus was closer to her house and easier to get to. The bonus benefit of treatment at Duke was getting to see Will. Later tonight, she'd take him and some of his friends out to dinner. She looked forward to their gathering.

Her phone rang. She glanced at the console, didn't recognize the number, and ignored the call. Probably a marketer. The next song was winding down with a guitar solo when her phone alerted her to a voicemail. She waited for an eighteen-wheeler to pass on her left before listening to the caller's message.

"This is Detective Brady from the Arlington Police Department looking for Catherine Bower. I'm calling about Phoebe Watson. She's missing. You're on her list of private clients and I'm calling all of them. I need to know when you saw her last, when you talked to her last, and if you know where she might have gone. Call me back at this number."

The recording ended with a click.

Catherine's jaw clenched. She snorted a bitter laugh. *You have got to be kidding me!*

Phoebe was "missing" because she was with John.

How ridiculous of Phoebe to throw away her business, to destroy her client relationships. That's what she'd done by skipping town without telling anyone, and all for a fling with John. Apparently Phoebe didn't know John's wealth belonged to Catherine and he lived off the income she provided. They didn't call it an allowance, though that's exactly what it was. Why she'd married someone so unambitious, she couldn't say. Maybe because in that respect, he was the opposite of her first husband. Yet they'd ended up having something in common. She hadn't been enough for either of them.

No. That wasn't it. She'd done nothing wrong. It was them. They were the cheaters.

Meanwhile, Phoebe was *missing*.

If the detective did his job well, he'd soon find her in Kiawah with John. Phoebe had better surface before then. If the search for her continued, if people found out…if Taylor and Will found out…that might be too much for Catherine to handle.

CHAPTER 26
One Year Ago - Catherine

Catherine was alone with her thoughts, and still an hour from Duke, when she got another call. It was Taylor. Which meant she needed something.

Catherine loved her only daughter with all her heart, but Taylor was irresponsible and only concerned with herself. Taylor's powerful sense of entitlement came from her spoiled upbringing. For that, Catherine blamed her first husband, Taylor's father. He'd doted on her. Gave her everything and expected nothing. His absence devastated Taylor, which is why Catherine had to coddle her daughter in so many ways. By the time Taylor had recovered, and Catherine tried to instill a sense of responsibility in her, it was too late. Taylor resented every attempt. More often than not, their interactions rubbed each other the wrong way.

"Hi, Taylor," Catherine said. "How are you?"

Catherine braced herself for what would come next. Maybe Taylor would surprise her and say she was just calling to check in, to make sure Catherine was okay.

"I've been better," Taylor answered. "Bud and I just broke up."

"I'm sorry, honey." Taylor went through so many boyfriends Catherine could hardly keep track. There'd been no long-term, serious relationships. She would have remembered those. Just a long string of dates that never seemed to work out. Short-term relationships that always seemed to leave Taylor feeling offended for a variety of reasons.

"I'll be okay," Taylor said. "It's not like we were serious or anything. I didn't like him much. I hated his breath."

Catherine heard a loud sigh and a smacking sound. Her daughter chewing gum.

"Also, I just got my AmEx bill, and I forgot about the Aruba trip with Lucy. I think I owe more than I have right now. Could you put more money in my account?"

"Sure," Catherine said. "I can't do it now. I'm driving. On my way to Duke. Send me an email and let me know how much you need." Taylor would add a few thousand to whatever she already owed. Catherine could handle it, although she worried her daughter would never learn to take care of herself or her own problems like Catherine had.

Taylor didn't ask the purpose of Catherine's visit. To be fair, she probably heard Duke and assumed her mother was going to visit Will.

"My fitness trainer is missing," Catherine said. She hadn't meant to share that information with anyone, and yet she'd blurted it out.

"What do you mean, missing?" Taylor asked. "Like someone abducted her?"

"I doubt that very much. All I know is a detective called me. They're calling all her clients."

"Weird," Taylor said, and that was all the time and attention she had for the topic. "Oh, something else I meant to tell you. If you still want me to get a job, I think I'd like to work for Clauss and Steinman. Do you know anyone there? Can you get me an interview with someone? I don't think it will be so bad. I told you Stacey Morgan works there, right? She's just not that smart, and she's been there a year already."

"I don't know anyone there. Why don't you ask Stacey to help you get an interview?"

"Definitely not. That would be so embarrassing. I don't want her to think I can't get a job by myself."

"Right," Catherine said, rolling her eyes skyward. Her daughter wasn't joking. As sad as that was, it was also somewhat amusing. "I'll see what I can do," Catherine said. "Send me an email about it so I don't forget."

"I'm doing it now," Taylor said. "I sent what I need for AmEx, and a note about the job."

Catherine only nodded, and Taylor couldn't see her.

"Mother? You there? Are you okay?" Taylor asked.

"As okay as I can be, honey."

"Will overheard you and John fighting. He told me what it was about. If John is cheating, you need to dump his ass. Get rid of him. You already have a lot going on without that awful crap. Kick him out. You don't need him. Dad would never have done something like that to you."

Taylor was wrong on so many counts. She held her father on a pedestal. As far as Taylor knew, he'd done nothing wrong. Catherine let her children believe the lie. It was her gift to them. In part, shielding them from the truth was also a selfish decision. She didn't want them to think of her with the pity or disdain she'd felt toward her own mother. She wished she'd never felt that way, but she had.

Catherine's father was a serial cheater. He had a long string of one-night stands and brief affairs. By the time Catherine started high school, she knew about them, and so did her mother. No way she couldn't know, the signs were so obvious. Yet she stayed with him. Catherine decided she would never let someone treat her with such blatant disregard.

Then came her mother's early-onset Alzheimer's. Unexpected. Unwelcome. Frightening and sad. In her mother's challenging final years, Catherine witnessed the unwavering devotion her father displayed as he cared for her. He orchestrated the best support system, providing an exceptional live-in nurse and a team of dedicated helpers. However, it was her father who assumed the role of the primary caregiver, feeding her when she could no longer do so herself, ensuring she felt loved and cherished. He tucked her into bed each night, whispering declarations of love until her last breath. Catherine's mother remained in the sanctuary of their home. Her husband's presence guaranteed she received excellent care.

Despite the challenges they faced as a couple, her father's dedication was a testament to his love and commitment. Catherine knew she wanted that same unwavering support, even if it came with infidelity along the way.

Catherine turned her attention back to the conversation with her daughter and said, "Actually, Taylor, I do need John."

But would he deliver what she needed when the time came?

CHAPTER 27

One Year Ago - Catherine

Just before noon, Catherine arrived at the Duke University Medical Center. She stepped out of her Mercedes onto the picturesque campus. Sprawling green lawns and stately neo-gothic buildings exuded an aura of academic excellence. She shielded her eyes from the sun's rays with a large-brimmed hat and sunglasses.

Catherine knew the way to the medical building where the presentation on the Neruvenax clinical trial would take place. Nervous excitement flowed through her veins. A potential lifeline awaited her.

Inside the grand assembly room, Catherine joined other prospective donors. She nibbled on fresh fruit, a finger sandwich, and a delicate petite-four. She couldn't help wonder who among the others shared her dual role as both a benefactor and a patient. Nothing motivated people to open their bank accounts more than a dire situation that directly affected their own well-being. Desperation could ignite remarkable acts of generosity.

The presentation was about to begin, and she positioned herself at the edge of her seat, her senses heightened. The Neruvenax clinical trial had given her hope, mingled with the ever-present potential for heartbreak.

Dr. Tarro, the director of the Neruvenax trial, introduced himself. A list of his credentials appeared on the white screen behind him: Harvard undergrad, Duke Medical School, and a list representing what seemed like two lifetimes of previous medical research.

Tarro's academic and research history disappeared, replaced by a single word—Neruvenax. The potential antidote to Catherine's kryptonite. The medicine she hoped would work magic in her brain.

Dr. Tarro turned sideways and aimed a red laser beam at the first line on the screen. He described the research for the drug, animal studies, and the recent human trials. Despite his impressive resume, Dr. Tarro droned on in a flat voice, failing to convey the excitement she wanted to experience. But if all his energy went toward his patients and delivering effective results, she didn't care that he had the personality of a houseplant.

"The intravenous therapy is for patients with mild cognitive impairment and mild dementia," he said, nearly monotone. "The FDA granted accelerated approval based on the reduction of beta-amyloid, a critical protein in Alzheimer's disease. Neruvenax works by preventing amyloid plaques from clumping."

Catherine knew the facts. She took notes, anyway, focusing as if her deep understanding would bolster the treatment's effectiveness.

A new list of information filled the screen behind Dr. Tarro. "In our first round of clinical trials, after nine months on the medicine, 62% of participants showed cognitive improvements," he said. "The side effects included vertigo, nausea, brain swelling, and micro hemorrhages. Repeated MRIs throughout the treatment protocol are necessary to detect those changes."

Catherine had an appointment with Dr. Tarro as soon as he finished his presentation. He hadn't officially accepted her into the trial yet. The protocol required people in the early stages—check. Otherwise healthy—check. Those with a close relative with the disease—check. Then there was the donation check she'd promised. They had to accept her.

Dr. Tarro turned back to the screen and adjusted the red laser beam. "Before treatment, patients meet with us for a baseline visit, which includes bloodwork, physical and cognitive testing. They're randomly assigned to either a treatment or control group. Patients assigned to the control group may receive a placebo, a medication or series of tests that have zero effect."

Catherine wrote *placebo* on her notepad followed by three question marks and an exclamation point.

When the presentation concluded, the director thanked everyone for coming. As the others gathered their belongings and rose, he made eye contact with Catherine. He joined her at the end of an aisle, and they left the room together.

"Can I get the bloodwork and other tests completed today?" she asked as they walked through an archway connecting one building to another. "I'm eager to get started as soon as possible."

"Yes," he answered. "When we get to my office, I need to have another look at your chart and ask you a few more questions."

They chatted, though Catherine did most of the talking, as they entered the next building, went up a flight of stairs, and entered his office. She told the doctor about Will, how he was finishing up his last year as an undergraduate, and how the location of the clinical trial worked out well for her. Now she'd have an excuse to see her son more.

Dr. Tarro was a terrible conversationalist. Rather than walk in silence beside him, Catherine persisted.

"You've made finding a cure for Alzheimer's your life's work. Why did you choose it as your subject of study? Did you have a family member with it? Is that what got you motivated to find a cure?"

Dr. Tarro merely nodded. They'd reached his office. Inside, he took a seat behind his desk and got busy on his computer. Catherine sat across from him, her hands twisting in her lap.

"I have the tests and diagnosis your doctors sent over," he said. "It seems you're in the very early stages of your disease."

"Yes, if it weren't for my medical history, my mother's experience, I might not have understood what was happening. I would have chalked things up to hormonal changes, and I wouldn't have a diagnosis yet."

"Are you struggling with depth perception or having any vision issue?" he asked.

"Yes. I'd say I've experienced some issues."

"Trouble recognizing faces?"

"No."

"Difficulty coming up with specific words?"

"A few times."

"Misplacing items?"

She hesitated. "No."

"Are you forgetting things? Losing minutes or hours of your short-term memory?"

"No," she said.

"Changes in behavior or personality?"

"No," she said, cringing inside as she saw herself yelling at John and hurling her wineglass at the living room wall.

"Not that you're aware of," he said. The doctor tapped his keyboard while his eyes moved from left to right and back again.

To stay calm, Catherine tapped out Frederic Chopin's Ballade No. 4 in F minor on her thighs. She played it from beginning to end as Dr. Tarro stared at his screen. "Any other information you need from me?" she finally asked.

"I'm reviewing the information you sent us. Everything you're currently taking. It's a long list."

It was. Herbal remedies, vitamins, and other supplements known to promote cognitive health. Vitamin E. Omega-3 fatty acids. Ginkgo. Turmeric.

"There's little evidence to support any of these things as effective treatments," he said, without looking at her. "Supplements can interact with the medicine from our trial. We'd like you to stop taking everything else."

"Oh," she said, thinking about the dozens of bottles and canisters now stocked in her pantry.

"And you haven't listed any alcohol or recreational drug use. Is that correct?"

"Only the occasional glass of wine," she answered, planning to cut back to give the treatment its best chance of working with no interference. "So, have you determined if I'm a fit for the trial?"

"Yes, you are," he said, offering a smile. "I apologize for not making that clear already."

She felt a giant release of tension. "That's wonderful. Do you really think it will help me?"

"The effects might be modest. There's really no way to know if your symptoms would be more severe without it. The benefits for memory aren't clear yet."

His response seemed miles away from the *yes* she so desperately needed to hear. Did the doctor believe in the treatment or not? It didn't seem like it. Not yet. Yet the research had convinced her the protocol was one of her best bets.

"I will get the actual drug, correct? Not the placebo," she said.

Dr. Tarro pivoted in his seat to face her. He tipped his head and stared at Catherine.

She knew it wasn't fair to expect to receive the medicine when no one else could be sure. But too bad. Nothing about life was fair, and everyone who didn't already know that had a rude awakening ahead.

Catherine batted her eyes, and though her voice dripped with charm, her intent was clear. "How many of your other patients are so generously funding your study?"

The doctor met her gaze. After a few seconds, he nodded.

"Good. I'm glad we have an understanding. I'd like to start as soon as possible. With the actual, *real medicine*," she added to make sure they were clear on that.

"You can start Monday," he said, with no trace of a smile. "Does that day work for you?"

"Yes," she answered.

Finally, she believed something in her life was about to take a turn for the better.

CHAPTER 28

Present Day - Deja

Will hadn't missed making a single video call to his mother since arriving in Europe. Deja could count on him. She took extra care with Catherine's hair and makeup, so she looked her best.

Deja checked the time. Five minutes until three. After wheeling Catherine out of the bathroom, Deja ducked back in to check her own reflection. She didn't want anyone to see her smoothing her hair down or applying a layer of lip gloss. She didn't usually do those things at work, and now she was doing them every day, right before Will's scheduled call.

Deja looked forward to three o'clock with a flutter of excitement inside her. Will radiated positive energy and an adventurous spirit. He shared entertaining stories about the sights he saw, his search for recommended restaurants and pubs, and his chats with random people. Will expertly managed one-sided conversations with his mother, never allowing awkward pauses. He acted like a television host narrating an improvised show called *Will's Travel Adventures*. Often he directed his questions to Deja, sparking a discussion between them.

If a day went by where Will got too busy and didn't have time to call, Catherine wouldn't be the only disappointed one.

Deja had the iPad ready when the video call came through just a few minutes after three.

"Hey, Mom. Hey, Deja," Will said.

"Hello," Deja answered as she propped the iPad on the desk in front of Catherine, then took a few steps back, out of the camera's view. Will's face filled the screen. He wore a gray cap and had a few days' growth of scruffy stubble.

"It's beautiful. Not a rain cloud in sight," he said. "Thought you might like to see London with me today."

He flipped his phone camera around and moved it for a panoramic view of a city street.

A sense of haunting familiarity enveloped Deja as she took in the historic buildings and storefronts flanking the road. This was the city where her mother's tragic death occurred.

Will flipped the camera view, switching it from the city streets to his smiling face. "What do you think?" he asked.

A sob caught in Deja's throat as terrible memories assaulted her. Her face contorted as she fought to maintain composure.

"Excuse me," she said, quickly backing away from the iPad. She had to choke back another sob and press her lips together. She missed her mother so much.

Deja hurried into the bathroom and closed the door most of the way. She needed to rid her mind of the terrible memories. On the brink of losing it, she filled the sink with soapy water. After gathering Catherine's makeup brushes, Deja began cleaning them in the same manner she'd watched her mother do years ago.

When Deja finished laying the brushes on a hand towel, she was in control of her emotions again. She'd pushed her earlier pain back to its usual state, a chronic sense of vague melancholy. In the main room, Will was still narrating a play-by-play of everything happening around him. He walked on a bustling street packed with pedestrians, cars, and a double-decker bus.

Part of Deja's face dipped into the camera's view as she moved to Catherine's side.

"Hey. Where did you go?" Will asked.

"I had to take care of a few things in the other room."

"What's the matter? Is everything okay there?"

"Just some painful memories," she answered.

"Of what? If you don't mind me asking."

Deja sighed. "It's a long, sad story," she said, surprised she'd even shared that much.

"Tell us. We've got time. I know my mother would want to hear what's bothering you. Unless you've already told her. I guess I don't know what you talk about when you're with her."

"I do the same things as you." Deja said. "I talk about what we're doing. What I'm thinking about while we're doing it. What we're going to do next."

"And what were you thinking about that made you sad?"

Deja's heart clenched as she stood behind Catherine's wheelchair, caressing her shoulders. A brief internal debate whirled within her. She worked for Catherine and shouldn't be going on about her personal life, especially her grief-laden history. It wasn't appropriate. But something compelled her to share. With a deep breath, she began recounting the day that forever changed her life.

Vivid details resurfaced from Deja's consciousness. The vibrant pink cursive sign of the gift store they had just left, the striped stick of candy in her hand, and the bag containing a present for their grandmother—all insignificant elements that now held immense weight. The present never made it home, lost forever in the unforgiving turn of events.

Deja's voice trembled as she painted a picture of their innocent journey.

Crossing the street ahead of her mother.

A car speeding around the corner, too fast for a pedestrian area.

Her father's screams from the other side of the road.

Deja remained frozen, fixated on the cherry red sports car. Through the windshield, she locked eyes with the driver. His drooping gaze met hers.

Then, a shocking jolt—an act of selfless sacrifice as her mother shoved her forward.

Deja winced, remembering the thunderous thud as the car collided with her mother, propelling her into the air. She landed on the sidewalk, arms and legs flung open, unmoving, drawing her final breath. That image, more than any other, haunted Deja's nightmares to this day.

"I'm so sorry," Will said.

Deja's eyes met his. "It's okay," she whispered, though her voice revealed a different truth. "There were no consequences for the person who took her from us. He never stopped. Three different bystanders captured his license plate. Later, we found out he was a foreign diplomat with immunity. Probably drunk. Nothing happened to him. No justice."

"I'm so sorry," he said again. "Why do terrible things happen to good people?"

Will's words resonated with her. Will and Deja shared the experience of loss. They were connected.

Deja found herself unable to answer. Instinctively, she wrapped her arms around Catherine's shoulders.

"Hey, Deja," Will whispered. "Look at my mom."

Deja let go of Catherine and stepped aside at Will's request.

Tears streaked down Catherine's cheeks.

Catherine, though hindered by tragedy, was still here. She was alive. Maybe she couldn't articulate or communicate, but she could share in the experiences and emotions of those around her.

Deja met Will's gaze again and an unspoken understanding passed between them.

CHAPTER 29
One Year Ago - Catherine

A few hours after meeting with Dr. Tarro, Catherine was exactly where she wanted to be—an opulent five-star restaurant near campus. Seated around her were Will and four of his closest college friends, including Nick, who shared an off-campus apartment with Will. The five of them possessed the bright glow of youth, strength, and energy.

Will had friends who were girls. At least Catherine thought he did. She couldn't think of any reason why he wouldn't. He just hadn't had a serious girlfriend in years. His studies took up too much of his time. Catherine hoped he'd meet someone special in law school. Everyone should have someone they trusted and could depend on. No one should go through life all alone.

Unless they wanted to.

If she'd discovered John's cheating before her diagnosis, she would have ended their relationship and embraced a solitary life. She'd have no regrets, aside from marrying him.

Catherine inhaled deeply. She needed to stop thinking about John and fully enjoy this moment with her son and his friends. To start off, she ordered several bottles of the restaurant's finest wine for the table.

"Order the best cuts of steak on the menu," she told the young men. "And you—" she said to Nick, who was vegan, "—tell them to fix something fantastic and special for you."

"Appreciate your generosity," Nick said, sounding very sincere.

A chorus of gratitude came from around the table.

Catherine didn't know if Will had told them the primary purpose of her visit, or about her condition, and that was fine. She wasn't going to bring it up. Instead, she asked them about their plans for the next year. The conversations included talk of financial positions in New York and Charlotte, and a graduate program in physics. Nick, like Will, was waiting to hear from law schools. They were fine young men. Barring unforeseen tragedies, they would have wonderful lives. Catherine enjoyed getting caught up in their plans. Listening to them provided a needed distraction from her troubles.

She sipped her wine, feeling buzzed by the alcohol and the positive energy around her. Catherine wanted to cherish this moment. She hoped she'd remember it two years from now. Or even a few months down the road.

"Anything new or exciting happening at home?" Will asked when Catherine got quiet, unable to think of anything more to say.

"Hmm," she said. "I have to find a new fitness trainer. Anyone you want to recommend? Did you go to school with anyone who does private training?"

"Nope. Sorry. I know students who offer training here. Not at home," Will said. "What happened to your last trainer? I thought you liked her."

"I heard she was hot," Nick said.

Catherine mustered a half smile. "We've parted ways," she said, wondering why she'd brought up the topic when she was having a good time. "How about dessert?" she asked, noticing Will and his friends had polished off everything on their plates.

Before they ordered anything else, their server approached the table. He carried a cupcake with sprinkles and a candle glowing in the center and placed it in front of Catherine.

"What's this?" she asked. Her forty-ninth birthday was still weeks away.

"Just celebrating you, Mom. Or you can call it an early birthday if you like. You've always been in my corner, and I'm in yours. All the way. Rooting for you. Supporting you. There is nothing you can't pull off."

Each of Will's friends got up from their seats to give her a hug. Will was last. He hugged her tightly and held on. "Love you, Mom, and I'm so proud of you. You've got this, and we've got you."

Catherine smiled. Tears formed in her eyes.

No matter what happened next, she needed to remember how lucky she was because of Will.

After saying goodbye to her son and his friends, Catherine checked into a nearby hotel. She left her small suitcase just inside the door and kicked off her shoes. With her journal, she sat cross-legged behind the desk and recorded details from the dinner conversation. When finished, she texted Will and asked him to forward his friends' addresses. She planned to send a care package and a graduation gift to each one. Already, she was rooting for their successes.

Catherine was shopping on a website that delivered care packages when John finally called. She hesitated before answering. She was still on a high from the dinner. Speaking with John would change her mood. Just seeing his name on her phone made the muscles in her face tighten, but she couldn't avoid him for too long. She blew out a puff of breath and pressed the green *accept* button on her phone.

"How did it go today? With the medical study?" John asked.

"It went well. I'm in."

"That's great. Sorry I couldn't be there with you."

"It's fine. I took Will and his friends out to dinner. That was worth the trip alone, and now I'm in the Washington Duke Inn."

"Oh, good. Relax and enjoy it."

"I'll stay here when I return for my treatments. The infusion process takes about three hours. Every other week. I'll get my first one on Monday."

"I'll go with you. We can stay there together."

"Wonderful," she said, dryly. "By the way, I received a call from a detective this morning. He's looking for Phoebe. I told you she didn't show up yesterday. Now it seems she's disappeared." There, she'd said it. She couldn't wait to hear how he would respond.

"That's strange. So, maybe you didn't fire her after all. What do they think happened to her?"

"I don't know what they think. They didn't tell me. What do you imagine happened to her?" Catherine tried not to have an edge to her voice. She didn't do a good job suppressing it.

John picked up on her sarcasm and sighed. "It's not something I'm going to think about. I don't know where your trainer is, Catherine."

Sure you don't, she thought, but held her tongue and said nothing further. She sat up straighter and lifted her chin, adopting the sense of self-control required to stick to her plan. She would get through the awful business of pretending her husband wasn't cheating on her and she would do it with grace and maturity. However, if Phoebe didn't get back to Virginia and back to work soon, if the detectives kept searching, the affair might blow up in all their faces.

Another call came in, the number scrolling across the top of Catherine's phone screen. Not recognizing the number, she ignored it.

"I better go," John said. "Early start tomorrow. I love you."

"I love you, too," she said, though she wasn't so sure anymore. She wanted to love him. He wasn't making it easy. "Have fun," she said, feigning sincerity. She had taken acting classes in high school and done a few shows in college. If she put her mind to it, she could pretend with the best of t hem.

A new notification popped up. The previous caller had left a voice mail. Catherine pressed play.

"This is Detective Brady calling for Catherine Bower again. I need to talk to you. You left a phone message for Phoebe Watson on Wednesday morning. I'd like to know what it was about. I also have some questions about your landscaper, George Martin. He was one of the last people to speak with Phoebe before she left work. Before she was last seen."

Catherine couldn't imagine her quiet gardener and her outgoing fitness trainer had anything in common. George was at least ten years older than Phoebe, which, now that Catherine thought about it, was less of an age difference than between Phoebe and John.

Perhaps Phoebe was a lot friendlier with everyone than Catherine realized.

She hovered her finger over the delete button for an instant, then changed her mind and left the detective's message on her phone.

CHAPTER 30

Present Day - Deja

Due to an accident, traffic wasn't moving. Inside her Honda, Deja tapped her gray polished nails against the center of her steering wheel. She'd never worn them super long, and now they were short. She needed to keep them that way so she wouldn't poke Catherine in the eye or any other area.

Deja checked her phone for an alternate route. They were all jammed. The coffee she'd brewed at home had long ago cooled to an annoying, barely warm temperature, yet she drank the last drops. Upon arriving at work, she always brushed her teeth, ensuring she didn't waft coffee breath into Catherine's face. Today she'd have to skip that task and rush straight to Catherine's room.

When she finally arrived at Atrium Gardens, she scanned her badge and signed in at the registration computer.

"Deja. Hey."

She turned to find Jasmine behind her.

"Stop in the office before you go to Catherine's room. The director wants to see you," Jasmine said.

Deja had only spoken with the facility's director a few times. Technically, Deja worked for the agency, not Atrium Gardens, but the director was ultimately responsible for every resident's care.

"Do you know why she wants to see me?" Deja asked.

"No," Jasmine answered. "But there's someone in there with her. Someone who looks important."

Deja walked at a brisk pace toward the office. She worried she was in trouble for arriving fifteen minutes past her usual time. The first time she'd ever been late.

The director stood next to her desk. Nearby, a middle-aged woman in a power suit watched Deja enter the office.

"Deja, we've been waiting for you," the director said. No smile.

Power-suit woman didn't waste a second before stepping forward. "I'm Larissa Carmichael. An attorney for the Bower estate. The Bower family is currently in the middle of a crime investigation because of your call to the police."

"Oh. I'm sorry, I—"

Larissa didn't let her finish. "What's done is done. Catherine's family wishes for you to continue in your position. We just can't allow anything like this to happen again. From now on, if you have a concern related to Mrs. Bower or her family, you are to call the agency first. You are not to offer up information to anyone. If a representative from the police department, the FBI, or anywhere else asks you questions related to the Bower family and their personal lives, you are to say no comment."

Deja nodded.

"We're clear?"

"Yes," Deja said.

"You agreed to and signed confidentiality agreements when you accepted your position," Larissa continued. "Any further breach of your contract will result in termination and legal proceedings against you."

"Oh," Deja said, her cheeks burning.

"You are responsible for the direct personal care of Catherine Bower. Nothing else. Understood?"

"Yes," Deja said.

Without lowering her gaze, Larissa opened a thin, silver box and held a business card out for Deja to take. "Here is my number. If anyone from law enforcement wants to talk to you, call me. Do not speak with them."

"I will," Deja answered, feeling like the attorney had just taken her down a few notches. All because she'd contacted the police. That call and her meeting with FBI Agent Heslin hadn't been worth the trouble it caused. They still hadn't found Phoebe Watson's killer.

CHAPTER 31

Present Day - Deja

At precisely three p.m., Will smiled up at Catherine and Deja from the iPad screen.

All Deja could think about was her meeting in the director's office. Someone in Catherine's family must have called their attorney. Was Will part of the decision leading up to that? Even though Deja had apparently broken her contract, she couldn't help feeling a little indignant about the reprimand.

If Will didn't mention the situation during the call, Deja wouldn't either. From here on out, she would mind her business.

"Hey, Deja," Will said. "Hey, Mom. You look as beautiful as ever. How are you doing?"

"She's doing well," Deja answered in a matter of fact, professional manner, absent the enthusiasm she'd shown for Will's recent calls.

"I'm not in London anymore. I'm on the train headed back to the Netherlands to get my stuff," Will said.

He flipped the camera around to show the crowded train before returning it to himself. He was grinning. "I have some news. Change of plans. I'm coming home in a few days. Only so many sights and so many pubs I can handle before I feel like a derelict. I need to get back to the grind before I forget what it's like to work my ass off." He laughed.

Deja couldn't stop herself from thinking he probably didn't work as hard as he thought he did. She left Catherine's side and went to fold her clean laundry while Will continued to point out the passing scenery from the train.

Over the last few calls, Deja had probably let herself get too comfortable. It happened naturally, since the calls often turned into conversations between her and Will. She started to feel as if Will was calling to talk to her. Then Deja had really let her guard down by sharing the story of her mother's passing.

From across the room, where she was putting clothes into the dresser, Deja kept an eye on Catherine.

"I'll see you as soon as I'm back," Will told his mother. "And maybe I can take Deja out to dinner for doing such a great job of taking care of you. If she'll go with me. What would you think of that?"

He must have wanted Deja to hear. What did taking her to dinner mean, exactly? A friendly thank-you dinner? If not for the incident this morning, Deja would have been excited. Instead, Larissa Carmichael's words came back to her.

Then Deja registered the unhappy expression on Catherine's face. Merely a coincidence, unless Catherine understood Will had just asked Deja out on a date. Did she think Deja wasn't good enough for her son?

Don't be ridiculous, Deja told herself. Catherine probably isn't feeling well.

"Deja, are you there?" Will asked. "Did you hear me?"

She crossed the room and leaned over Catherine's shoulder until she appeared in the video frame. "I heard you."

"And what do you think? Are you up for having dinner with me? The least I can do is treat you to a nice evening out, since you've been subjected to all my travel stories. Or is that just adding insult to injury?"

"I appreciate the offer, Will. Really, I do. But dinner isn't necessary. I enjoy taking care of your mother, and it's my job."

"And I appreciate your attitude," he said. "But you still didn't answer. If it wouldn't kill you to go out somewhere nice for dinner with me, I'd really like you to say yes."

Deja hesitated before saying, "I don't know if it's appropriate."

Will peered at her from the iPad screen and his voice dropped. "If you don't want to go, that's one thing, and I promise I won't ask again. However, the appropriateness of the matter is not anyone else's concern."

Deja stayed silent for a few seconds. She should say no. Yet there was that flutter inside her again. She wanted to go. "The thing is…your family attorney came by here this morning. She sort of reminded me of my place."

"Your place?" Will sounded incredulous. "What did she say, exactly? You know what, don't tell me. I'll have a word with her. Is that the only thing making you uncomfortable?"

She nodded.

"And if I were to resolve that area of uncertainty for you and then ask you again, do you think you might say yes?"

"I don't know, Will."

He looked so earnest, as if he was waiting for her to change her mind.

"Maybe," she said.

"Okay, then. I'll get back to you." His smile had returned. "What do you think, Mom?" He laughed. "Can't believe I have to ask you out with my mother listening."

When the call ended, Deja couldn't stop thinking about it. She hadn't dated in months. Will was different. It wasn't because of his wealth, which made her uneasy, and her father would surely distrust him because of it. Will stood apart from other guys his age because of his exceptional care for his mother. Checking in on her every day now that he wasn't in school. Sharing his life. Maintaining a cheerful attitude and acting like Catherine's circumstances were normal, when in fact, the situation was incredibly sad and unfair.

Deja hoped Will would ask her out again and convince her to say yes.

CHAPTER 32

One Year Ago - Catherine

With John still on his golf trip, Catherine faced an empty house on Saturday. After her dinner with Will and his friends, she'd considered staying an extra day in Durham, maybe taking him out for lunch and shopping. He probably needed some new clothes. She decided against it because he was busy with schoolwork and an event at his friend's fraternity. Since she planned to see him again on Monday after her first infusion treatment, she didn't want to wear out her welcome. Not that Will had ever made her feel like an imposition, but she respected that he was a college student with a lot going on.

Sunlight streamed through the windows as Catherine walked through her living room wearing a thick white robe over her black bathing suit. It was a beautiful day. She would make the most of it.

George had parked his truck in the driveway. It was not unusual for him to work on a Saturday.

Catherine's thoughts flew from George to Phoebe. The detective had mentioned a connection between them. He hadn't mentioned *John* and Phoebe in his message. He'd asked about *George* and Phoebe. Ever since then, that mention had piqued Catherine's curiosity. Could George have anything to do with Phoebe's supposed disappearance? Catherine wondered and also hoped so. Phoebe and George together presented a better situation than Phoebe and John.

After her swim, Catherine planned to find George. She'd ask if there was anything she should know about her property. She'd ask about his family's wellbeing. He had moved his mother into his house a few years ago, after his father died. Catherine hadn't heard much about the situation since. Then, after their small talk, maybe she'd casually ask him about his relationship with Phoebe.

George hadn't started up any of his machines yet, and the only noise in the backyard came from the lively conversations of birds in the treetops. Catherine headed across the patio to the pool house. The building used to bustle with activity, hum with the chatter and laughter of teenagers when Taylor and Will lived at home. Their friends slept over often. They'd wake up around noon and lounge poolside. Catherine used to order platters of sandwiches, fresh fruit, and cookies and set them in the pool house kitchen. Music played late into the night. No worries about disturbing neighbors when the nearest were acres away.

No one except Catherine used the pool these days. That's why she stood inside the French doors, staring ahead at the interior and feeling completely puzzled. The place was a mess. Not ransacked with overturned furniture or broken objects. Nothing that extreme. It just wasn't perfect as usual.

In one of the guest rooms, the duvet hung off the side of the bed, touching the marble-tiled floor. The pillows were askew. One lay on the floor nearby.

Had George come in and taken a nap since the cleaning crew's last visit? No, he wouldn't. Christian, however, *would* do something like that. In her opinion, no one should nap at their place of work, and he should have left the bed the way he found it.

She begrudgingly straightened the bed. She didn't want to look at it in its present state. Taylor and John left messes nearly everywhere they went. But they were family.

On her way into the adjacent bathroom, something in the corner of her eye drew her gaze to the beige stone tiles on the floor. She stopped in her tracks and peered down at smudges of dirt. Not just dirt, dirty footprints. The big toe and the heel were clearly visible. Someone had walked through the guesthouse with filthy feet. That was too much! It wasn't from a houseguest or a family member, which would be an entirely different situation. Irritating maybe, not outrageous.

Just as Catherine's face was twisting with disapproval, vague memories came back to her. She felt a sudden coldness spread over her skin.

George hadn't caused the disorder. Neither had Christian. It was her. She had slept in the guest house just a few nights ago. She'd passed out, hadn't she? Woken with dirty feet and rinsed them in the shower. She hadn't remembered how her feet got dirty then. She still didn't know.

Another chill snaked through her body. This was how it started. Bits of forgetfulness mired in confusion, and nothing she could do about it. For a long moment, she stood in the bathroom's corner, hugging her body, staring at her reflection in the mirror without seeing.

The loud whoosh of a machine pulled her back to the present. That would be George, blowing bits of debris from the driveway or garden paths.

Catherine returned to the bed she'd straightened. She pulled the covers off. Dirt coated the sheets beneath. She stripped the bedding and left everything in a pile with the soiled bathroom linens. Then she stood by the door, trying to remember why she'd come into the guest house in the first place. She stood there for at least a minute, shaking her head, before it came to her. With a loud huff of breath, she grabbed one of the large navy and white striped towels from the closet stack.

More than ever, she needed a good hard swim.

After forty minutes of laps, she stretched out on one of the chaise lounges. The exercise had done its job, and she felt good. At peace even. Her mind and body had relaxed. She'd feel even better with a glass of wine by her side. But it wasn't even ten a.m. She needed to wait.

The sun's rays massaged her skin. She admired the vines with large white flowers spilling over a stone wall and the white petunias bursting from large pots surrounding the pool. She closed her eyes and tipped her face up to the sky.

Catherine was just dozing off when George ambled past, rolling a wheelbarrow full of tools. Without stopping, he let go of one handle and pointed beyond the pool house, telling her, "I'm going to edge the garden paths."

She nodded and said, "Wonderful."

George mostly decided what he would do and when he would do it. It took a lot of work to keep up her property. He took pride in his efforts, and Catherine appreciated that.

Gardening wasn't in Catherine's blood. The previous owners, a retired couple, were exceptional, certified gardeners. They'd created something very special on the property. A true labor of love. Stepping-stone paths wove through lush potted plants and vibrant flowers. Engraved signs on little silver posts labeled plants and bushes. Catherine had destroyed some of the former owners' legacy when she built the guest house. On the other side of the building, now blocked from view, the gardens flourished. At least Catherine assumed they did.

She couldn't say when she last went back there to appreciate the gardens and George's efforts. It was long overdue that she have a look at the pollinator garden of his. A cultivated natural area with native plants to attract bees, birds, and butterflies, is what he'd told her.

Heading along a path by the pool house, George bent down and plucked something from the bushes. A weed, probably. No. Not a weed. When he straightened, he held a wine bottle. He set it in his wheelbarrow, bent down again, and retrieved two empty mini bottles.

Catherine's mouth parted in horror. She couldn't explain how those bottles ended up there, just like she couldn't explain how she ended up in the guest room bed with dirty feet. Yet a stab of shame told her she was responsible. George kept her property looking beautiful, and her most recent contribution was to toss empty liquor bottles into the bushes. That was her prerogative as the owner, yet it didn't make her proud.

George continued on. Catherine slid her feet into her sandals, wrapped her towel around her body, and followed him.

Wisteria vines arched over iron trellises. She'd forgotten how beautiful the plantings were in late spring and early summer. The lush leaves. The purple heavy-hanging flowers.

She spotted George in a corner of the yard by the well. With his back to her, he cut a hard and muscular profile. He held a shovel in one hand. The other gripped the top of the well. The house had city water, so it wasn't a real well. Constructed of stone and cedar siding with a pitched roof, the structure was merely decorative. A part of the former owners' garden vision, as far as Catherine knew. Actually, she didn't know. Like everything else back there, she didn't have a clue about it. She'd never asked George or lifted the lid to look inside. It wasn't her concern. She trusted if there was an issue with anything on her property, George would let her know, though more likely, he would simply fix it.

This was as good a time as any to ask him a few questions.

"Hey," Catherine said as she headed in George's direction.

His free hand flew to his chest as he spun around. His mouth hung open in surprise.

"Sorry, didn't mean to startle you," she said, smiling. "I came back here to check things out. What are you doing?"

"Uh. I'm sealing this top in place. It wasn't completely closed. Rain would have gotten inside."

"Then I guess it's not an actual well with water in it, is it? What's down there?"

George shrugged, nudged the rim of his hat, and said, "It's a cement hole. Airtight when the lid is in place. The previous owners used it to store bags of birdseed for the feeders."

"Do you keep anything in there now?" Catherine asked.

George removed a handkerchief from his pocket and wiped his forehead with it. "There's nothing in there. I cleaned it out years ago."

"I'd like to see," Catherine said, her eyes on the well. Though the structure was over a decade old, it showed no signs of moss or mildew. As with everything else outside, George maintained it.

"There's really nothing worth seeing. Like I said, it's just a cement hole," George told her, still standing in front of it.

Catherine marched the last few steps to the well. George finally moved over.

She grasped the metal handle with both hands and dragged it to one side. It was heavier than she expected. With her hands on the edge, she peered in.

What the—?

Her breath caught in her throat.

It can't be....

She jerked back and let out a blood-curdling scream.

CHAPTER 33

One Year Ago - Catherine

Catherine jumped away from the well. Her towel fell off her body. One of the plant labels scraped her ankle, tearing the skin as she stumbled backward into the bushes.

She tried to process what she'd seen.

Hair. Long red hair. Presumably attached to a body, though she wasn't sure. A striped towel from the pool house covered everything below the head.

Catherine stood transfixed, one foot still in the middle of a prickly bush. She stared at George, and the moment stretched on as he stared back. Neither moved.

Catherine had left her phone by the pool. She glanced in that direction for a split second, just long enough to judge the distance. Could she make it to her phone? Did she have time to race inside, lock the doors, and call for help? Was she faster than him?

George started moving toward her, eyeing her strangely. He still carried the shovel.

Catherine held out her arms. With more courage than she felt, she snapped, "Don't come near me."

George cocked his head and furrowed his brow. "What did you see?"

Catherine didn't answer.

"Did snakes get in there?" he asked.

Catherine slowly shook her head, not taking her eyes off George. Then she started to question what she'd seen. Maybe it was something that only looked like red hair—string or rope bunched together. Maybe it *was* a swirling mass of thin baby snakes. Except what she saw wasn't moving. It was deathly still.

Finally, George turned away from Catherine. She felt her breath come back as he went to the well. He stood a few feet from the structure and stretched forward to see into the opening.

This was her chance to make a run for it. She flicked off one sandal and was about to drop the other so she could sprint across the yard. Before she did, George gasped. His eyes grew wide. Slowly, he backed away. "Was that...is that Phoebe? Your trainer?"

When Catherine still didn't answer, he looked her straight in the eyes. With a shaking voice, he asked, "What happened?"

"I don't know! How would I know? I haven't come back here in months. Maybe years. You were doing something at the well when I came around the house."

She instantly regretted accusing him. He still held the shovel. It would only take a second for him to close the short distance separating them. She'd gotten defensive because he implied *she* knew something about the awful find. As if she might somehow be responsible.

George shook his head, blinking rapidly. "The cover wasn't all the way on. Someone moved it."

George seemed more shocked than Catherine about the discovery. Only for those reasons had she not already taken her chances and raced toward the house. Still, she kept her distance. Standing in the bushes wearing only her bathing suit, near Phoebe's lifeless body and with George holding a shovel, Catherine felt exceptionally vulnerable. She shivered, though it wasn't cold. Then something occurred to her.

"Any chance she's still alive?" Catherine asked.

George's face had contorted into a permanent wince. "She's dead. It's been a few days."

"How do you know?" Catherine asked, still wary of him. He looked completely shocked. Though his reaction might result from getting caught, rather than from discovering a dead body.

"The smell. I can tell from the smell," he said. George rocked forward and back on his heels. He didn't seem to know what to do with himself.

"Why did the police question you?" Catherine asked, narrowing her eyes.

George answered without hesitation. The words practically spilled from his mouth in an agitated torrent. "I was one of the last people to see her. I took her class at the gym. Didn't even know she worked there. I said hello when it was over. Then I left. That's all. I don't know what happened to her. The police suspected me. Now that we found her, they'll think I did this."

If the police suspected George before, they had plenty more reasons to suspect him now. Catherine had caught him back here with his hands on the cover of the well, in an area of the property where only he and Christian ever went.

But witnessing George's panic and anguish, Catherine believed him. She knew George. She didn't think he had it in him to fool anyone. Especially not her. But if George didn't put Phoebe in the well, who did?

A likely explanation surfaced like the tip of an iceberg, leaving Catherine momentarily paralyzed with dread. It was so obvious. John was having an affair with Phoebe. Now Phoebe was dead in the backyard. Something must have happened. Had Phoebe threatened to reveal their affair? Did they get into a violent argument? Or was it innocent? Maybe Phoebe had a terrible accident that John was too afraid to report.

Or maybe Catherine was mistaken about who was inside the well. A towel covered most of the corpse, including the face. Maybe the dead person wasn't Phoebe after all. Phoebe wasn't the only woman in Virginia with red hair. Catherine had to take another look.

She stepped up to the well, opposite George. With the well's diameter separating them, she peered into the cement interior again. She had to cover her nose while her eyes took in every visible detail. Hair length and color. Shape of the head. A slim hand protruding from under the towel. Short fingernails with clear polish. All of it was unmistakably Phoebe. She wasn't missing any longer. She was inside the fake well, and she was definitely dead.

While Catherine struggled to process her shock, George dug into his back pants pocket, pulled out his phone, and tapped the screen.

"Who are you calling?" Catherine snapped.

"The police," he answered, though his fingers grew still, no longer moving across his screen. He lowered his phone. "What do I do if they don't believe me?"

At that moment, Catherine should have said, *That's something we'll have to worry about later. We need to call the police now.*

Everyone except the guilty would agree—calling 9-1-1 is what you do after finding a dead body. But Catherine wasn't ready. That call could permanently alter her future. First, she needed to understand what had happened.

She held up a hand. "Wait. Don't call anyone yet. I need to think about this." She scooped her towel from the ground, draped it around her body, and tucked the corner in at her hip. "*We* need to think about this. Because you're absolutely right, George. If you're already on their radar…and now this…they probably won't believe you."

CHAPTER 34

Present Day - Deja

The MRI machine, a metallic beast, dominated the room. Clad in a pale hospital gown, Catherine lay on the narrow table, her head inside the tunnel.

Separated from Catherine by a thick pane of glass, Deja stood in the observation room. Her eyes never wavered from Catherine's figure. As Catherine's limbs twitched spasmodically, Deja felt a surge of empathy. The machine made loud and unsettling sounds. For anyone even slightly claustrophobic, the tunnel was terrifying. More so if the person inside didn't really understand what was happening. Deja wished she could stay in the room with Catherine, hold her hand, and offer her some reassurance.

A rustling sound behind Deja made her turn around.

John Murdock approached the glass. He wore a polo shirt with a Quail View Country Club insignia, shorts, and a belt.

He flashed a smile at Deja. "How is it going?" he asked. "Did they just get started?"

"She's only been in the machine for a few minutes," Deja said. She didn't know Catherine's husband planned to join them for the doctor's visit. Deja hadn't seen John since the birthday party. As far as she knew, neither had Catherine. He hadn't come to visit.

"I want to hear firsthand what the doctor has to say," John said.

Deja turned to peer through the barrier again and keep watch over Catherine.

There was plenty of room at the window. The glass spanned several yards. Yet John stood so close his arm brushed Deja's side. She expected him to apologize and scoot over. He didn't. She quickly backed away, pretending to get something out of her purse.

"How long did they say the scan would take?" John asked.

"About twenty minutes, if she stays still inside the machine."

"She doesn't look still to me," John said.

He sat down on one of the waiting chairs and stared at his phone. Deja remained by the window to keep an eye on Catherine.

Thirty minutes later, the radiology technician slid the table and Catherine out of the machine and beckoned Deja inside.

"I'm her husband," John said, entering the room with Deja. "What did you see? Any changes?"

"You'll have to wait for her doctor to read the scans," the technician answered. "He's going to look at them and speak to you as soon as he can."

That was unusual. In Deja's experience with her grandmother, who hurt her back and needed an MRI, it took days for a doctor to look at test results and get back to them.

The technician helped Deja get Catherine off the table and into her wheelchair. Deja brought her into an exam room, got her dressed, and put her jewelry back on. Per the MRI instructions, Catherine's face was makeup free. Deja took a small makeup bag out of her purse and added some color to Catherine's cheeks and some liner on her eyes.

When she wheeled Catherine out to the waiting room, John moved away to the far corner of the room with his phone to his ear and spoke in a hushed whisper.

"She looks better now," he said a few minutes later, after putting his phone into his back pocket and rejoining them. He tilted his head as if he was trying to figure out what had changed.

"She's wearing a little makeup," Deja said, smiling at Catherine. "But I think she's beautiful, with or without it."

"Yes. She's always been a beauty," John said, and went back to doing things on his phone.

Deja put Catherine's earbuds in her own ears to test the volume. She pressed play on the current audiobook, listened for a few seconds, rewound a minute, then switched the earbuds to Catherine's ears.

Not much later, Catherine's doctor called them into another room and Deja removed Catherine's earbuds.

The doctor pivoted his computer monitor around to show them the images of Catherine's brain.

"What does it mean as far as changes?" John asked. He stood next to his wife and now held her hand.

Something about him touching Catherine made Deja uncomfortable. As if it were her job to protect Catherine from this man pretending to know her. Which made little sense. John was Catherine's husband. Nonetheless, the unsettling feeling persisted.

"There are minor changes from her last visit," the doctor answered. "As expected, those changes are not positive. The Alzheimer's is progressing, and the damage to her brain from lack of oxygen looks mostly the same."

"So...nothing to report, is what you're saying?" John asked.

"Only that her disease is progressing as we would expect. Have you noticed any signs of lucidity where she's communicating clearly?"

"No, not really," John answered.

"Sometimes she has moments of lucidity," Deja said. "Where she communicates with me."

John frowned at Deja as if she'd spoken out of turn. As if she was wrong. She wasn't. There had been definite moments, brief as they were.

"Can you give me an example?" the doctor asked.

There were many things. Yet Deja couldn't think of anything aside from Catherine correctly identifying Phoebe Watson from the news story.

The doctor didn't wait long before continuing. "Emotional connections and hormonal changes can trigger those incidents. They're part muscle memory, part invoked instinctual responses," he said.

"Glimpses of her personality poking through, right?" Deja asked.

"Absolutely," the doctor answered. "We can't know for sure what Catherine is experiencing, how much she hears or processes of what is happening around her. As a result of the oxygen deprivation, she's mainly in her own world, lost to us. Having said that, the brain is an incredible organ. Every so often she might break through the barriers."

"But according to the scans, there are no signs of any improvement, correct?" John asked.

The way John phrased the question, leaning forward, looking more eager than disappointed, Deja could have sworn he wanted the doctor to say no.

CHAPTER 35

One Year Ago - Catherine

George didn't look well. Leaning against Catherine's Viking stove, he took a loud, gasping breath. "How did she...Who could have..." He couldn't finish his sentences.

"You have to calm down. You're hyperventilating," Catherine told him. She sensed his weakness and struggled to contain her frustration, fighting the urge to raise her voice and shout, *Pull it together, George!*

He closed his eyes and said, "We have to report finding her."

"We will."

And they would. Just not yet. First, Catherine had to know who had killed Phoebe and left her in the well. Assuming it happened in that order.

George didn't seem to know anything about John and Phoebe's affair. It would serve his interests to mention the illicit relationship and cast suspicion away from himself. Instead, when not expressing his shock and horror at Phoebe's death, he'd declared his own innocence and worried about what the police would do with him.

Catherine poured herself a shot of whiskey and tossed it back. She offered the bottle to George. He refused. She drank another.

George moved from the stove to the window. One hand fidgeted with his earlobe, the other clutched his phone. "We better call them now. We shouldn't wait any longer," he said. He turned in her direction and settled his gaze on a random spot to her left. He hadn't made eye contact since she told him not to call the authorities.

"There's no urgency now. Phoebe is already dead," Catherine said.

She sat down and pressed her fingertips against her temples. If only George hadn't been around when she'd found the body. Now she had him to worry about, too. If she didn't take charge, things could get out of control quickly. For Phoebe, the worst had already occurred. Calling the police wouldn't bring her back. It would wreak havoc in Catherine's life. A criminal investigation. A trial. All of it centered on Catherine and her family. She didn't want to endure that. She had her health to consider. Her weekly treatments. She didn't want John to go to jail. How could he take care of her while serving time in prison? Or worse, facing a death sentence? She had to figure everything out so she could stay in control of the outcomes.

She forced herself to figure out who had been on her property over the last few days. Three people she knew of for certain. John. George. And Christian. She'd almost forgotten about him.

"Where is your brother-in-law?" she asked. "Is he here with you today?"

The second she finished asking that question, Christian walked into view outside the kitchen window. He stopped by the pool. With his hands on his waist, he looked around, probably searching for George. Another partial rotation of his neck and he plopped down on a chaise lounge.

"Would he do that to her?" Catherine whispered, though Christian couldn't possibly hear them. Not through the triple-paned windows and across the yard.

George spun around. "No. He wouldn't."

Catherine wasn't about to dismiss Christian as a suspect so quickly. She barely knew the man. Maybe Phoebe arrived early on Wednesday morning and ran into him. It was possible. Anything was possible. But if that's what happened, where was Phoebe's car?

"Christian is not a killer," George added.

Catherine hadn't thought John was either. A liar and a cheater—yes. Not a killer. And yet someone had stuffed Phoebe inside the well.

Catherine leaned toward George and kept her voice low. "When you first asked me about bringing Christian on to help you, you said you'd monitor him. I did a little research. I know why you were worried. He has a criminal record."

"For petty theft. Not for murder," George said. "I have to talk to him."

"Talk to him about what?"

"About Phoebe."

Catherine gripped the edge of the table. "You don't know if he'll tell you the truth. For now, no one else should know."

She wondered if John would tell her the truth if she asked him. He'd lied about having an affair. He would lie about murder. A profession of innocence counted for nothing if she couldn't trust him. She certainly didn't want to hear him say *yes*. She was better off not knowing. Which took her right back to Christian.

"Maybe Christian doesn't have anything to do with Phoebe's death, but do you think a jury will believe him?" Catherine asked, deciding she needed to be the voice of reason. "He already has a criminal record. He's one of the few people with access to my property. If the police question me, I'll have to say I saw him watching Phoebe the other day. While you were working, he was staring at her for a long, long time, watching her record a video. Maybe he made a pass later, and she rejected him. He got angry. Maybe he tried to rape her."

"No." George's voice shook, and so did his hands. "That didn't happen. He has a wife and children."

"That has little to do with anything. Marriage doesn't stop a man from wanting someone else. Rape is about power and control. Listen, the police will find evidence. Maybe DNA. They'll find out who did it. That person will be in jail for life. Is that what you want for your brother-in-law?"

"If he killed her...then yes," George said. "He deserves to be locked away."

Ah, there it was. *If.* The representation of doubt. A part of George, maybe a small part, but a part, nonetheless, believed Christian might have killed Phoebe.

"If they don't find evidence proving Christian did it...they'll think it was you," Catherine said. "You would go to prison and lose everything."

George sunk into a chair. He leaned his elbows on the table and dropped his head into his hands.

Catherine's gaze remained fixed on him as her thoughts raced. If they involved the police, the investigation would naturally begin with her own family. Given Phoebe's lifeless body lying in the backyard, and John's affair, both John and Catherine would look guilty.

"Stay there for a moment," Catherine said. She grabbed her journal from the bedroom and took it back to the kitchen with her. She could not afford to forget anything. Nor could she write *Found Phoebe dead in the backyard.* Instead, with a slight tremor in her hand, she scrawled, *Found a dead racoon in the well.*

The electric whirr of an edging machine came from the front of the house. Christian had resumed working.

George still gripped his phone. He hadn't made any calls. Not yet. Catherine was in charge. He was waiting for her instructions.

"Christian is going to wonder what happened to me. I have to let him know I'm in here talking to you," George said.

"Don't say a word about this," Catherine told him. "And come right back."

George went out the back door. When he was out of sight, Catherine scanned her journal. Her eyes came to rest on a note she'd written the previous day.

The detective.

He'd already called twice. He might come to the house to question her in person. It could be any minute. She couldn't delay calling him back. She had to return his call before he came looking for her. Not quite yet though. Not until she had some info on the status of their investigation.

She scrolled through her phone. It didn't take long to come across Phoebe's name. Catherine clicked a news link updated only minutes ago. She waited for the story to open. Her heart was already racing. She braced herself to see an image of her house. Or a picture of John. Something that meant it was all over for them. After a few seconds, which felt like minutes, the article appeared. One of Phoebe's professional photos filled the top. The news below it was brief.

Authorities are looking for information on the disappearance of twenty-six-year-old fitness trainer Phoebe Watson. She was last seen leaving the Edgemont location of Fitness World at 7:30 p.m.

Catherine's shoulders relaxed a bit. The police were clueless.

Thankfully, the detective's message remained on her voicemail. She pressed his number. The phone rang once, twice, then three times. Concerns swarmed her thoughts. Had she and George closed the well completely? Could George keep his mouth shut? Did the detective already find out about Phoebe's affair with John?

"This is Brady," the detective said after the fourth ring, when Catherine was eyeing the driveway, her panic rising again.

She inhaled deeply before speaking. She had to sound normal. "Hello. This is Catherine Bower. The other day, you left me two messages regarding Phoebe Watson. I'm a client of hers. My apologies for just getting back to you now. I was traveling, and I didn't recognize your phone number. I just listened to your messages. Phoebe hasn't shown up yet?"

"No. She hasn't. You said you were an exercise client of hers?"

"Yes. That's correct. One of her clients."

"Hold on," he said.

A distinct clunk came from the detective's end. Shuffling noises followed, giving Catherine the impression he had so many people on his contact list that he wasn't sure who was who. Another good sign.

The line quieted and Brady said, "Glad you called Ms. Bower. Saved me a trip out to see you."

Instead of relief, she felt horror. She'd come so close to having him on her property. She took a shuddering breath and tried to steady her hands. Her whole body trembled inside, a sickly vibration coming from too many nerves firing at once.

"You left a message on Phoebe's phone last Wednesday," he said.

"I don't remember that."

"You don't remember leaving her a message?"

"I have some memory issues." So far, she'd held off on telling anyone who didn't need to know. She'd told her family and medical providers. Will's roommates. No one else. Now, it seemed honesty was the best policy, at least in this one small regard, so she could figure out what she'd said in the message to Phoebe.

"I'm not sure what you mean by memory issues, ma'am," he said.

"I have early onset Alzheimer's. For the most part, I'm fine. Sometimes it affects my short-term memory. Little things. My message to Phoebe must be one of them. Can you remind me what I said?"

"You said, and I quote, 'How dare you?' You sounded angry."

"Oh. Goodness," she said, intending to sound embarrassed and harmless. "I was upset because Phoebe missed our training session without canceling."

"Starting last Thursday, she missed a lot of training appointments. None of her other clients left messages quite like yours."

"I was having a difficult day. My condition, you see. I feel embarrassed now and realize how awful I must have sounded."

"From what I've learned about Ms. Watson, she never missed appointments and was extremely punctual. It never occurred to you that something might have happened to her?" His question sounded more like a reprimand. To Catherine's ears, he wasn't suspicious, only judgmental.

"That's right. Phoebe was always on time. Obviously, I didn't know she was missing. It never crossed my mind. I don't know what I thought. In hindsight, I regret my message and feel just awful about my lack of concern, considering you still don't know where she is. You really have no idea?"

"Did she ever mention leaving town?" he asked, leaving Catherine's question unanswered.

"No. She didn't. Not to me."

Detective Brady seemed to accept Catherine's explanation. "You have my number. Call me back if you think of something."

Catherine tapped her pen against her notepad. One crisis averted. She expected it might be the first of many. She took a few minutes to determine what needed to happen next, specifically how best to handle George. Quickly, she made a mental list of everything she knew about him.

Without knocking, he entered the kitchen through the back. Under any other circumstance, the action would have been inappropriate. Considering all else, it hardly mattered.

"The police don't know where she is. They don't seem to know anything," Catherine said. "Did you say anything to Christian about...about what we found?"

George held on to the back of a kitchen chair with both hands. "No."

"Good."

He let go of the chair and paced the kitchen, his eyes darting to the pool house and what they both knew lay beyond it.

Catherine was a bundle of nerves wound up tight, but when she spoke, she sounded calm and professional. She might as well have been delivering instructions at a Smartbox board meeting. She was in control of this agenda.

"How long have you worked for me, George?"

"Twelve years," he answered without hesitation.

"That's right. You started at my house on Valenterra Circle. Do you still take care of your mother?"

He nodded.

"And your sister and her family live with you, don't they?"

"Yes."

"All of them depending on you. Hmm. I'm proposing a retirement plan."

George stared at her, clearly confused about why she would bring that up now.

"I'm going to take care of that today. It will start off with a hundred thousand. I'll set up monthly payments. A fifteen percent match on whatever I've been paying you. That's what we do for the executives at SmartBox. It's the least I can do. So you won't have to worry about yourself or your family." She met his gaze then. "So neither of us will have to."

"Why are you doing this?" he asked, without specifically defining *this*. Maybe he meant the retirement plan. Or maybe he already understood what the money really represented.

He hadn't asked who else Catherine suspected of killing Phoebe, and Catherine wasn't about to tell him.

"We have to get it out of there," she said. *It* being Phoebe's dead body. "Just trust me on this. It's the only way. We have to get it off the property."

George dropped his head into his hands again and let out a soft moan. She expected a similar response, considering the type of man he was. He nurtured dead plants back to life rather than rip them out of the ground. George had convinced her to stop using the Mosquito Troop spray treatment, even though it was uncannily effective. He'd explained that it also poisoned the birds and bees and other wildlife. Someone like him would not handle a murder or its cover up well. However, from over a decade of employing him, she knew one thing for sure: George would do what she told him.

"Come back tonight and we'll take care of everything then," she whispered, though they were still alone in the house. "We'll get rid of the racoon. I know a good place."

CHAPTER 36

One Year Ago - Catherine

The sky darkened ominously over the course of the afternoon. By nightfall, the thick clouds had unleashed a torrent of rain. Catherine sat by her front window with her legs tucked underneath her. She stared outside as heavy raindrops slashed against the glass.

An unsettling sensation had permeated every cell of her body. She knew it would be like that for some time. She would get used to the feeling, as with so many other things in life. However, one thing she could not get used to was keeping a dead body on her property.

Moving Phoebe's corpse was risky, but necessary. Even if they moved it from the well and buried it in the wooded area beyond the yard, Catherine would always know it was out there. Someday, a detective might show up with cadaver search dogs. Hence, the corpse needed to disappear somewhere else—permanently. A place where buried secrets remained hidden.

Catherine gripped the zipper on her black hoodie and moved it up and down. She turned to the arched mirror to study her reflection. Dressed in black from top to bottom, she did not look or feel like herself. She would blend into the night. They were headed to a place of utter darkness.

Headlights appeared at the end of the driveway. George's truck with the trailer behind it. He parked and walked to the front of the house with his head down. By the time he got to the door, Catherine had it open.

He hesitated on the doorstep. Catherine motioned for him to come inside.

He entered the foyer and dripped rain onto the stone floor. "It's not too late to call the police," he said, gripping the edge of his hat. "Say we just found her."

Catherine let her mouth hang open for a second. She had to talk some sense into him. "You came over at midnight and we just happened to find her? Why would anyone believe that story?"

George bit into his bottom lip. "You could say you found her and called me because you didn't know what to do."

Catherine's exasperation rose. This was not the time for second thoughts. She needed George on board and fully cooperating to pull this off. "I wouldn't have any reason to look inside the well in the middle of the night. Even if I did, I wouldn't have called you. I would have called the police."

"Then why didn't you?" George asked, his voice soft.

Catherine had to bite the inside of her mouth. She'd never admit to another soul that she was a terrible, selfish person who didn't want her husband to go to jail, even though he cheated on her and murdered his mistress. All because Catherine would need him later when she could no longer take care of herself. That truth was hard enough for her to live with, she wasn't going to share it.

She locked eyes with George. "This is what we agreed to do. It's what we're doing. It's what's best for all of us."

He averted his gaze. "I brought the tarp like you asked."

"Perfect," she responded, without the charm or excitement normally accompanying her use of that word.

George went to get the tarp, and Catherine pulled on rubber Hunter boots. She stared into the coat closet at her black Burberry raincoat. It was the logical choice for this weather, but not for what they were about to do. She pulled one of John's golf raincoats from its hanger. Water resistant, not waterproof. Black. Yet when she discarded it later, he'd never miss it.

George came back carrying the tarp and wearing gardening gloves.

Catherine shut off the floodlights around the front of the house, planning for the unlikely event of an unexpected, late-night visitor. Then she slid on her own gloves. Black leather lined with cashmere. The best option from the choices she had.

"Let's go," she said, slinging her bag over her shoulder and heading for the back door. Outside, they hurried to the pool house. Under the awning, protected from the rain, George rolled out the tarp.

"Come on," Catherine said, pulling the raincoat's hood over her head.

When they got to the well, she pulled the lid aside and let George do the rest. Leaning in, with his hands under Phoebe's armpits, he pulled her out and gently placed her on the wet ground. The towel that had covered her head had slid to her ankles. Catherine grabbed it and draped it over Phoebe's face. A face she couldn't bear to see.

Phoebe wore a blue sheath dress and strappy wedged sandals. Not an outfit she would have worn for their exercise session if she'd come to the house on Wednesday morning. Which seemed to rule out Christian as her killer. It was the type of cute dress she would wear for a night out. A date, perhaps.

Even outside, in the fresh falling rain, the smell of the decaying corpse filled the air. Catherine tried not to notice anything more, but Phoebe's lifeless body was lying directly below an overhead landscape light. The towel hadn't covered her neck. A red line of chafed skin circled the pale blue skin there. The type of line that would result from a rope tightening and squeezing the life out of her.

George had seen it, too. His eyes lingered on the ugly red line.

Was it a rough sex thing? John liked to be in control whenever they made love. He'd wrapped his hands around Catherine's neck once. She thought it was more about trying something new than fulfilling a secret desire. As far as she remembered, neither of them had enjoyed the choking sensation enough to repeat the act.

Catherine shook herself back to the task at hand. "Let's do this," she said, grabbing Phoebe's ankles. She waited for George to take hold of the opposite end.

"Oh, God," George said, stumbling away from the corpse. "The back of her head. It's crushed." He jerked his head to the side and vomited into the bushes.

Catherine waited for George to recover. She wanted to tell him to man up. He could vomit when it was all over. She held back because that strategy might backfire. She had to be patient with him.

George finally trudged back to her, and they scooped the corpse off the ground. With George walking backwards, they made their way back to the tarp and set Phoebe's body down. After covering Phoebe's face and neck with the towel, Catherine undid Phoebe's sandal clasps and slid the sandals off.

"What are you doing?" George asked.

Grasping the bottom of Phoebe's dress, Catherine answered, "Taking her clothes off, in case there's evidence on them."

"I thought we were taking her somewhere no one would ever find her."

"We are, and they won't. It's still best to be as careful as possible. This way, there will be nothing to connect her to anyone."

"You mean…" George didn't finish his sentence.

Catherine didn't know what George was thinking. All that mattered was he followed her instructions.

She pulled Phoebe's dress up, revealing a peach-colored cotton bra with eyelet lace trim. Phoebe wore no panties. Her Brazilian wax was on display. Catherine remembered a previous conversation about underwear visibility.

"You know, there's nothing more unrefined than having your underwear lines peeking out under yoga pants," Catherine had said. "I don't want to see that on anyone."

"Maybe, but I can't stand thongs," Phoebe had answered. "Besides, they're like a breeding ground for bacteria." Phoebe's smile disappeared and her lips formed a small o. "Oops! Do you wear thongs? I'm so sorry."

Catherine had smirked and replied, "No. I don't do thongs. I prefer to go commando."

Phoebe's nose scrunched a bit, as if she didn't understand. Then she dipped her head back and laughed. Her ponytail danced in the air behind her. Catherine could picture it now. In her mind, Phoebe was real again, not a lifeless figure but the spirited young woman Catherine had enjoyed spending time with.

She could not afford to get emotional. She had to focus. Otherwise, something might get overlooked. They'd already moved the body. They'd taken off the clothes. There was no turning back now. Catherine would see this endeavor through to its ugly finish.

You didn't kill her, Catherine told herself.

Someone else did.

You're simply taking steps to protect your own life.

Catherine stuffed Phoebe's dress, shoes, and bra into a black trash bag.

Together, Catherine and George rolled the corpse on its side toward the edge of the tarp. As it settled face down, something on Phoebe's right buttock caught Catherine's attention. A dark patch of skin. It was about two inches wide in the shape of a sharp-edged square. Something like a tattoo. No. It was dark with blood. Someone had neatly sliced the top layer of skin away from her leg. There wasn't much blood, so it must have happened after she died. Catherine didn't understand what it meant. She didn't want to think about it.

They rolled the tarp like carpet, with Phoebe inside, then lifted the bundle off the ground.

"We're going around the house because this is not coming inside," Catherine said.

In silence, they trudged around the house in the pouring rain, carrying the tarp between them. The package grew heavier with each step. Catherine's shoulders and lower back strained. She kept moving. She didn't want to delay their efforts. They needed to get this job done as quickly as possible.

They made it to the driveway and put the bundle in the back of George's trailer, wedged between a wooden side panel and a lawn mower.

Drenched from the rain, Catherine ran to the passenger's side and peeled the magnetic *George's Landscaping* sign off the door.

George got into his truck, holding the other sign. He dropped it in the space behind the front seats. Looking straight ahead, he wiped a finger across his cheek. Catherine couldn't tell if he was crying or wiping raindrops from his face.

"Let's go," she said as their breath fogged the windows.

Once they were out of the neighborhood, Catherine told George where to go and when to turn. Splattering raindrops, the scrape of the windshield wiper blades, and the rattle of the trailer formed the soundtrack for their journey. Catherine was emotionally exhausted, but adrenaline kept her alert. She recited the facts to herself, only to confirm they were true and she wasn't just having a bad dream.

We rolled Phoebe in a tarp and stuck her in the back of the truck.
Someone strangled her.
She was dead inside the well at my house.

Catherine didn't know what had happened, yet she'd taken care of the problem. No room existed for seeds of doubt.

An hour later, they passed a sign for an upcoming exit. "Not much further," she told George.

Off the highway, after a few more miles and a series of turns, the roads changed from pavement to gravel. "Slow down," Catherine said. She peered through the rain-streaked side window at the dense forest, yet almost missed the turnoff. "Here!" she shouted. "Take a right here."

"What is this place?" George asked as they pitched in and out of water-filled ditches on a winding road barely wide enough for his truck.

Madison Creek Woods, she thought, but said, "Nowhere. It's private property. No one comes out here. Never did and probably never will."

"Then how do you know about it?"

"I just do," she said.

The road was in worse condition than she remembered. No one cared for it. Without proper maintenance, time took its toll on everything.

George's trailer clattered in protest at each steep dip in the rough terrain. They hadn't seen another vehicle since long before they turned off the main road, yet Catherine worried someone would hear the noisy rattling.

George slowed further. Ahead of them, an old and rickety bridge spanned a creek. The creek wasn't wide, it was deep, and the bridge looked like a raft someone had pieced together on a deserted island.

"I don't know about crossing that thing," George said.

Catherine had forgotten about the old bridge. It was in terrible shape a decade ago. She wasn't sure it would hold the truck's weight now.

"Keep going," she said. She tensed up as they rolled over the bridge until they made it to the other side. The structure only needed to stay together for their drive back. If it fell apart after, all the better.

"We're almost there," she said as the truck rattled around another bend.

An enormous tree trunk blocked the trail ahead. George slowed to a stop and said, "I have a chain saw in the back."

"No. It will make too much noise. Here will have to do," Catherine said. She unscrewed the top of a silver flask. After several long gulps, she held it out for George.

"I don't want any," he said, as a wind whipped a dead branch in front of the headlights.

"Suit yourself," she answered.

A bolt of lightning zig-zagged through the sky, followed by a clap of thunder. The relentless rain continued to splatter the roof and windshield. At least the ground would be soft.

Catherine guzzled more of the liquid before returning it to her bag. She pulled her wet gloves onto her fingers. Over her boots, she slid booties left behind by the cleaning crew. She dropped a pair onto the seat beside George. "Just in case," she said. "So we won't leave footprints. And don't even think about vomiting here and leaving your DNA behind."

George still stared out the front window. "We don't have to do this. It's not too late."

"Yes, it is," she answered, her gloved fingers wrapped around the door handle. "Get your shovels."

CHAPTER 37

Present Day - Victoria

After her meeting with Christian, Victoria called the Federal Correctional Institution and asked to speak with the director. She waited through a full ten minutes of elevator music before he came on the line.

"This is Victoria Heslin. I'm a special agent with the FBI. I'm calling about one of your case managers, Maria Ruiz."

The director sighed loudly. "What's the issue?"

"I needed to schedule an emergency interview on short notice. Part of a murder investigation. Maria made it possible. I just wanted to let you know how much I appreciate her help. From our meeting, it's obvious she really looks out for her assigned inmates."

"Oh," he said. "I'll make a note of our call and put it in Maria's file. All day long, I hear from people who are angry or have problems. Getting positive feedback is a nice change."

"I'm grateful for her help. Please make sure her boss knows."

"I will. Thanks."

"Thank you. Have a nice day."

With that small gesture accomplished, Victoria focused on the investigation again. Her boss wanted indisputable evidence proving Dan Sullivan had killed Phoebe. Victoria hadn't found that. Instead, she'd discovered a roundabout connection linking Catherine Bower to Dan Sullivan. Bridging the gap between them lay a web of people holding knowledge and secrets. George, Christian, and John. One of them might have killed Phoebe.

Unless...what if it wasn't *one* of them? Perhaps *all* had played a part in Phoebe's death. Unfortunately, Victoria didn't have any proof. She only had a trail that started with Catherine and kept leading back to her.

Victoria merged onto the highway and called Rivera. She hoped he'd found something new from the crime scene. Maybe a commonality between Phoebe Watson and Diane Johnson, the woman they'd found in the back of Sullivan's van.

"Did you just call me?" he said.

"Yes." She chuckled. "Obviously. We're speaking."

"That's weird. I called you at the same time."

"Good timing then," she said. "I was checking if forensics gave you any more information on the fibers they found."

"Yes. I've got something, but it can wait. I've got major news. Unless you already heard."

"What is it?" Victoria asked.

"They found another body."

Victoria's grip on the steering wheel loosened. Her hand instinctively flew to her chest. "Where?"

"Madison Creek Woods. Near to where they discovered Phoebe. The forensics team is expecting the remains to arrive late tonight. They'll begin their analysis tomorrow morning."

A wave of unease washed over Victoria. "Did Sullivan lead them to the body? Did he provide another tip to the police?"

"No. During the previous search, a fallen tree blocked the road. It had been there for years, so they didn't bother searching beyond it. Then, after the initial crime scene didn't yield much, they went back and expanded the search area using cadaver dogs. That's how they discovered the remains."

"Jeez. That place is turning into a graveyard. Who owns the land?"

"It belongs to a family named Madison, which makes sense," Rivera said. "Over a hundred acres passed down through generations. Used as a hunting ground. The current owners live in California now."

"I'd like to call them. I have some questions of my own related to this angle I'm pursuing with Catherine Bower."

"I'll send you the contact information. Now, about the fibers they found with Phoebe Watson. They come from a high-end line of beach towels called Château de Mer. French name. American company. They're sold at upscale department stores around the world. They're also sold online. I'll send you the details."

Victoria waited until she was home to check the information Rivera sent her. It included the phone number and address for a woman named Linda Madison, who had inherited the Madison Creek acreage from her family. There was more. Catherine's parents' address, the house where Catherine lived until she went off to college, was located a few miles from the Madison family's home. It's possible they knew each other.

Victoria phoned Linda Madison.

"Is this about my land in Virginia again?" Linda asked. "Don't tell me they've found a *third* body?"

"No. They haven't." Not that she knew of.

"As the police are aware, it's been ages since I last set foot in those woods," Linda said. "It's astonishing how private property can become a free-for-all for people to do as they please. I always assumed people used it for hunting, despite the *No Trespassing* signs posted everywhere. Never could I have imagined it was being used as a burial ground."

"Yes, it's certainly a regrettable situation," Victoria murmured, though that was an understatement. "The reason for my call is to find out if you know Catherine Bower." Victoria used Catherine's maiden name. Catherine had kept it, not changing it for either of her marriages.

"Who?" Linda asked.

"Her family used to live a few miles away from yours in Virginia."

"A few miles away from which house? Our main house? Wait, do you mean Missy Bowers? Her father, or maybe her grandfather, was the CEO of Smartbox, wasn't he? Her parents lived in a home that used to be a plantation?"

"Yes."

"We called her Missy back then. Haven't seen her since we were teenagers. She used to drive around in a blue Porsche convertible."

"So, you and she were friends?"

"Acquaintances. I'm not even sure how I knew her. Maybe from the country club? We partied together a few times during the summer. We used to go out to my grandfather's woods to get drunk and make a ton of noise."

"The same woods where police found the bodies?"

"Same place. I haven't been out there since high school. Once we got fake IDs, we had other options. Before then, we'd take a convoy out to the woods. I can picture us sitting on the old bridge, feet dangling in the air, drinking whatever we confiscated from our parents' liquor cabinets."

Linda couldn't know how damning her recollections were for Catherine Bower.

"What do you remember about Missy?" Victoria asked.

"She was a lot of fun. Smart, I think. A music prodigy. Violin?"

"Piano," Victoria said.

"Right. Right. Not someone you'd would want to mess with either."

"Why do you say that?"

"I'm remembering this one night. We were probably drinking. That was the only reason we went out there. Missy accused someone of flirting with her boyfriend. Missy was so mean about it. I can't remember for the life of me what she said or did, but the whole mean vibe stuck with me. Too bad that's what I most remember about her. Unfortunately, it's the truth. She left me with the impression of someone you don't want to cross. What is this about? Don't tell me she's also missing. Oh, I hope she's okay."

Linda obviously hadn't heard Catherine was physically and mentally compromised now.

"She's not missing. Thank you for your time. I appreciate it," Victoria said.

The evidence was building. The deeper Victoria delved into the investigation, the more confident she became. Catherine was not merely an accidental observer of Phoebe's death. She was an active participant. Maybe even the orchestrator. Catherine didn't just know *something*. She might know *everything*.

And if Victoria wasn't mistaken, someone hadn't wanted Catherine to share that information.

CHAPTER 38

Present Day - Victoria

Victoria Heslin sat at her modest desk in a corner of the FBI building. It was a far cry from her beautiful home office, and less private, yet served as a home base if she was in the office for meetings. She discarded a crumpled post-it note, dropping it into the bin alongside her Starbucks cup from earlier that morning.

Catherine's son, the elusive Will Montgomery, hadn't returned Victoria's calls. Unlike the rest of Catherine's family members, whom Victoria had interviewed, he was unreachable. She couldn't pop over to Europe to ask him a few questions. Though he hadn't lived at home in years, Victoria still wanted to speak with him. Maybe he had insight into what was really going on with his mother and the landscapers. Perhaps he might be the one person who wouldn't withhold information. Though Victoria wasn't counting on that happening.

Her chair creaked as she reached for the phone. She called Will and was preparing to leave another message. He surprised her by answering.

"Hey, sorry didn't get back to....later today...my sister...talked..."

"You're breaking up," Victoria said. "I can't understand you."

"Oh. I've got my earbuds in. One moment." A few seconds later, the line cleared. "Is that better? Can you hear me now?"

"Yes. Thank you," Victoria told him.

"This is about Phoebe Watson, right?"

"Yes," she answered and waited to see what would come next from him.

"I heard you're looking into George the landscaper," Will said. "My sister mentioned it. I want to share my perspective on him. From what I know, he's a genuinely good guy. Admittedly, I don't know him as well as I should, considering how much he did for my family. Boarding school kept me away from home for most of the time. Then college. However, my mother liked him and trusted him. He worked for us for years, and I can assure you, if he had ever crossed any boundaries, my mother wouldn't have tolerated it."

"What about his brother-in-law? Christian? Do you know him?"

"I know even less about him. I've seen him around my mother's house. We say hello in passing. That's about it."

"Would you know anything about the large payment your mother sent George in May of last year?"

"No. How much are we talking about?"

"Over ten times larger than the usual payments he received."

"I don't know what that payment was for, but George's role extended beyond landscaping duties. Did you ask John about it? On second thought, never mind. He won't know. I'm pretty sure he's not involved in financial matters. My mother or her accountant handled everything. Intentionally."

It was a little unusual that John wasn't involved in any of the household financial decisions. Though if Catherine took care of all expenses related to her estate before she married John, it made sense. Most people in Victoria's own family relied on accountants and attorneys to handle everything.

"Your questions about the large payment give me the impression you suspect something else," Will said. "What are you thinking?"

"The timing of the payment aligns with Phoebe's disappearance."

Will chuckled. "I'm not sure what you're getting at. If you think my mother played any part in what happened to Phoebe, that's just ridiculous.

I'm sure she was just helping George out. Perhaps extending him a personal loan."

"He says she was setting up a retirement account," Victoria said.

"That sounds about right. My mother was a savvy businessperson, well-versed in treating valued employees with respect. Undoubtedly, she valued George. Let me clarify something, Agent Heslin. Are you or anyone else attempting to create trouble for my mother? Are you making accusations against her?"

"Your mother knows what happened to Phoebe. Somehow, she's involved."

"Agent Heslin, I must respectfully disagree with your assessment. Even if, hypothetically, you could prove her involvement in something unlawful, she wouldn't face legal consequences due to her condition. She lacks the ability to defend herself or present her side of the story. Her attorney would argue incompetence to stand trial. She is incapable of committing any crime at this stage, and there is no chance of her regaining competence. I suggest you stop wasting your time investigating her through us. It's a truly reprehensible approach."

Will already sounded like an attorney.

"Where were you when Phoebe disappeared the night of May fourth?" Victoria asked.

"I was at Duke. I'm in law school there now. My first year. Last year was my senior year of college. I remember when Phoebe disappeared."

"Why would you remember if you were at school?"

"My mother was with me for one of her first medical treatments. My friends and I took her out to dinner to show our support. She told us her trainer was missing and asked if we could recommend a replacement. Naturally, I remembered that conversation the first time I heard the news about Phoebe's disappearance. I have an excellent memory. It's rare I forget anything. No matter when or what."

"Then you'll probably thrive as an attorney," Victoria said.

"That's the plan. Thank you," Will answered.

When their conversation ended, Victoria tapped her pen against her desk for a few seconds as she mentally reviewed the list of names she'd compiled. Then she rechecked her email.

The video recording from John's golf trip at the Winston Retreat waited in her inbox. Excellent. If Catherine knew something, chances were good it involved her husband.

John Murdock's golf trip alibi had checked out but didn't tell the entire story. This new footage presented a chance to see what he was up to when he wasn't golfing. Most crimes occurred in the dead of night when people were asleep. Fewer witnesses and the cover of darkness provided criminals with advantages.

The recording came from the hallway outside John's room. Victoria sent the files to an app that flagged movement.

In the video frame, John left his room at seven in the morning wearing golf clothes. He returned in the late afternoon. An hour later, he emerged in different clothes, and came back for the night a little after ten p.m. He followed a similar routine the second day. Day three, his routine changed. When he got back to his room in the evening, he wasn't alone. A woman accompanied him. She was young, late twenties maybe. She wasn't Phoebe. They didn't leave the room until the morning. The leggy blonde went in and out of John's hotel room for the remainder of John's trip. They spent the evenings together inside the room, with multiple visits from room service.

Though John had failed to mention his female companion, his alibi held. He was in Kiawah when Phoebe disappeared. He didn't sneak out of his room during the night. But Taylor was correct. He was having an affair.

John had referenced Catherine's paranoia. Considering his affair, the paranoia appeared justified. If she had been aware of her husband's infidelity, if she suspected Phoebe was his mistress, that gave Catherine a motive for murder.

Victoria pondered Catherine's character. The knowledge came from interviews with friends and family, each of whom might have their own agenda. Was Catherine capable of murder?

It wasn't only Catherine's marriage to John Murdock that tugged at Victoria's thoughts. She also had to consider Catherine's first husband, Charles Montgomery. Who was he and what was their marriage like?

Victoria conducted a quick background search on him. The results, when added to what she already knew and suspected, sent a shiver down her spine.

Victoria couldn't shake the feeling that she was on the edge of a revelation where the line between victim and perpetrator blurred.

"This is Agent Heslin from the FBI," Victoria said when Taylor answered her phone.

A few seconds passed before Taylor responded. "What do you want, detective?"

Sensing something had changed since their last conversation. Victoria let the misnomer slip. "I have a few more questions for you."

"Did you find out who killed my mother's trainer yet?" Taylor's voice had a cold, almost cruel edge.

"Not yet."

"It's weird how you keep calling my brother and me. When you came to my house before, I thought you were interviewing everyone who might have known Phoebe, and since my mother couldn't talk...But now I don't think that's the case. My family isn't involved. And we don't know who killed Phoebe."

"You said your father died in a boating accident," Victoria said.

"That's right. Why would you ask about that? What could it possibly have to do with any of this?"

"Do you remember when it happened?"

Taylor scoffed. "That's not a thing you easily forget."

"Is it true your family never recovered his body?" Victoria asked.

"Yes. That's not unusual with someone lost at sea. The Coast Guard searched for days. My family hired divers, too. We didn't want to stop looking, didn't want to give up. Eventually we had to. My mother waited an entire year before having a funeral."

"Did you find any evidence of his death?"

"Evidence? Are you suggesting he might still be alive? You think he faked his death?" Another huff of breath. "My father is dead. He had way too good a life to walk away from it, and he loved us. Especially me. We had a bond." Taylor sniffed, and it sounded like she was crying. "You probably think he's lurking around killing people now, don't you? This is ridiculous. I don't have to talk to you. I'm hanging up."

Click.

The line went dead.

CHAPTER 39

Present Day - Victoria

Victoria marched into the Atrium Gardens Facility and got in line behind a couple waiting to sign in at the registration desk. When they finished and moved on, Victoria stepped up to the desk, her identification in her hand. "Victoria Heslin with the Federal Bureau of Investigation. I'm here to see Catherine Bower."

"Oh," said the woman behind the desk. She sat there long enough doing nothing that Victoria wondered what was going on. "Just one minute, please." The woman finally got up from her chair and spoke into the partly open doorway behind her. "Someone from the FBI is here to see Catherine Bower." The woman left the desk area and Victoria didn't hear the rest.

While she waited, Victoria had time to think about the reasons she'd returned to Atrium Gardens for another crack at getting information out of Catherine. There was the timing of Catherine's suspicious accident, and the connection between Dan Sullivan and Christian, her landscaper. Victoria had also discovered Catherine's substantial payment to George Martin, and her familiarity with Madison Creek Woods. Not to mention that Catherine had correctly identified Phoebe. Perhaps Catherine understood more than her family seemed to believe.

The door behind the desk opened again. "I'm sorry," the woman said. "Catherine can't receive visitors without her lawyer present. You'll need to schedule something. This is their attorney's number." The woman handed Victoria a business card with the name Larissa Carmichael on it.

Lawyer? When did that happen? Catherine, who supposedly couldn't communicate, now needed a lawyer present to have visitors? And not just a family attorney. Larissa Carmichael. One of the best and highest paid criminal attorneys in the state of Virginia.

Victoria left the facility. Outside the main doors, an Atrium Gardens van blocked the road. A man in uniform completed the raising of a wheelchair ramp and shut the van's door. Beside him, a dark-haired woman hoisted a bag onto her shoulder and turned the occupied wheelchair around. It was Deja and Catherine.

Deja smiled. A brief instant of recognition. Then her expression clouded, and her mouth clamped shut.

The driver had gotten back into the van. Only Victoria, Deja, and Catherine were outside.

"I'm sorry, I can't talk to you," Deja said softly, definitely sounding apologetic.

"I heard," Victoria answered. "Glad you called us when you did."

"Except I shouldn't have done that." Deja cast a sidelong glance at the front of the building. "I signed a privacy agreement with my employers."

"The information you provided was critical to this investigation," Victoria said. "I just have a few more questions."

Deja shook her head. "I'm sorry. I can't. Everything to do with the investigation has to go through the Bowers' attorney. I can give you her number."

"No need. I already have it," Victoria said.

Before Deja could walk away, Victoria crouched in front of the wheelchair. She was only inches away from Catherine. "Do you know who killed Phoebe Watson?" Victoria asked.

Catherine focused on Victoria. They locked eyes.

Victoria repeated, "Do you know who killed Phoebe Watson?"

Catherine nodded, her head bobbing vigorously up and down. Her hand rose to her chest, and she seemed to tap her heart.

Deja gasped and drew the wheelchair backward. "She doesn't know what you're asking. That means nothing." Deja's voice rose as she took long strides away from Victoria, pushing Catherine toward the facility's entrance. "I made a terrible mistake by calling you. Contact Catherine's family attorney if you have questions. Please don't come back here."

Victoria met Agent Rivera at the rooftop café of an office building overlooking the cityscape of D.C. They had a panoramic view of the city and its iconic landmarks. The open-air seating area held sleek tables and chairs. They opted for a corner table under a wide umbrella, affording some privacy and shade from the afternoon sun. A light wind carried the faint sound of the traffic below and blew a few strands of Victoria's hair across her face.

Rivera leaned over their table toward her as they exchanged their notes and theories.

"Nothing in Sullivan's vehicle or apartment matches the evidence collected from the crime scene or Phoebe's remains," he said.

Victoria was glad to hear that. It meant her own theories regarding Catherine, though vague, remained sound. "Any word on the second set of remains from Madison Creek Woods?"

"We know they're older. The victim has been deceased for at least fifteen years. All we have is bones. No signs of trauma. But obviously the body didn't bury itself out there."

"Do you think one person is responsible for both victims?" Victoria asked.

"We don't have enough to say," Rivera answered.

"But likely it's one person who knows about Madison Creek Woods. I'm sure it's Catherine. I think George and Christian saw something and she was paying them off in the form of an unusual retirement plan. Unfortunately, I have no proof. It's all circumstantial. Their stories line up. Catherine isn't saying anything. She can't."

Victoria stopped short of telling Rivera how Catherine nodded when Victoria asked her point blank. That wouldn't hold up in any court of law. Nor was it reliable, given Catherine's mental state.

"Your instincts count for a lot," Rivera said.

"Yeah. It's my gut feeling against a woman who can't defend herself. Though she's got attorneys preventing us from seeing her now."

"She's helpless now but wasn't when Phoebe disappeared. Why don't we get her phone records? And also find out if she kept a diary."

"Excellent idea. She did write in a journal. Her daughter mentioned it." Victoria sighed. "We'll need a warrant to search her property."

"If we put everything we have together, and you present it, we'll get one. Building cases is your forte, Ms. State debate champion," Rivera said.

Victoria grinned. She'd also need a pro-prosecution judge.

CHAPTER 40

Present Day - Deja

"I think the Waldorf chicken salad is one of your favorites from the lunch menu," Deja said to Catherine as they rounded the corner headed toward room 104.

A woman from the housekeeping staff came out of Catherine's room with the soiled linens.

"Thank you," Deja said, as if the woman had done her a personal favor. It was like that now whenever anyone assisted her with Catherine's care. Deja viewed her responsibilities as more than a job. When she wasn't at Atrium Gardens, she worried about Catherine.

Deja used her butt and shoulders to push the door open and enter the room backwards. When she turned the wheelchair around, a fresh bouquet of white and lavender colored flowers greeted them. Someone had arranged them in a tall vase on the table by the door. She had just enough time to wonder how they got there before Will came out of the bathroom, running a hand through his hair.

"Hey," he said, heading straight to his mother. He gave her a hug and a kiss on the cheek. Then he straightened and smiled at Deja. "It's nice to see you again in person."

Already she felt herself blushing. A tingling warmth spread inside her. It was the way Will looked at her. He wasn't leering by any means, yet his gaze conveyed appreciation.

"Am I interrupting anything?" he asked.

"No," Deja answered. "We just got back from lunch."

"What's next on the agenda?"

"We usually go outside for a walk, if it's not too warm."

"Great. It's not too warm. Let's do it. I'll go with you."

Deja went to the closet to get a hat. She was grateful Will couldn't see her face right then. His unexpected visit made her a little giddy, and she didn't want him to notice. From the top shelf, she took down a lovely straw hat with black ribbon and placed it on Catherine's head to protect her from the sun.

"Okay. We ready?" Will asked, his hands gripping the wheelchair handles.

"Almost," Deja said. She took a bottle of water from the mini-fridge and tucked it in the back of the wheelchair so she could offer Catherine a drink later.

Outside, Deja chose a shaded trail leading to the ponds and gardens in the center of Atrium Gardens.

An elderly couple ambled toward them on the path. The man wore a dress shirt and a tie complimenting the woman's long-sleeved floral dress. They were coming from the direction of the formal dining room, which had a dress code even for lunch.

"Good afternoon. Enjoy your day," Will said as he moved the wheelchair toward the edge of the path to make more room for the couple.

Deja admired Will's confidence and his manners, which seemed to come naturally to him.

Will did most of the talking as they walked. He told them about his trip back to the States, reminding his mother of trips their family had taken together. After a few minutes of that, most of his questions were for Deja. First, they related to his mother's schedule and daily activities, then they were about Deja's.

She kept drawing the conversation back to Catherine to keep things professional, but Will had a way about him that made Deja relax. By the time they reached the pond and crossed the bridge, Deja had forgotten about holding back and was simply enjoying her time with Will.

He stopped moving near a small waterfall. "Want to sit here for a few minutes?" he asked.

"Sure," Deja answered.

Will pulled the wheelchair into the shade near a bench.

Deja checked to make sure Catherine wasn't drooling or needing her nose wiped. As Deja stepped in front of Will, she felt the warm weight of his hand against her lower back. Just as quickly, it was gone. Deja thought she might have imagined it, except for the tingling sensation his touch had left behind.

Will took a seat on the bench. "Great day," he said as a breeze rustled the tall feathery ornamental grass beside them. "Not too hot or too cold. Not raining like almost every day when I was in London." He looked at Deja, then at the space on the bench beside him. Deja smiled as she sat down, leaving ample room between them.

"So, I wanted to tell you I spoke to Larissa Carmichael. Our attorney," Will said. "You'll never hear anything from her to make you uncomfortable again. I promise."

"I hope you didn't..." Deja didn't finish because she wasn't sure about her exact hopes. She simply didn't want to cause any trouble.

"Larissa works for me, so she has to respect my wishes," Will said. "I'm my mother's trustee and the one who hired you."

"I didn't know you hired me." Deja imagined Will reading her application and looking over the photographs she'd had to include. It surprised her to learn Will was in charge of his mother's care. She'd assumed Catherine's husband was the one who made those decisions.

"My mother and I were really close," Will said. "We really understood each other."

Deja nodded. "Seems like you still are close."

"Yes. Though obviously it's different now." He sighed. "So, something else I wanted to ask you. I should have asked you this before. Are you seeing someone?"

"You mean, like...?"

Will grinned. "Like a boyfriend who would mind if I asked you out again."

"No. I'm not seeing anyone."

"That's hard to believe, although I'm glad to hear it," he said. "What about your father? Would he care if you went out with me, do you think?"

"Why would he care?" Deja asked, though she could think of several reasons. But she knew he'd change his mind if he got to know Will.

Will shrugged. "Just trying to cover all my bases so I won't be too hurt if you say no again. I think we get along well, and I'd like to get to know you better."

Deja felt her skin flush. She looked toward the pond where two ducks had separated from the others and floated at the water's edge.

"So, how about tomorrow night?" Will asked.

She turned back to find him staring at her with his eyebrows raised, and she couldn't help but smile. "What do you have in mind?" she asked.

"Depends on what you like to do. Dinner? Dancing? Another walk?"

"Dinner sounds good. Could be fun."

"Could be? It will be. I promise you an evening you won't forget." Will got off the bench and jumped in front of the wheelchair. "You hear that?" he asked his mother. "She said, yes!"

Deja laughed. She also had a strange feeling. Sitting there with Will, flirting with him, she'd forgotten something, and she knew what. She'd forgotten Will's mother was with them, hearing every word. That was certainly a first, getting asked out by someone in front of his mother.

Deja studied Catherine's face for signs she'd understood any of the conversation.

Catherine stared blankly, as she often did. She didn't look happy or sad. Then Deja noticed Catherine's fingers. She gripped the edges of her wheelchair so tightly she was cutting off the blood flow.

Deja gently uncurled Catherine's fingers and set her hands on her lap.

As much as Deja loved Catherine, because she really did, it might be nice to spend an evening with Will. Just the two of them alone for once. She was looking forward to it.

CHAPTER 41
One Year Ago - Catherine

If only she knew the circumstances. Every story had at least two sides. Catherine didn't know any other version of this one. She'd only speculated. What truly happened to Phoebe remained a mystery.

From the living room couch, she glared up at John in the portrait over the fireplace. It was raining again. Not as hard as the day before, but the dampness seemed as if it had come to stay. John might come home early because of the weather. He hated golfing in the rain. Catherine wasn't ready to see him. She needed more time to process the recent turn of events.

The previous night barely seemed real. More like a bizarre bad dream where she was miserable and wet and had spent hours in a truck with George. Since then, she'd relived every detail, making sure they hadn't overlooked anything. She remembered digging. The ache in her back and shoulders wouldn't let her forget. The dirt was soft yet heavy with the rain.

Following Catherine's instructions, George had stuffed the tarp in a dumpster behind a restaurant with a neon green *Pasta and Pizza* sign. A place she wouldn't eat at unless she was literally starving. They'd stashed the black trash bag with Phoebe's clothes in a different dumpster twenty miles away at an Arby's. Their gloves and John's raincoat went into a separate bin at a convenience store. They never stopped for gas. George had refueled his tank from a container in his trailer.

The best thing either of them could do now was to pretend none of it ever happened. Catherine wouldn't have a problem doing so. Would George?

Trembling, she poured whiskey into a tumbler and took several desperate gulps. Her phone rang, vibrating the coffee table's glass top. It was John. How surreal would things get when he came home? Would he sense she knew? What if he hadn't intended to leave Phoebe's body in the well indefinitely? What if he checked on her? Would he ask, "Hey, Catherine. By any chance, did you move the dead body I stuffed in the well?" Or would he suspect she'd taken care of the situation, as she had done with almost every matter affecting their lives? After all, she'd acted to protect him. To protect her future.

The ringing of her phone persisted. She finally picked it up. "Hello?" she answered, wincing at a sudden and unwelcome image of John standing behind Phoebe, the muscles in his arms straining as he pulled a rope tighter and tighter.

"How are you doing?" he asked.

Exhausted because I only got a few hours of sleep. I was in the woods burying the woman you strangled and left in the backyard, she thought as she swallowed and answered, "Fine. Are you on your way back?"

"That's what I'm calling about. We lost two days to the rain. The course flooded. We're all planning to stay another day. The weather is supposed to be clear this afternoon. We already got a late tee time for tomorrow. Should be dry enough by then."

"Sounds good," she said, and meant it, grateful for the delay. "I hope the course clears up for you. I'm headed to Duke tomorrow for my first treatment. I can handle it."

"Oh, damn. I wanted to go with you. You know what? I don't need to stay. I'll come home."

There wasn't a lot of conviction in his claim. He wanted her to say it wasn't necessary for him to come back and he should stay. For now, having John stay away from home worked best for her. She wasn't ready to see him.

"No, really, John. It's no problem. I'll get time with Will afterward. If this treatment goes well, there will be a lot more."

"All right, if you're sure you don't mind."

As she expected, he didn't insist.

"I'm sure," she said. "Don't worry."

"Okay. I'll call you later. I love you," he said. "Thinking about you every minute."

Catherine wasn't disappointed when she said goodbye to him. She felt relief. Now she had more time to sort through her feelings. To figure out how she felt about having a killer take care of her for the rest of her life.

If John knew what she'd done for him, surely he would appreciate it. Maybe she'd tell him some day. At the least her efforts and silence should buy her years of gratitude, trust, and goodwill. If she told him, if they discussed Phoebe's death, Catherine would finally get the chance to learn what happened.

Now that she knew what her husband was capable of, she had other worries to consider. What would happen if John tired of taking care of her someday? Would she end up in the well like Phoebe? Perhaps she should have thought these scenarios through more carefully before moving Phoebe's corpse.

Not for the first time, she wondered how George was dealing with things. She'd told him what to do, and he'd obeyed her. But he wasn't comfortable with what they'd done. That much was obvious. He was her landscaper. Not a mafia bodyguard for whom discarding bodies was a way of life.

Because of the pounding rain, George wasn't likely to come by her house to do any work. She'd better check on him. There wasn't any reason she shouldn't. He was her landscaper. Nothing suspicious about reaching out to him over the phone. It wasn't as if their calls were being recorded.

First, she finished her glass of whiskey. By the time she called him, a pleasant numbness had taken over her body.

"It's me," she said.

"Uh, is everything okay?" he asked.

"Everything is fine," she said, sounding like her normal, confident self. "I'm just calling to see how you're holding up today."

He didn't respond right away, and Catherine was about to speak when he blurted, "Christian didn't do it."

"What?" Another layer of worry leaped into her consciousness to join the heavy folds already there. "How do you know?"

"Because he told me. I believe him."

Catherine balled her hand into a fist and spoke through clenched teeth. "Why would you say anything to him? Why?"

"He doesn't know we found her. I just…I had to confront him. I had to know what happened. For the sake of my sister and my nieces. How could I let him live in my house if he'd done that?"

His question cut straight into Catherine's core. Her stomach felt sick and heavy, as if the whiskey she drank was about to gush out. "Whatever he might have told you, you can't believe him. He's not going to confess after what he's done."

"I believe him," George said. "He knows nothing about her."

"But you didn't tell him anything else?"

George hesitated, then said, "No."

He lied. There was no doubt in her mind. Lies seemed to be the currency of those around her. John. Christian. Now, even George. It was like a rapidly spreading epidemic. Everyone said whatever they needed to say to cover their misdeeds and safeguard their interests. With enough repetition, they also convinced themselves. Their fabrications became their distorted version of reality. Catherine understood this all too well because she had done it, too.

"Don't you want to find out what happened?" he whispered. "Don't you need to know who hurt her?"

"No. I don't," she said. "It's done. I don't want to think about it again. You should be grateful neither you nor Christian has to go to jail for something you didn't do."

"But do you know who did it?" he asked.

"No. Absolutely not." His question left her stunned. Did he have suspicions about John? He must. Because George couldn't possibly think she'd done it. Not after witnessing her genuine shock at finding the body.

"We probably shouldn't be talking about it," George said.

"Exactly. We shouldn't have said anything about it to anyone. Not ever," she hissed. "That's what we agreed on, and why you have a bulging bank account now with more to come."

"He won't tell anyone," George said again. "But don't you think we should find out—"

"No," Catherine said, cutting him off. "Don't ask me again. Learn to live with what you've done, George. Or you won't like what happens next. You and your brother-in-law are the ones who stand to lose everything."

Her whole body was trembling when she slammed her phone down.

CHAPTER 42
One Year Ago - Catherine

Two days after burying *the racoon*, Catherine's arms and back still ached. Her workouts, even the "multi-functional exercises" Phoebe designed, had never included shoveling dirt to dig a grave. Yet it was Catherine's hangover that proved most unforgiving. She'd tried to drown her troubles with whiskey. It was not her friend now. All night she'd worried George had told Christian about moving the body. He must have. No one mentioned finding a dead body without getting asked, *what did you do next?*

Catherine wasn't sure how to handle the situation with George and Christian, though anything they said would be their word against hers. She firmly believed hers carried more weight.

Worrying about something that might happen had never been her style. As always, she would forge ahead with confidence. For now, she needed to focus on herself.

She made a superfood-packed smoothie, minus the supplements, and swallowed three ibuprofen.

Until the moment Catherine walked out the door into the garage, she considered canceling her first treatment. She wouldn't mention nursing a hangover. She would simply say she felt unwell. But every time she went to call Dr. Tarro, she reminded herself that any treatment postponement allowed her condition to worsen. The infusions offered a chance to stay well for as long as possible. Perhaps even long enough for someone to develop a cure. And while she was at Duke, she'd get to see Will.

She put an overnight bag in the back of her SUV and texted her son to see if he could meet for dinner again. Just the two of them this time.

She had only made it as far as the end of the driveway when Will responded to her text.

I'll meet you at my apartment after you're done. Good luck!

As she gave Will's response a thumbs up, a second message from him arrived.

Do you need someone to pick you up after the treatment? I can get you.

She smiled as she typed her answer. *I should be fine. I'll let you know. Thank you!*

Then she began the three-hour drive to Duke. Three hours to pull herself together. To get George and Christian and John and dead Phoebe out of her mind. She could do her deep breathing exercises. Her health depended on it. So did her sanity.

As she drove, the sun's rays illuminated the windshield, revealing a hazy film of dirt. She'd meant to have the car washed. Spraying the windshield fluid only smeared the grime more.

A jolt of horror shot through her as a memory returned.

Waking up in the pool house. Feet caked in filth.

How had her feet gotten so dirty?

Was it possible? Could she have killed someone and have no memory of it?

No, she tried to convince herself. It was inconceivable.

Committing murder was not an act a person could forget.

Yet a gnawing uncertainty spread within her.

John must have done it. He must have.

What if she was wrong?

CHAPTER 43

Present Day - Victoria

With his front door ajar, John glowered at Victoria, Rivera, and the two-person evidence team.

"You can't come in here," John said. "I'm calling our lawyer."

Victoria wanted to laugh at his misguided confidence, instead she held it in as she brandished the warrant. "Allow me to clarify how a search warrant works. We have the authority to enter. You are required to vacate the premises."

John moved to shut the door. Victoria wedged her foot in the narrowing gap. It felt as though the iron edge collided with her bone. She hid her wince and the surge of anger that accompanied it. "Don't make this more difficult than it has to be, please. Kindly wait outside while we conduct the search."

"This is outrageous!" John said, directing his piercing glare at Victoria.

"In fact, it isn't," Victoria said with all the professionalism she could muster, despite the searing pain in her foot. "This is standard procedure when we have probable cause."

She pushed her way inside, and John finally stepped back.

"You can help us make less of a mess here if you tell us where Catherine's phone is," Victoria said.

"Her phone? I don't know. Obviously, she hasn't used it since her accident."

"That's okay, we'll find it. If we don't, I've already sent the warrant to your carrier. We should have those records soon."

John just shook his head.

"Taylor said Catherine kept a journal. Where is it?" Victoria asked.

"She had one," John answered. "But I don't know where it is now."

After searching the house, the evidence team found three consecutive model iPhones. Two in a kitchen drawer, and one inside a bedside table. They'd filled multiple bags with towels and blankets.

"Enough linens for a small army," Rivera said. "And they still have to search the guest house."

Victoria stepped wearily into her mudroom, the dogs swirling around her. Their wagging tails and huffs of greeting lifted her spirits, providing a brief respite from the weight of disappointment. Despite the search team's best efforts, they hadn't found Catherine's journal and the answers that might lie inside. While the discovery of the iPhones held promise, someone had deleted the messages. The FBI's communication experts could retrieve them. It would take time on their part and patience on hers.

After locking her bureau weapon in the hall safe, Victoria wrapped her arms around Myrtle and rubbed her neck. Her alpha dog loved getting snuggled.

"Hey," Ned said, his voice filled with empathy and concern. "Tough day?"

Their eyes met and a silent understanding passed between them.

"Just a long one. I'm glad to be home," she said. She tossed her phone onto the nearby counter and fell into Ned's open arms.

Barely a few seconds had passed before her phone rang. She lifted her head from Ned's chest and glanced at her screen. For the slightest beat, she considered not taking it since she'd just walked in the door. She longed to leave the case behind for the rest of the night and enjoy the sanctuary of her home. But the call held the promise of crucial information or a breakthrough in the case. She'd just spent the entire day with Rivera. He wouldn't call her now unless it was important. Her excitement and curiosity took over.

"One second," she murmured apologetically to Ned.

"Sure. No problem. I'll be waiting, though." He kissed her forehead and left the room.

She answered the call. "Hey, Rivera. What's going on?"

"I just heard from Rebecca. She identified the recent remains from Madison Creek Woods with a dental match."

There was no mistaking the excitement in Rivera's voice. "Who is it?" Victoria asked.

"Charles Montgomery."

"Catherine's first husband," Victoria whispered.

CHAPTER 44

Present Day - Victoria

The agents met in a windowless conference room at the FBI headquarters. The room held a large rectangular table, polished to a shine, surrounded by comfortable leather chairs. A few FBI emblems adorned the white walls.

Rivera grabbed a water bottle from a small refreshment station tucked away in a corner, then sat down next to Victoria. As they delved into the details of the case, their voices filled the otherwise quiet room. They discussed their evidence. Of one thing they were certain, they hadn't found anything new pointing to Dan Sullivan as Phoebe's killer.

Murphy joined them ten minutes later. District Attorney Harold Walker followed him.

Murphy facilitated the introductions and told Walker that Victoria was the lead agent.

Walker, a seasoned district attorney known for his no-nonsense approach, wasted no time in getting to the heart of the issue. "What did you find?" he asked. "Did Sullivan do it?"

Victoria met Walker's gaze. "Sullivan didn't kill Phoebe Watson," she stated.

Rivera spoke next, presenting the avenues he explored to rule out Sullivan as the killer. Mainly there was a lack of evidence, no matter what angle he pursued.

"Then how did he know where to find her?" Walker asked, his voice tinged with disbelief.

"We believe Sullivan got the information from another inmate. His name is Christian Davis. He never disclosed Phoebe's name to Sullivan, though."

"So Christian Davis killed Phoebe?" Walker asked.

"Christian may have played a role in the cover-up or had knowledge of it from his brother-in-law. They worked for a woman named Catherine Bower. She's our primary suspect," Victoria said.

At the mention of Catherine's name, Walker's reaction was immediate. He did a double take and pulled his glasses off. His response made Victoria pause as a flicker of doubt crept into her mind. Then she pressed on.

"We have evidence Catherine Bower's second husband was having an extramarital affair," Victoria said.

Walker's face lit up. "With Phoebe Watson?"

"Someone else. Though it's possible Catherine suspected Phoebe to be his mistress. Catherine left an angry voice mail for Phoebe. The message said, 'How dare you?'"

Walker folded his arms. "I know the Bower/Montgomery family. I knew Catherine's first husband, Charles. Tragic about what happened to him. Then her own tragedy. Unable to speak or communicate, is my understanding. You must be absolutely certain before you accuse someone like Catherine Bower."

"We are consulting with our legal department on the best course of action," Murphy assured him. "But the evidence we've gathered points to her. The towels from the Bower's pool house match the fibers found in Phoebe's hair. We suspect she was bribing her landscaper, who likely holds critical information. Multiple interviews with family members and her employees mentioned Catherine's struggles. Drinking. A serious health condition. There's also the reason behind our investigation's initial focus on her. According to her caregiver, Catherine said Phoebe's name during a news report—before anyone else knew the remains in question were

Phoebe Watson's. It's as if Catherine Bower wanted to make sure someone knew of her role in Phoebe's death."

"All circumstantial evidence," Walker said.

"We have her phone in our possession, and forensics is working to retrieve the messages. It may provide us with concrete evidence," Victoria said.

"Still, that's all you have?"

"Catherine was familiar with Madison Creek Woods, and we confirmed the identity of the second body we found there," Victoria added.

"Who is it?" Walker asked.

"Charles Montgomery," Victoria answered.

The DA gasped and covered his mouth with his hand. "But Charles died in a boating accident."

"And his body was never recovered," Victoria said. "We can't say for certain if Catherine is responsible for his death. Not yet. Though it looks that way."

"I assume you'll deal with this information carefully," The DA said. "No need for it to get out yet." He sat back against his chair and rubbed his chin. "You're sure Dan Sullivan lied to us about killing Phoebe Watson?"

"Yes," Victoria answered.

The DA shifted his attention to Murphy. "Then he's lying to us about his other victims. I did not want to make a deal with a killer. Now I don't have to. Well done."

"The credit goes to my agents," Murphy remarked.

"Thank you, Ms. Heslin and Mr. Rivera," the DA said. "I'm well aware of your impressive track record. I truly appreciate this."

"They consistently deliver," Murphy said.

Yet Victoria couldn't shake her unanswered questions. Was Catherine's near drowning truly an accident, a consequence of her declining health and excessive drinking? Or was there something more sinister at play?

Victoria believed it was no accident. However, the theory didn't make sense if Catherine was the killer.

As Victoria's mind whirled with possibilities, a new one emerged. Perhaps the incident was never about silencing her. Instead, someone wanted to punish Catherine Bower.

CHAPTER 45

Present Day - Victoria

Victoria felt a sense of anticipation mixed with unease. This was a crucial moment, a make-or-break point in the investigation. The evidence against Catherine was damning, and Victoria was determined to unravel the truth. To do that, she'd brought George Martin into the FBI's office for questioning. George hadn't come alone. He'd brought an attorney with him, and not just any attorney. Larissa Carmichael. Everyone in law enforcement in the D.C. area knew who she was. There was no way George could afford her exorbitant fees unless the Bower family was paying them.

With everyone seated in the conference room, Victoria presented the evidence they had against Catherine. She gave them a few seconds for the information to settle. Then she focused on George. Her voice cut through the charged silence. "Catherine Bower was paying you to keep quiet, wasn't she?"

Larissa's interjection was swift. "Mr. Martin pleads the fifth," she said, invoking her client's right to remain silent. It was a tactical move to shield George from self-incrimination.

Undeterred, Victoria pressed on. "Did you tell your brother-in-law where you buried Phoebe?"

George didn't answer. His eyes shifted under the weight of what she believed was overwhelming guilt and fear.

Victoria pushed further. She was inching closer to the core of the investigation and needed George to take her there. "Tell us, did you help Catherine bury Phoebe in the same place where she buried her first husband?"

Still, George offered no answer. A flicker of anguish twisted his features.

"The fifth," Larissa said.

"Did Catherine Bower murder Phoebe Watson?" Victoria asked.

George's response came out as a long, gasping breath and one word. "Yes." It resonated through the room, leaving a chilling silence in its wake.

Larissa scowled, and Victoria fought to maintain her composure. Though his admission confirmed her belief, hearing it stunned her.

"And then she couldn't live with what she'd done," George said, in a voice capturing the weight of his regret.

The truth was finally emerging.

CHAPTER 46

One Year Ago - Catherine

Catherine's Neruvenax infusion treatment lasted two hours. During that time, her headache returned. Was it her hangover persisting, or was it a side-effect of the treatment?

She tried to relax and get caught up in the novel she'd brought along. After only reading the same paragraph again and again, she finally closed her book and her eyes. The machine pumping medicine into her veins made an intermittent noise, a soft squelch that grated on her nerves. It sounded like her shovel plunging in and out of the wet earth to dig Phoebe's grave.

Before she could dismiss the disturbing recollection, another image intruded. A vivid scene of unrolling Phoebe's naked corpse from the tarp and into the dark void below as a lightning strike illuminated her crumpled body.

With an involuntary shudder, Catherine forced her attention to comforting thoughts of piano concerts and seeing Will after her treatment.

She arrived at Will's apartment in the late afternoon. Nick answered the door. He was on his way out with a backpack slung over one shoulder and car keys in hand.

"Mrs. Bower," he said. He smiled and gave her a hug. "Will said you were having your first treatment today."

"Yes. It went well."

"You're feeling okay?"

"I think so. They had me wait an hour to make sure before sending me on my way. I feel a little strange. Not quite myself."

"Good news. Well, uh, I'm on my way to a seminar. I'm not sure where Will is."

"He's in class." Catherine held up her phone. "I can check his location."

"Okay. Make yourself at home while you're waiting," Nick said.

"I will. Thank you." She thought Nick was a nice young man, and Will was lucky to have him as a friend.

Inside the apartment, Catherine looked around the kitchen. It was remarkably clean, considering two college students lived there. Catherine paid for a cleaning service, but they only came bi-weekly, so the boys had to do some maintenance between those visits.

Since she'd left the treatment, Catherine's headache had only intensified. She went to Will's bathroom, opened the mirrored medicine cabinet, and took three pain killers.

How could she make herself useful until her son came back? She hadn't done much of anything for him lately. Not since her diagnosis. She'd been too busy with her own needs. This was a good opportunity. While she was waiting, she could check on Will's clothing situation and see if any items needed replacing. Taylor shopped constantly. In contrast, Will never asked for anything and he'd never been one to go shopping on his own. Some of his shoes and clothes probably needed updating and replacing.

Catherine opened Will's closet and scanned the space. Athletic shoes and a pair of boat shoes lay scattered across the floor. They all looked worn. She snapped photos of the sizes printed on the insides so she could replace them.

Two stacks of shoe boxes lined the back of the closet. Pushing her son's clothes aside so she could get to the boxes, Catherine selected a stack of three and carried them to Will's bed.

The first box contained brown dress shoes in excellent condition. The next contained black dress shoes. She remembered buying them and an identical pair for John. They were scuff free and gleaming. One glance at the soles told her Will had never worn them.

The box at the bottom of the stack weighed less. That's when it first hit her—perhaps she shouldn't have removed anything from his closet. What if the boxes contained something other than shoes? Personal items. The thought came too late, as she was already opening the third box and lifting the white tissue paper covering the top. She peered down at a lacy black pair of women's underpants from Victoria's Secret.

As far as Catherine knew, Will didn't have a girlfriend. Apparently, he hooked up with a girl or girls who accidentally left their underwear behind. It happened, and it was none of Catherine's business. She felt bad about invading her son's privacy. She hadn't considered she might be snooping and truly hadn't intended to find anything except shoes.

She was about to close the box when a patch of color inside caught her eye. There was something else in there.

Catherine nudged the black panties aside and stared down at what lay beneath them. Her eyes widened, her chest tightened, and she gasped.

CHAPTER 47
One Year Ago - Catherine

Inside the box, tucked under the black underpants, was another pair of women's underwear. Peach colored with eyelet lace.

A lump formed in Catherine's throat. She recognized them. They were an exact match to the bra she'd removed from Phoebe's corpse.

Horrible, previously unimaginable images invaded Catherine's mind.

Will tightening a rope around Phoebe's neck. Her fingers clawing to relieve the pressure.

Catherine berated herself for letting her mind stray down that path. There were alternative explanations. Perhaps the same bra and panties set was a popular choice among young women. Maybe the pattern wasn't the same as the bra Phoebe had been wearing when she died.

But why is Will keeping them in a shoe box in the back of his closet?

Again, so many possible explanations. Her son collected women's underwear. He had a fetish. That's all it was. Yes, it was a little creepy. Maybe a little strange. But there were worse things. So much worse. She cringed, because she couldn't stop imagining those much worse, ugly things.

Will had nothing to do with Phoebe's death, Catherine told herself. He was at school when Phoebe disappeared.

Except…wait…no. Catherine took her journal from her purse, opened it to a page from a few days ago, and scanned her notes. *Argument with John. I lost control and hurled my wineglass. Will overheard.*

A sick feeling flooded her body. She remembered her strange alcohol-fueled dream in the early morning hours inside the guest house.

I have to leave you now.

The whispered voice lingered in her mind. Perhaps it hadn't been a dream at all. It had been Will saying goodbye. And it had happened the morning of Phoebe's disappearance.

But Will wouldn't hurt anyone.

Taylor was the one with the unforgiving, cruel streak. Cross her once and she might never forgive you. Catherine had seen it many times ever since Taylor was a child. Will wasn't any of those things. He was a good person. The best.

Catherine stood in the center of Will's room, shaking.

John killed Phoebe. Catherine needed that to be true.

She stepped into the hallway to make sure she was still alone. The apartment was silent. There was no one else. She retreated to Will's bedroom and called John. Her hand shook as she listened to her phone ring. Once. Twice. Three times. Then John answered.

"Hey. I was just going to call you to see how things went," he said. "Did you have your first treatment?"

"John, I need you to tell me the truth, or I will call my attorney right now and have him draw up divorce papers."

John responded in a hushed whisper. "Whatever it is, darling, I can explain. You know I love you. Please, you need to calm down."

Too late. She couldn't pretend things were okay now. She needed to know for sure, without a doubt, if he killed Phoebe.

"Did something happen between you and Phoebe?"

"Your trainer?" John asked, sounding incredulous. "Are we back to this again?"

"I promise nothing will happen to you. You will not get in trouble. I promise I'll protect you. You don't even have to explain. I don't need to know the details. I'm sure it was an accident. Just tell me the truth." It wasn't just Catherine's hands shaking now. Her entire body trembled.

John didn't answer right away.

"Did you do something to her?" Catherine asked, silently begging him to say, *yes.*

"We talked about this already. I told you, no."

"I don't care if you and she were having an affair. I need to know if something else happened. Something bad. Tell me, John. Please, tell me." She pleaded, desperate to hear him admit he'd killed Phoebe.

"For the last time, I've talked to Phoebe maybe a few times in passing. That's it. There's nothing else. Nothing between Phoebe and me. Never has been and never will be. I know she's missing. I have nothing to do with that. I don't know where she is."

As John spoke, a murmur came from somewhere near him. Distinctly feminine.

Catherine's breath froze in her chest. She strained to hear the sound again and to make sure she hadn't imagined it.

For several seconds, there was only silence.

"What was that in the background?" she finally asked, so tense someone could pluck her like a guitar string.

"What was what?" John answered.

"I thought I heard something."

"Why don't you finally just tell her about us?" said a female voice, followed by a huff of derisive laughter.

John must have tried to cover the phone. What came next was muted. Catherine heard the woman say, "You said she wouldn't remember soon."

The pieces clicked. There was a woman with John. His mistress.

As fast as she could, Catherine mashed her finger against the end call button.

She leaned against Will's bedroom wall, her chest heaving.

CHAPTER 48
One Year Ago - Catherine

Standing in Will's bedroom, staring at the open shoebox, Catherine's whole body went numb. She felt empty.

John really *was* having an affair.

But not with Phoebe.

That knowledge had left Catherine dizzy with legs so weak she could barely stand. A side-effect from the treatment? Or the emotional rollercoaster slipping off the rails inside her?

She didn't know what to do. She told herself to stay calm. Don't jump to conclusions.

The peach eyelet panties in Will's closet might not have any connection to Phoebe. Should she ask Will about it? No, she couldn't bring herself to do so. If only she hadn't looked through his belongings.

In a feverish daze, Catherine sat on her son's bed next to the open shoebox. She had to return everything to the closet. As she put the panties back, trying to remember just how she'd found them, she spotted one more item inside the shoebox. A plastic sandwich baggie with something dark inside. Something about the size of a quarter that weighed almost nothing. She lifted the bag out for a closer look and immediately wished she hadn't. If only the bag contained weed or drugs. If only it were anything else.

The plastic baggie held a square-shaped piece of clotted, dried flesh. Just like the missing chunk of skin on Phoebe's buttocks.

Then things got worse. Another bag hid below the first. Inside it, another square of flesh.

There had to be a mistake.

There had to be.

An idea came to her—it was the wrong closet! This was Nick's room, not Will's. Her eyes darted over the walls, desperate to see something unfamiliar. Instead, the room contained photographs, banners, and framed art she recognized. Many of the items were gifts she'd given. The closet held familiar clothes, and she sat on the bedding she'd chosen and purchased for her son. It was Will's room.

No. No. Please, no.

If she hadn't looked inside the well, she might never have known.

If she hadn't removed Phoebe's dress.

If she hadn't opened the shoebox.

All those things had happened. It was too late to undo any of them.

Catherine stared at the box's contents again. She'd read enough thrillers and watched enough true crime shows to know serial killers kept souvenirs and trophies to remember their victims. If the pinkish panties belonged to Phoebe, who owned the black ones?

Catherine cursed herself for conjuring the word *serial killer*. Will did not belong in the same stratosphere as the connotations accompanying that term. Yet, how could she explain what she'd found?

A strangled cry escaped her lips. She began to sweat and shiver at the same time. Racing out of Will's room, Catherine made it into the bathroom with not a second to spare before throwing up.

A minute later, feeling as if she'd had her stomach ripped out of her, she gripped the edge of the sink and stared at her reflection in the mirror. There must be a mistake. A misunderstanding. A strange coincidence. Something she was missing. Another explanation. One that removed all blame from Will. Because Will could not have done something so horrible. Not her perfect, sweet, kind, flawless Will. People like Will, the best amongst us, did not do terrible things.

Catherine flushed the toilet and rinsed her mouth in the sink. She'd been so certain John had done it. With little hesitation, she'd believed and accepted her husband had strangled the life out of Phoebe. But not her son. Not Will. Even with the glaring evidence, she could not believe it. Yet she couldn't unsee what she'd found.

It was her fault. It had to be. She was Will's mother. Something must have gone terribly wrong in his life for him to have…Catherine squeezed her eyes shut, unable to finish the dreadful thought.

"Hey, mom," Will said. "You're here."

Heart racing, Catherine spun around to face her son. She hadn't heard him come inside. Nor had she heard him walk through the kitchen and into the hallway.

From the bathroom doorway, she could see across the hall to his room. The shoe box and its contents were in full view where she'd left them on his bed.

Will's eyes followed Catherine's to the panties next to the box.

After several pounding heartbeats, he said, "Kind of awkward you finding those, huh?" He laughed then, a convincing mixture of good-natured humor and embarrassment.

Catherine didn't laugh, and she didn't smile.

They stared at each other, Will searching her face, most certainly wondering if she understood what she'd uncovered. Her response provided the answer. Under any other circumstances, she would have laughed, apologized, joked, asked if she'd get to meet the owner of those underpants someday. She didn't do those things. In the shock and horror of the moment, she didn't have it in her to pretend.

Will looked down at his shoes and scuffed one across the carpet.

Catherine seemed to snap out of her shock then, overcome with the sudden need to escape Will's apartment and sort through her horror in private.

"I'm sorry, Will, I'm not feeling well. The treatment…" she stammered, looking over her shoulder at her ashen face in the mirror. "I have to take a rain check on our dinner."

"Okay. I understand. Do you want to take a nap here in my room? I'll stay in the kitchen and study."

"No, I better go back to the hotel."

"I can drive you."

"I'm good. Really. I'm fine."

His eyes roamed to the box on his bed, then back to Catherine. He smiled. A sheepish smile.

Catherine forced one foot in front of the other, eyes focused on the front door.

Will spoke from behind her. "Don't worry, Mother. We'll each have our secrets."

Shocked and confused, she kept moving.

"I know what you did to protect us," he said, his voice gentle.

How did he know? No one except George knew. Maybe Christian. So, what was Will talking about?

Still several yards from the door, Catherine's vision blurred. The dizzy sensation intensified, gnawing at her. She needed to get out of there.

"The infusion…I just don't feel like myself. I have to go. I'll call you later," she said, her hand reaching for the door's handle.

For the first time in her life, she left Will without hugging him goodbye.

CHAPTER 49
One Year Ago - Catherine

With the sun still low in the eastern sky, Catherine drove from Durham to Virginia, her stomach weighed down by a heavy, sick feeling. Since her discovery in Will's apartment, she hadn't uttered a word to anyone. She was still struggling to make sense of what she'd found. There was one thing she knew. She would never divulge his secret to another living soul. Never. Her son's secret remained safe with her forever. However, she and Will needed to have a long talk. No matter what compelled him to do what she believed he'd done, he had to stop.

She'd already ensured his protection, though she hadn't known whom she was protecting. No one would ever find Phoebe's remains. Without a body, there could be no murder investigation. If Will ever got caught—*because who did those black panties belong to?*—Catherine would hire Larissa Carmichael to gather a team of the best attorneys. They would argue insanity if necessary. They'd get therapy for Will rather than prison time. Because to do what he'd done, something inside him must be broken.

Her phone buzzed again. John was also on the road, driving home from Kiawah. Since yesterday, he'd left a dozen worried-sounding messages for Catherine. She'd ignored all of them. She had bigger problems.

When she stopped to refill her gas tank, she typed *Phoebe Watson, missing* into her browser, and clicked on a news clip. A woman who looked a lot like Phoebe faced the camera with tears welling in her eyes. It was Phoebe's mother, Sharon Watson.

"I know Phoebe is out there and she's okay," Sharon said, the tears now streaming down her cheeks. "I can feel it. She's going to come home."

That wasn't going to happen. Sharon could repeat those words until she believed them, if that's what she needed to keep going. Still, it wasn't going to happen.

Sharon's eyes, filled with desperate pleas, bore straight into Catherine's soul. "If you know anything, if you have any morsel of information, anything at all, I beg you, please come forward and share it with us," Sharon said.

Catherine couldn't bear to witness the woman's pain. With a heavy heart, she turned her phone off and set it face down on the console of her Mercedes. She fixed her gaze on the giant Shell sign looming ahead. As cruel as it seemed, sometimes mothers were better off not knowing the horrifying truth about their children.

CHAPTER 50
One Year Ago - Catherine

Catherine typed key search words into her laptop.

Unsolved murder of a woman in Virginia
Mysterious unsolved murder of a woman in North Carolina
Murder victim with missing undergarments, North Carolina.
Murder victim with peculiar square-shaped incision on her skin
Any instances of female murder victims found without underwear and with skin removal?

The results were disheartening, though not unexpected. News about missing women and unsolved murders populated her screen. Yet none of the information mentioned the specific details she was looking for. Not surprising. Law enforcement often withheld certain facts from the public. Usually, facts that were strange or disturbing. They had to distinguish true perpetrators from false leads.

Having learned nothing useful, Catherine cleared her search history. She stood and stretched before opening the refrigerator and peering inside. Despite having eaten nothing all day, she wasn't hungry. She had no appetite for food or anything else. Images of Sharon and Phoebe Watson randomly assaulted her, yet the most distressing thoughts centered on Will. He'd always been her greatest source of joy. He was the best motivation she had to fight her disease for as long as possible. Now all of that was ruined.

She walked away from the fridge empty handed and poured a drink instead. She took a long sip of the amber liquid and placed it on the table beside her. From the built-in cabinets beside the fireplace, she took out the scrapbooks with pictures of Will's childhood. She hadn't looked through them in years. Now she wanted to know when her son became something other than the wonderful, near-perfect person she'd thought he was. Were there clues hiding in plain sight and she'd missed them?

The first pages of the book she selected had snapshots from Will's middle school days. Will smiling with a lacrosse stick. Laughing on a sailboat. Beaming at the camera from under his football helmet. With each turn of the page, Will filled out more, growing taller and stronger, going from cute to undeniably handsome. Not one photo caught him smirking. There were no cocky grins. No sinister stares. He looked so happy, like someone you could trust.

Catherine opened another scrapbook. The pictures in the center pages caught Will playing rugby. On one side of the layout was his All-American certificate. A few pages later, and he was wearing a cap and gown, graduating as the salutatorian of his high school class. After Taylor's less than stellar boarding school performance, anything above a C would have made Catherine proud. Will had done so much more and all while excelling at sports, serving as senior class president, and completing hours of community service. He was her baby. Her pride and joy. What she'd found yesterday, it just didn't make sense.

Catherine refreshed her drink and opened a third album. In this one, Will was an irresistibly adorable toddler with a smattering of freckles across his face and a touch of sunburn on his nose. With the sun on the horizon, he stood on the front porch of their beach house, holding a giant conch shell. Beside him, his father leaned against the white railing. Charles wore a white polo shirt and Nantucket red shorts.

A flush of adrenaline quivered through Catherine's system as she recognized that outfit. She'd taken the photo *that* day. Had she really included the picture in a scrapbook? What had she been thinking?

She didn't want to revisit that part of the past, but the memories flooded back to her. Eighteen years ago, Catherine, Charles, and Will were spending a long weekend at their beach house while Taylor attended horseback riding camp. As Catherine rummaged through Charles's windbreaker pocket, hunting for the spare car key, his phone chirped. She slid it out and saw a new message from his assistant. Then Catherine's whole world spun.

Catherine wasn't clueless. She'd suspected her husband's relationship with his attractive assistant went beyond the professional. There were small hints and clues. Late night hours at the office. More work dinners and out-of-town trips than usual. A growing distance between herself and Charles.

Catherine planned to confront her husband once she had actual evidence. If her hunch was right, she'd planned to give him two options. One, end the affair immediately and fire his assistant. Two, pack his bags and say goodbye to his marriage forever. Catherine would not follow the same path as her mother. She wouldn't look the other way while Charles screwed someone on the side. Because that's exactly what she assumed would happen if she didn't give her husband an ultimatum. His affair was a meaningless fling. Of course it was.

But the messages on his phone proved her wrong.

Let me know as soon as you tell her about us. Good luck. I love you.

Catherine felt dizzy and disoriented. Her hands shook as she read through the other texts. They went back months. Flirtatious comments at first, then giving way to more caring and meaningful exchanges.

The ultimatum she'd planned wouldn't matter. The messages made that clear. Charles had already made up his mind.

Catherine returned his phone to his pocket, then locked herself in the bathroom to cry and to think. When her tears dried, she had a plan.

That evening, three-year-old Will slept in the upstairs bedroom, wiped out from a long and fun day in the sun and ocean air. Downstairs, with the sound of the waves crashing near their beach-front home, Catherine mixed cocktails for herself and her husband.

Charles asked for a double. Perhaps he was going to tell her now, and he needed the extra courage it would provide.

Catherine braced herself for the end of their marriage as she prepared their drinks with precision.

His cocktail contained an infusion of nut oil, a lethal concoction that could kill him.

CHAPTER 51

Eighteen Years Ago - Catherine

Charles got through half his drink before his face reddened and he collapsed on the marble tile. He clawed at his throat. He choked out her name.

Catherine. Help.

"For better or worse," she whispered as he writhed on the floor. "I guess this is the worse part, Charles."

Each breath he struggled to inhale became a desperate rattle when she left the room, taking their phones with her. Charles kept EpiPens in the house for his severe nut allergy. Catherine had removed them. She hoped the end would come quickly for him, and it did.

After replacing the EpiPens in various drawers, she tugged Charles into the back of her SUV. He weighed a hundred and eighty pounds. She met the physical challenge with sheer adrenaline and the benefit of years of grueling workouts.

From the end of the dock, Catherine tossed her husband's phone into the ocean and watched as it disappeared into the dark water. After putting his windbreaker and the boat keys in the boat, she untethered the vessel and gave it a big shove, praying the current would carry it far away. If it didn't, no matter. Statistically speaking, most accidents happened close to home.

Before leaving the beach house, she woke her sleeping toddler and strapped him into his booster seat.

"We're going home because we have to get Taylor from the stables in the morning," she told Will.

"Why are your hands shaking, Mommy?" he'd asked.

She gripped the steering wheel tighter to make the trembling stop. "I drank too much coffee, sweetie. It's making me jumpy." What she needed was a good stiff drink or two. But she didn't drink and drive, especially not with Will in the car. She'd take a Xanax at the next stop.

"Don't have too much again. I don't want you to feel shaky," Will told her, his lips slightly puckered, and his little brow furrowed with concern. His look of pure love melted Catherine's heart.

"I won't sweetie," she said, smiling back at him in the rearview mirror.

Will turned on his tablet and watched a movie about dinosaurs.

"Where's daddy?" he asked after they'd been driving for over an hour.

"He's staying at the beach house another day," Catherine told him.

"Oh." That's all Will said. Even as a toddler, he never questioned his mother. Never argued with her. He was curious, but always accepted what she told him. He trusted her.

Catherine had pangs of regret for her children's sake. Taylor loved her daddy because he spoiled her. Yet children were resilient. They would be fine. Charles wasn't home much. He'd always spent more time in the office than anywhere else. Especially since he'd incorporated time for his mistress into his already busy work schedule.

All Catherine needed to temper any rising guilt was to remember Charles's final text message from his mistress. *Good luck. I love you.* It made Catherine's stomach turn and motivated her to see the endeavor to its end.

Catherine couldn't dispose of Charles's body in the ocean and risk divers or anyone else finding it soon. A dead husband with nut oil in his system might point straight at her. Charles needed to rot somewhere no one would ever find his remains. She knew just the place. On the way there, she called his phone a few times and left messages.

Driving just above the speed limit and avoiding all toll roads, Catherine drove to the deep and secluded woodlands where she used to party as a teen. About a quarter mile from the rickety old bridge, she parked her SUV. While Will slept soundly in his booster seat, she single-handedly dug a shallow grave and buried her husband. From there, she drove home, showered, and took care of her son.

As luck would have it, an unexpected storm hit the beach only a few hours after she left. Raucous waves and thunder could only help her get away with what she'd done.

The next morning, on her way to pick up Taylor from the stables, Catherine called their beach-house neighbor.

"Would you mind going over to our house and seeing if my husband is there?" Catherine asked. "It's just not like him to go so long without checking in with me and the children."

Her neighbor called back twenty minutes later. "Your boat isn't in the slip. Charles probably went for a ride."

"Oh. He must have left his phone behind." Catherine said, making sure she sounded uncertain. "Thank you so much for checking," she added. "I appreciate it. I probably shouldn't worry. I just can't help it."

To calm her nerves, Catherine took her children to lunch and played the piano in the afternoon. Then she drove back to the beach with Taylor and Will.

As expected, the boat slip remained empty. Catherine called her parents and told them how worried she was. They encouraged her to call 9-1-1.

From there, it was a whirlwind of nerve-wracking days playing the part of a grief-stricken wife, which she did convincingly well. She hired divers to search the area near their dock for Charles's body. They never found him. The ocean was a long way from Madison Creek Woods.

Eventually, with no evidence to the contrary, authorities concluded Charles died in a boating accident. They officially declared him dead. Life went on for Catherine as a widow. Raising two children on her own, even with nannies, left little time to dwell on what she'd done. She visited her parents often and learned her mother had early onset Alzheimer's.

Between the children, her Smartbox obligations, and visiting her mother, Catherine kept busy. Her husband's accidental death came up often enough, usually in the form of condolences from friends and acquaintances. Eventually, like everyone else, Catherine came to believe her own lie. Charles had indeed perished in a tragic boating accident.

That illusion shattered in an instant.

On an ordinary day, Will and a friend from his kindergarten class were playing in his room. From the hallway, Catherine overheard their conversation.

"My grandmother has a sickness where she doesn't know who we are," Will had said in a matter-of-fact manner. "She doesn't know who anyone is. She's dying."

"My grandpa already died," the friend said. "Do you know what happens when people die?"

Will hesitated, then answered, "Your family digs a hole and buries you in the ground."

Catherine covered her mouth as a gasp escaped her lips. She slumped against the wall, overwhelmed by a sickening mix of emotions, yet needing to hear what came next.

"Nah. That's not how it happens," Will's friend said. "I saw a show about people who…you know…the ones who take dead people when they die. It's not your family who does it. It's guys who work at the cemetery. Grave diggers."

"It's not always strangers. Sometimes it's your family," Will said. He didn't sound defensive. His words carried an unwavering certainty, conveying the spirited confidence that was already the trademark of his personality.

That brief exchange had occurred over a decade ago. Catherine had forgotten it. Suddenly, what Will had told her when she last left his apartment made sense.

Don't worry, Mother. We'll each have our secrets. I know what you did to protect us.

Will knew what she'd done. He must have seen her, though he'd never said a word to her about it. He'd seen his mother bury his dead father in the woods, then pretend like it never happened. The experience had traumatized his little mind. Now, because of her, Will was a killer, too.

All those years ago, Catherine believed she'd taken care of her problem. She'd taught Charles a lesson for betraying her. Killing him had preserved her dignity, and she'd gotten away with it. No regrets. Yet her decision had come back to haunt her, shattering her world and destroying all she held dear. What she'd done had created a much worse situation. Catherine didn't know how she could live with it. She wasn't sure she wanted to.

CHAPTER 52

One Year Ago - Catherine

The Director of Atrium Gardens guided Catherine through a grand dining area with luxurious amenities.

At one table, a frail woman sat slumped in her seat with a vacant gaze. Her trembling hand brought a spoonful of food toward her mouth. Green beans slid off, cascading onto her lap. Her empty spoon tottered in the air, inches from her lips, as if she'd forgotten what she was doing. She wore a lovely string of pearls over a pale blue cardigan set. She had perfectly coiffed silver hair, but she was old and fragile. So much older than Catherine.

Catherine looked away; her gaze moving to a man in a wheelchair, leaning to the side, gnarled hands in his lap. He sat with a man dressed in the white Atrium Gardens uniform. The older man opened his mouth expectantly as the caregiver fed him. It was a glimpse into a future Catherine wanted to avoid. This couldn't be her fate.

Atrium Gardens boasted the reputation of being the most expensive, and therefore, the finest facility in the state. Yet Catherine prayed she would never have to call it home. The visit had merely been a precautionary measure, an exploration of her options. Now, standing within the facility's walls, she was certain this was not the solution she desired. She didn't want to spend her final years in this place surrounded by people who had already lived such long lives. Yet she worried if she could trust John to honor her wishes. What were the chances of counting on him when she couldn't take care of herself?

Catherine followed the director through the well-lit hallways with their perfectly curated artwork. As she passed stranger after stranger, memories of her mother's battle with Alzheimer's filled her mind. Her mother had gradually lost her personality, abilities, and memories. Yet, even amidst the sadness, she'd been able to remain in the familiarity of her own home, surrounded by familiar comforts. Her Persian cats. Breathtaking views from the balconies. Joyous visits from grandchildren—despite the confusion and disarray in her mind.

Catherine was determined to ensure her own final years followed a similar path. Shortly after her diagnosis, she had attempted to broach the subject with John. She tried to explain the importance of hiring in-home care, someone to live in the guest house. He had been dismissive, avoiding the conversation. Probably because it made him uncomfortable. He claimed they had ample time to address those issues, failing to grasp the urgency of the situation. When the time came, it would be too late for discussions. Catherine would be incapable of making rational decisions regarding her own care.

She had to take matters into her own hands, to establish a plan while she still had the capacity. Home care, specific criteria, multiple caregivers, and legal directives—all details she needed to arrange with her attorney to ensure her wishes.

Catherine sat in Larissa Carmichael's elegant office. Shelves held stacks of leather-bound books and legal documents arranged with precision.

Larissa, dressed impeccably in a tailored designer suit, smiled at Catherine from behind a large desk. A collection of awards and diplomas adorned the wall behind her.

"I appreciate you taking care of this for me," Catherine told the attorney. "I know it's not your area of legal expertise, however, I trust you can handle it or make sure it's handled correctly."

"Absolutely," Larissa said. "As soon as you decide what you want, send it to me. Those forms will help guide you."

"You can expect something back from me this week," Catherine said.

As their conversation drew to a close, Catherine reached into her bag and retrieved a package—an eight by twelve-inch envelope sealed in wax. It contained her journal. She'd made carefully chosen, subtle adjustments to it.

"In the event of my incapacitation or death, I'll need you to read this and proceed as necessary," Catherine said.

She should have felt a devastating sadness then. She didn't. Only strangely detached, her emotions buried beneath an impenetrable numbness. The weight of her most terrible secret was crushing her.

CHAPTER 53

One Year Ago - Catherine

Catherine canceled her infusion treatment and hadn't left the house in days. Tired of watching her sleep, John went to play golf. As soon as he was gone, Catherine got out of bed and started drinking.

An engine rumbled to a stop in her driveway. She turned toward the front windows, almost lost her balance, then steadied herself in time.

It was George. She wasn't expecting him. His presence was well timed. She needed to tell him something. Best to do it in person. She opened the door and called him over. He trudged toward her with his shoulders hunched forward.

"I trust you got your retirement plan," she said, propping herself against the doorframe.

He nodded, studying her face. "Are you sick?"

"I'll be fine," she said, pulling her shoulders back, straightening her posture. "Please listen. This is important." She waited for him to come closer. "If they ever find, you know…the racoon, and start asking questions, tell them I did it."

George gave her a blank look. "You said no one was ever going to go out there."

"They won't. But if something completely unexpected happens and somehow, it's connected to us, you absolutely must tell them I did it."

"That you went out to those woods and…"

"Tell them I did all of it. I'm the reason the raccoon ended up in the well."

George narrowed his eyes and scanned her face as if searching for something there. "It's not...you didn't," he said, not sounding entirely convinced.

"You know I'm sick, don't you? My disease has a cruel way of changing people, making them forget things."

George looked skeptical. "My mother has dementia. She'd never—."

"It affects everyone differently," Catherine said, shutting down his argument. Debating the symptoms of dementia with George was not part of the day's agenda.

"Is that why you didn't want to call the police? You thought you could be responsible?"

Catherine bit into the side of her cheek as she answered. "Yes, it might have crossed my mind. I believed Phoebe was having an affair with my husband."

"You never really thought it was Christian?"

"I wasn't sure then, and I'm still not sure."

George looked dazed, though nothing should have surprised him about a pseudo confession at that point. Not after a murder, a cover up, and hush money.

Catherine softened her voice again. "Can you do that for me, George? Can you do what I asked you?"

"Why?"

"Because it's best for all of us. If the time ever comes that it's necessary, I might not be able to do it for myself. You won't be alone. I've ensured you will have the best attorney representation to help you sort things through...if it ever comes to that. It shouldn't. All you need to do is keep going on with your business. Enjoy your life. Forget what happened. Okay?"

They stared at each other for several seconds. A bitter taste rose from Catherine's throat. She leaned harder against the door, needing more support. Whether George answered, she had to trust him.

He turned his head toward the side of the house. "I'm going to trim the viburnums."

"You don't have to tell me. I trust you to do what needs to be done. I always have."

He opened his mouth as if he might say more. Instead, he nodded without meeting her gaze. Then he walked away.

Catherine watched him go. She didn't know if she could count on him after what he'd told his brother-in-law, and yet she trusted him more than anyone else. What did that say about her life?

With a loud sigh, she shut the door and returned to the living room, where she slumped against the sofa cushions, feeling truly exhausted. So many factors compounded her situation. Her early-onset dementia—it was changing her, draining her energy and her ability to think. The wine and the whisky—her drinking was out of hand, but she needed it. John's affair and his lying hadn't helped any.

Yet none of those issues had affected her like the matter with her son. An overwhelming sense of guilt weighed her down with a force so heavy she didn't have the will to climb out from underneath it. She was ultimately responsible for turning Will into something terrible, just like herself. Perhaps he was even worse. Did he even have a reason to kill those women?

He was so handsome.

So helpful.

So intelligent.

And apparently he had an extra-curricular hobby she'd never once suspected.

Catherine couldn't even think about him now without choking back a sob and reaching for another drink.

She knew what she wanted to do. Going through with it meant never having to work out the legal directives or arrange for her future care, and not having to worry about her future with John. She could be done with all of that.

Her decision wasn't a sudden one. Months ago, when she'd received her diagnosis, she'd contemplated going out on her terms rather than gradually yielding to Alzheimer's. Not when she was still barely symptomatic. Later. Much later. Yet as she sat alone with no good reason to struggle through the next few days, never mind weeks and months and years, the timing seemed right.

Nothing about the decision seemed cowardly. It felt like the brave thing to do for herself, allowing the gift of mercy. The right thing to do, considering all she faced.

Catherine sent a message to her son, choking up as she typed and deleted and revised. She didn't want him to think her decision was his fault. There were so many other factors. Yet the truth—she wanted her Will back. The innocent Will.

Finally, she hit send.

A brief though critical exchange of texts followed.

In one wobbly motion, she stood from the couch, the decision fully made.

She placed the first sleeping pills on her tongue and gulped them down dry. She took more and quickly chased them with the remaining whiskey.

In a sluggish daze, she trudged to the pool. Her vision blurred. The backyard spun around her. The pool house dipped to her right, then soared toward the sky. She needed to lie down, close her eyes, and surrender to sleep. Ignoring the urge, she forced her feet to shuffle forward, one after the other, in a dream-like state. Stretching out her fingers, she searched for the iron rail snaking up the pool's steps.

She descended the stairs, her eyes barely open. The warm water rose to her waist, then to her chest. It lapped at her skin, embracing her, beckoning her into oblivion. When it reached her neck, she let her eyes fully close, and her legs gave way beneath her.

As she settled to the bottom, she felt no self-pity. Not when she'd buried two bodies in Madison Creek Woods and her son was not the perfect person she had always believed him to be.

CHAPTER 54

Present Day - Victoria

"Are you coming to bed soon?" Ned asked.

"Yes. I just need to check something," Victoria said, leaning toward her laptop. Her eyes focused on a new email with *E-Z pass* in the subject line.

A toll road ran between the Bower family home and Madison Creek Woods. For that reason, Victoria had requested E-Z pass records for the five vehicles registered to the Bower's estate.

Victoria scrolled through the records, starting with the Mercedes SUV John said Catherine used to drive.

The Mercedes hadn't traveled through a toll check point in over a year, which made sense. Nor had it registered on any toll readers between the time of Phoebe's disappearance and Catherine's accident. That lack of evidence hardly mattered. Not when so many other signs pointed to Catherine.

Victoria checked the other vehicles registered under Catherine's name. Only one of the five had passed through a toll area during the time in question. It was the Jeep Grand Cherokee Limited. The car Will drove. The toll report showed the Jeep traveled southbound on June second. It returned through the toll reader at five am on the morning of June fifth.

Will hadn't told the truth regarding his whereabouts on June fourth, the evening Phoebe disappeared. He wasn't at school in North Carolina. He was in Virginia.

What else had he lied about?

Shortly after her second cup of coffee, a notification from a forensics communication technician propelled Victoria out of her chair. She hurried through the corridors of the FBI building. They'd recovered the deleted messages from Catherine Bower's phone—messages that might hold critical information as to what really happened.

As Victoria walked, she greeted the colleagues she passed with a nod. Inside the Digital Forensics Department, technicians hunched over screens, scanning lines of code and data patterns, their faces bathed in a bluish glow.

Victoria approached the analyst who notified her. He handed her a tablet with the recovered messages. She moved to a desk in the corner of the room and swiped through the screens, fixating on the last messages. Will and Catherine had sent them the morning of her accident.

Catherine: *I love you with my whole heart and soul. Nothing can change that. I will own your misdeeds. Let them become mine.*

Will: *Are you drinking???*

Catherine: *I did it.*

Will: *Did what? Are you talking about the thing with the underwear?*

Catherine: *The underwear. The square cuts. All of it.*

Will: *Thanks. Not necessary for you to own anything. We're fine.*

Catherine: *I know. Just in case, in the future, some day.*

Will: *Umm...okay???*

Catherine: *I need you to make me a promise. You have to stop.*

Will: *I don't know if I can.*

Catherine: *You can, and you will. It's all I ask of you.*

Will: *Okay. You're weirding me out. Doesn't sound like you.*

Catherine: *I'm sorry I did this to you. I love you.*

Will: *You didn't do anything to me. Right now, you're really freaking me out. Are you drinking? Is John there with you?*

Victoria read through the messages again. What had Catherine asked her son to stop doing? What was the 'thing with the underwear' and the 'square cuts'? Were those references to Phoebe's murder? Killers didn't allude to what they'd done via text. Not unless they were supremely confident they'd never get caught. Perhaps Catherine and her son were just that confident.

Back at her desk, Victoria logged into the VICAP database. She searched for unsolved murders within a hundred miles of Virginia and North Carolina.

She focused on keywords from the text conversations and found a hit.

A few months before Phoebe disappeared, a couple vacationing in Miami found the body of a young woman from Alabama. She'd visited the city for her spring break. During the night, she'd gotten separated from her friends. They didn't know who she'd gone off with, or who had taken her, only that she was gone. When the couple found her half buried in the sand dunes, days after she went missing, she wore a bra and no underwear. Someone had strangled her and carved a square-shaped piece of flesh from her buttocks.

Victoria noted the date of the woman's disappearance. Then she went to Will's social media account. His profile picture portrayed a serene moment captured on a sailboat—an image of him and his mother, their radiant smiles forever frozen in time. But something dark loomed beneath those smiles. Victoria was sure of it.

Will's online presence was minimal. His infrequent posts featured landscapes from distant corners of the world. No one had tagged him in any pictures. It seemed he had taken precautions to prevent them from doing so. He'd left no obvious digital breadcrumbs to follow. It was a smart move, one befitting a future attorney.

Victoria clicked through Will's list of friends, starting with his fellow students. April of the previous year served as her starting point, the time when the woman had vanished in Miami. One by one, Victoria dissected the images and anecdotes shared by Will's friends. The first friend she chose had traveled to the vibrant streets of Tokyo during spring break. Her second choice had shared snapshots of a lively group frolicking in Cancun. The third friend, a Duke senior named Nick, had posted several group photos on the sun-soaked beaches of Miami.

Thousands of college students descended on the Florida beaches for spring break trips. Still, Victoria's pulse quickened as she enlarged each of Nick's group photos and painstakingly scrutinized each face. Until—there he was—Will, his presence unmistakable. Enveloped in a swirl of Hawaiian shirts, brightly colored board shorts, and beers, his arm draped causally around his companion.

Coincidence that he was in Miami when the woman from Alabama disappeared? Victoria didn't think so.

If someone had found Phoebe's body soon after her death, rather than a year later, would she have had a similar cutout on her body? Based on the text messages between Will and his mother, Victoria was sure of it.

After the interview with George, Victoria had written up a case to prove Catherine Bower murdered Phoebe Watson. At that very moment, the legal department was determining how to proceed.

Now, Victoria wasn't so sure she'd gotten the facts right.

CHAPTER 55

Present Day - Victoria

"I don't think Catherine killed Phoebe," Victoria told Rivera.

He tilted his head, listening.

"It was her son. I started to suspect him when I learned he lied about his whereabouts at the time Phoebe disappeared. I think I found another victim of his. A girl in Miami."

Victoria handed Rivera a printed list of the text messages. "These are from the morning of Catherine's accident. It sounds like Catherine knew what he'd done. She wanted to take the blame if it ever got out. She wanted to protect Will."

"If Will killed Phoebe, what was his motive?" Rivera asked.

"I don't know. Maybe he's like Dan Sullivan and just enjoys hurting women," Victoria said. "I kept hearing how wonderful Will is, how his mother adored him. I think when she learned what he did, she couldn't live with it. From these messages, it sounds like she's planning to end her life."

"It does," Rivera agreed. "But weren't you sure her so-called accident resulted from someone trying to punish her?"

"Yes. And I was right. That person was *her*. She felt responsible for Will's actions. Suicide was her own form of punishment." Momentarily lost in her thoughts, Victoria snapped out of it. "We need to search his car. It's still registered under his mother's name, so our warrant covers it. He might be in Durham. If he knows we're on to him, he'll have a lawyer at his side and we'll never find evidence, if there's any to find."

"We've got Catherine's phone right?" Rivera asked. "If her son is still on her phone plan, we might be able to see his location. Let's try that first."

Without wasting a moment, the agents darted back to Digital Forensics and checked Catherine's phone out of the evidence room. They accessed the contacts, navigating to the favorite's sections and Will's name. Victoria pressed the info icon. The screen transformed into a map with a solitary blue dot in the center—Will's current location.

Will was not basking in any tropical paradise, nor had he returned to Durham. The map revealed he was in Virginia—at Atrium Gardens.

Victoria clutched Catherine's phone tighter as she figured out her next move.

CHAPTER 56

Present Day - Deja

Deja spotted Will's white Jeep in the back of the parking lot where he told her he'd be waiting. Funny how he still didn't have her number. They'd only communicated through Catherine's iPad or the phone in Catherine's room.

"Hi. You look amazing," he said when Deja walked up to his open window.

"Thank you." Normally she would have said, you don't look so bad yourself. With a haircut and a white linen shirt, all his travel scruffiness gone, he'd never looked so handsome before. They'd already shared so much over the video calls, yet still she felt shy. A little voice in her head kept reminding her they inhabited different worlds.

"Ready for dinner?" Will asked, without getting out of the Jeep.

"I am," she replied.

"Do you want to leave your car here and go together? I'll drop you off later."

"Sure," she agreed, making her way to the other side of his vehicle.

"You really do look great," he said again when she got in.

"You mean out of my uniform?" She hadn't gotten all done up by any means, only added a touch more makeup, a cute dress, and some low heels.

Will turned on music and glanced away from the road to smile at her and ask, "Did you tell anyone you were with me?"

"No. I didn't say anything to anyone." She answered with a shrug, as if to say *why would I?* She'd only mentioned something to her grandmother, telling Gran she had dinner plans at The Palm with a friend who just returned from traveling.

"It's probably good you didn't tell anyone," Will said. "Since you work for the agency. I told you I spoke with our attorney. I should also talk to the agency and find out what your contract says. It has so many restrictions, intentionally, to protect my mother's privacy. Whatever it might say, I can work around it. I can rewrite it to say whatever works for...you know...whatever we might have going here."

"Oh," Deja said. Why did her employment status keep coming up?

"You're so good for my mother," Will said.

"Thank you," Deja answered. She'd almost added, "I love her." It was true. They'd spent so much time together. Deja felt a strong connection. But Will might think that was strange.

Music filled the car, and they were silent until Deja said, "Your mother and I communicate sometimes."

"Oh, yeah?" Will asked. "Has she said anything more about her former trainer? Phoebe Watson?"

"No. She hasn't spoken a word since then. It's more in her facial expressions and her body language."

"Has the FBI agent come back to talk with you again? Agent Heslin. The one from the airplane crash."

"Is that who she is?" Deja asked, surprised. She'd known there was something familiar about Victoria Heslin. That explained her missing fingers. "She came back a few days ago. I told her to call the attorney. I can't believe they still haven't found Phoebe's killer. Whoever it is, he's still out there and he could be anywhere. Can you imagine someone doing something so terrible?"

"Pretty wild," Will said, raising his eyebrows. "The weather is perfect. What do you think about having a picnic instead?"

She hadn't dressed for a picnic, though she could make it work. "Did you have a place in mind?" she asked.

"Yep. I have a cooler in the back with takeout. A bottle of wine. I thought it would be nice. If you were up for it."

"You already bought the food?"

"I like to be prepared."

Deja turned to look in the back of the car. A large cooler bag sat in the center of the seats next to a black duffel bag and coils of rope.

"What if I'd said no because I don't like picnics or eating outside?" Deja asked, laughing.

He shrugged. "I'd take the food home and eat it later."

"What is the rope for?" she asked.

"Line. For the main sheet and the jib sheet."

"I have no idea what that means," she said.

Will chuckled. "For my sailboat. Check out the food I brought. See if you like it."

"Now?"

"No sense having a picnic with food you don't like."

The car was slowing for a stop sign. Deja pivoted around again and reached into the back. She unzipped the cooler bag. Will had tucked a chilled bottle of wine inside. Plastic containers of food filled the rest of the space—cold deli salads from Troutman's, an upscale eatery not far from Atrium Gardens.

"This is exactly the sort of food I would pick out," Deja said. "Everything looks great."

Though she hadn't seen everything yet. She lifted a smaller container from the bag. It wasn't from Troutman's. It had a Trader Joe's label on the side. Her favorite couscous salad.

"Oh! This is one of my go-to favorite meals," she said. Slowly her delight changed to discomfort. Was it just a wild coincidence? If not, how did he know?

CHAPTER 57
Present Day - Victoria

With Rivera at the wheel, the agents sped toward Atrium Gardens, their surroundings whizzing past in a blur. Crowded buildings and city streets gradually gave way to peaceful tree-lined suburban roads while Victoria used Catherine's phone to monitor Will's location. By the time the agents arrived at Atrium Gardens, the pin still hadn't moved.

They approached the front desk, holding up their badges.

"We're looking for Will Montgomery. Catherine Bower's son. He's somewhere within the building or on the property," Rivera said.

The woman behind the desk stared from one agent to the other, then glanced at her computer screen. "I saw him come in. He hasn't signed out, so he might still be here. Though not everyone remembers to sign out when they leave. If he's not with his mother, Mrs. Bower's caregiver might know where he went...unless she already went home for the day."

"Thank you," Victoria said, leading the way to Catherine's room.

Catherine was lying in bed with her eyes closed. The television played across from her, a smiling young woman announcing a mega-sale on all new Toyotas.

"We're looking for your son," Victoria said, struggling to reconcile the seemingly helpless woman in the bed with the things she'd done.

Catherine's eyes flickered, her grip on the blanket tightening. She remained silent.

The agents split up, moving through the corridors, checking the gathering rooms. Still no sign of Will. Yet the pin showing his location hadn't moved.

It was worth checking with Deja. Maybe she'd seen Will before the end of her shift and knew where he was. Victoria retrieved Deja's number and dialed. The call went straight to voicemail.

"If her shift is over, she probably went home," Rivera said. "The facility must have an emergency contact for her. A parent or roommate. Someone who is with her now or knows how we can get in touch with her. I'll see if the front desk has the info."

Victoria retraced her steps back to Catherine's room. Inside, everything was tidy. With no mess, there were few places to leave a phone where it wouldn't get seen, unless someone had intentionally hidden it. Victoria slid her hand between the sofa cushions and behind the throw pillows. Nothing.

Catherine's stare was no longer vacant. Her eyes followed Victoria around the room.

Heart pounding with anticipation, Victoria retrieved her own phone and dialed Will's number. Her phone rang first. A split second later, she heard the muffled echo of another.

She followed the sound to a dresser. She opened the first drawer and moved aside the top layer of neatly folded clothing. Her eyes locked onto a black iPhone. She scooped it up. The device was password protected.

Victoria felt a surge of adrenaline. She didn't know why Will had left his phone behind, hiding it under his mother's clothing. It seemed a deliberate move to mislead someone about his true whereabouts.

Rivera entered the room clutching a sticky note with Deja's emergency contact number—Ramone Torres, her father.

Victoria dialed the number, told Ramone who she was and said, "I'm looking for your daughter. Do you know where she is?"

"Is this related to the murder investigation she called about?" he asked.

"Yes. I need to speak with her and she's not answering her phone."

"She silences it when she's at work. Sometimes she forgets to turn the ringer back on. If it's in her purse, she won't know anyone is calling. She should be home any minute."

Victoria heard murmurs in the background and then Ramone said, "I made a mistake. Deja went out to dinner with a friend. To The Palm."

"Did she say who the friend was?"

Another muffled conversation ensued in the background before Ramone responded. "All we know is that the friend was recently overseas."

That sounded like Will. Victoria was worried, but she didn't want to alarm Deja's family unnecessarily. The agents had traced Will's phone location using Catherine's device. Maybe they could track Deja using her father's. Victoria asked, and in a matter of seconds, a screenshot appeared from Ramone, revealing Deja's last known location. It wasn't The Palm, a place Victoria had recently dined with her family and Ned. Deja was nowhere near the restaurant's vicinity. Victoria recognized the map on her screen. A forest area with winding trails. It was a lovely location few people knew about. The last time Victoria visited to hike with Ned and their dogs, they'd practically had the whole place to themselves.

Deja was somewhere inside those secluded woods with Will. The agents had no time to lose.

Before leaving Catherine's room, Victoria said, "I don't know what your son is up to, or what sort of game he's playing, but we're about to stop it."

CHAPTER 58

Present Day - Victoria

The sun had dropped beneath the tops of the trees lining the entrance road leading to the seventy-five acres of trails. A sign at the park's entrance read, *Area closes at dusk. No admittance after dark.* The rule wasn't enforced. No one patrolled the park. There was no gate to close.

Two cars were parked in the first visitor parking lot. Neither was Deja's Honda or Will's Jeep.

Rivera kept driving, heading deeper into the secluded area. Victoria scanned the dense trees. Her left knee bounced uncontrollably as she imagined worst-case scenarios where Will had dragged Deja into the woods. At the next parking area, she spotted one car. A white Jeep Cherokee in the corner, tucked under the trees.

No sign of Will or Deja.

The agents parked and got out of their car.

The Jeep was empty.

There were two trail heads nearby. A three-mile loop and a longer out-and-back trail. Rivera and Victoria separated, and Victoria set off in a jog down the longer trail.

She hadn't gone far when the trail opened to a clearing with two picnic tables. A couple occupied one of them. A woman with shiny black hair, and a man with the build of an athlete. Victoria felt relief as she recognized Will and Deja. Deja was all right, spooning food from a container onto the plate in front of her. She wore a dress and heels, more suited for a nice restaurant than an outdoor picnic.

Deja laughed. So did Will. They sounded like they were having a pleasant time. That was about to change.

Victoria approached the pair, her steps deliberate, her hands positioned near her weapon.

Deja stared in confusion when she spotted Victoria. "What are you doing here?" she stammered.

Will stood. His face held a confident smile.

"Will Montgomery, I need you to come with me," Victoria said, her voice left no room for negotiation.

Will's smile faded. "Why?"

"You're under arrest for the murder of Phoebe Watson." They hadn't planned to arrest him yet. Ensuring Deja's safety had forced Victoria's hand.

Deja gasped.

Will's hand moved toward his pocket.

"Don't move! Get your hands up!" Victoria commanded, her gun drawn and trained on him.

"Don't get all worked up," he said. "Just looking for my phone to call my attorney."

His nonchalance only fueled Victoria's suspicions.

"Do not move. You'll get your call later. Besides, you don't have your phone. You left it in your mother's dresser," Victoria said.

"Why would you do that?" Deja asked, her voice shaking.

"This is preposterous." Will scoffed, finally raising his hands. "You're going to be sorry."

Victoria didn't think so. Not sorry the way she would have been if something had happened to Deja.

Rivera raced into the clearing from the trail. He seemed to gain a quick understanding of the situation, and secured handcuffs around Will's wrists.

Will went on and on, insisting they'd made a terrible mistake and his family's attorneys would crush them.

"As for who gets crushed, let's entrust that outcome to a judge and jury," Victoria said, eliciting an approving smile from Rivera.

CHAPTER 59

Present Day - Will

Will left the psychiatrist's office, accompanied by Larissa Carmichael. A line of photographers waited for them outside. As they snapped pictures, Will shielded his face, though his expression revealed nothing.

Another battery of tests was behind him. Tests that could potentially prove him insane and incompetent to stand trial, just like his mother. That was only the fallback plan, a contingency if all else failed.

Will wasn't insane. He was fully aware what he'd done was wrong. He knew a lifetime in prison was a deserving punishment. Though rarely did anyone get what they deserved, be it good or bad. Thanks to his mother and the unexpected involvement of Dan Sullivan, prison time wasn't in Will's future.

Before his mother's accident—Will still clung to that term, aware it was a euphemism for her attempted suicide—she entrusted Larissa Carmichael with a journal. Within its pages, his mother hinted at her involvement in Phoebe's death, alluding to feelings of jealousy and betrayal, and a blackout period she couldn't account for on the night Phoebe disappeared. Not an explicit confession, the admission was far more subtle, and therefore believable. It was a skilled manipulation of the facts. Her journal cast significant doubt on the identity of Phoebe's killer.

George had admitted to his part in burying Phoebe's body. Fibers from the crime scene matched fibers from towels in the guesthouse. Chemicals found in Phoebe's hair matched chemicals in George's truck bed. With so much doubt and confusion, no jury could convict, and Will had no intention of accepting any plea deals.

Will's mother was an amazing woman. He had to give her that. Though he was merely four years old at the time, he remembered when she'd buried his father. Her composure was striking, as if nothing out of the ordinary had occurred. She'd acted so calm, so normal, that Will had never really questioned what was happening. She'd loaded her husband's lifeless body into her car and then left it in the woods. What followed truly left a lasting impression on Will—the way she'd concocted an alternate reality, claiming they'd left Will's father at the beach house. Even then, Will instinctively understood not to challenge his mother's narrative. He watched her shed tears and fabricate lies, year after year, until he had a hard time believing what he'd seen with his own eyes. It was an education in deception, and he'd learned from a master.

Will didn't think he was a psychopath. He was capable of love. He loved his mother and probably his father, too. He loved Taylor in the same way you can love a family member without actually enjoying their company or liking anything about them. Will appreciated his friends and was grateful for their presence in his life. But something inside him was different. The something that compelled him to squeeze the life out of Phoebe. And the girl before her. And the first girl.

Having witnessed his mother's behavior, the way she got away with things; those things didn't seem so risky. They seemed almost normal.

The first time it happened, Will hadn't planned for the event, and hadn't known there would be others. She was a young runaway, weighing a mere hundred pounds, give or take a few. A hitchhiker. Hard to believe anyone would hitchhike when Ubers were nearly everywhere. This girl clearly couldn't afford one. Will learned that when he used her ID to find out where she lived. A decrepit double-wide in the rural North Carolina mountains. Ironic how her final and forever resting place was in the woods behind Will's family home, an estate valued at over ten million.

He'd gotten rid of the young woman's backpack, her purse, and her clothes, everything non-biodegradable. He hadn't kept a single item to remember her by. Later, he regretted that.

Will met the next woman in Miami. After tossing back a few cocktails, she'd gone off for a walk with him in the dark, and that was the end of her.

Those first two opportunities fell into his lap. Nothing connected him to those women, which made them safe choices. Phoebe was a different story.

She was leaving a training appointment with his mother when they'd struck up a relaxed and flirtatious conversation. Will had asked her out. It was that easy. He hadn't planned to kill her. Although, if he were being honest, when they were flirting, he wasn't thinking about things with Phoebe leading to eventual sex or a relationship. Instead, he'd imagined something much more satisfying—wrapping a rope around her fair-skinned neck, then twisting. When Phoebe laughed in response to something he'd said, Will smiled and appeared thoughtful, wondering if it would be difficult to hold her down when he tightened the rope. Phoebe was a fitness guru, after all. Strong and agile.

That same night, he picked her up near her apartment. A new resident was moving into the complex, and their U-Haul truck blocked the entrance. Phoebe met him down the street. They were supposed to go out for drinks. She looked amazing in a sleeveless black dress. He thought about showing her off in the bar where a few of his friends were meeting later. Then Phoebe turned to look at him from the passenger seat. What she said next changed everything.

"Did you tell your mother we were meeting?"

"Why?" he'd asked, before answering her question.

Phoebe shrugged and moved a little black purse onto her lap. "I didn't tell anyone I was going out with you tonight. I wasn't sure if it was a good idea to see you."

Will cocked his head. "You having second thoughts about grabbing a drink with me?"

"No, it's not that." She smiled. "Your mother is one of my best clients. What if she doesn't approve of us going out together?"

Will laughed. "You mean she won't think I'm good enough for you?"

Phoebe had a beautiful smile, and it grew larger. She tipped her head back and laughed. "Let's just have fun and see where this goes before we mention it to anyone. Okay?"

"Sure. No problem," Will answered, realizing he hadn't told anyone either.

Another opportunity.

A few days later, Will found out Phoebe was true to her word. She hadn't mentioned Will's name to a single soul, or the police would have been at his door as soon as someone realized she was gone.

Will hadn't left anything to chance. Immediately after strangling Phoebe, he'd met up with his friends at the bar as planned. Told them he'd just woken up from a nap. He hung out with them for hours, nursing a few beers. He was in a great mood the entire time, pulsing with exhilaration and anticipation, while Phoebe slept an eternal sleep under a blanket in his car.

Killing wasn't his endgame, he'd realized. The biggest thrill came with getting away with it. The giddy sensation lasted for months. Knowing everyone was looking for someone, and only he knew where she was. God, that was satisfying. The knowledge cheered him up when he was stressed or burned out from his schoolwork, and that wasn't all. Will took pride in knowing that, just like his mother, he could keep enormous secrets. The type of secrets that might slowly but surely eat others up from the inside until only a dark void remained.

On the evening of May fourth, after parting from his friends at the bar, making sure he was the last to leave, he stuffed Phoebe in the well behind the house. No one would look there. Unlike with his first two victims, Will could check on her again.

The next time he came home, immediately after his mother's near drowning, he looked inside the well. Phoebe wasn't where he'd left her. He knew that had to be his mother's doing, though it was too late to get answers from her. Besides, he was so upset about her near-death experience and condition, he hardly cared Phoebe's body was missing.

A year passed. The police dug up Phoebe's bones and identified her. That was a shocker, and yet it shouldn't have surprised him. In fact, he should have known if his mother was involved, Madison Creek Woods was exactly where Phoebe would end up.

When law enforcement and the press resurrected Phoebe's investigation, Will got a real kick out of watching them try to put the pieces together and repeatedly sticking them in the wrong places.

The way he saw it, thanks to him, Phoebe was famous now. She was on the news. Her video views were on fire. A prime-time crime program featured her in an episode.

Will could live with what he'd done. No problem there. Just like his mother.

Unfortunately, they'd be watching him now. He had no choice. He had to stop. In that way, he was honoring his mother's last wishes.

CHAPTER 60

Present Day - Deja

Deja sat alone in her car, stealing a few precious minutes before heading into work. Her eyes skimmed the news highlights on her phone, and her heart skipped a beat. Will's face stared back at her. The same photograph had haunted her for months—the one used repeatedly in articles about Phoebe Watson's alleged killer.

William Montgomery, Duke University law student from a prominent family, arrested for the murder of fitness trainer Phoebe Watson, the headlines screamed.

Will's voice echoed in Deja's mind. "I didn't do it. I believe in our justice system. The legal process will show I'm innocent."

Deja still struggled to comprehend the events that unfolded after Agent Heslin arrested him. Three months had passed, and she still couldn't fully grasp all that happened, or figure out the truth. Had Will truly cared for her, or did he plan to make her his next victim?

Will wasn't the only one from his family in the news. Catherine's face also graced the trending articles.

Tragic millionaire and Smartbox heiress implicated in multiple murders.

The authorities had also arrested their landscaper, George Martin, for obstructing justice and aiding Catherine.

The family's sinister deeds continued to captivate the public's attention. Deja couldn't escape their smiling faces as she remembered them from the family portrait above Catherine's bed. That image had seared itself into Deja's mind. It infiltrated her thoughts at the most unexpected moments, evoking a visceral sense of disgust. To make matters worse, a recent revelation from Agent Heslin now haunted Deja. Will had placed a camera inside the frame of that very portrait, recording both video and audio.

Maybe he'd placed it there to make sure his mother received proper care, or maybe he wanted to make sure she never told anyone his awful secrets. Either way, the camera had enabled him to spy on Deja. She'd spent so much time talking to Catherine, thinking it was just the two of them. The thought of anyone witnessing their private conversations made Deja twitch with discomfort.

A puzzling question lingered in her mind, one that could never be answered. Why had Catherine uttered Phoebe's name, leading law enforcement straight to her and her family? Was it her guilty conscious surfacing? Did she not realize what she was saying?

No matter which version of the stories prevailed, Catherine was not the woman Deja had believed her to be. That's why Deja had requested a new client.

Shelby was ninety-eight years old, needed help with daily tasks like dressing and preparing meals, yet in possession of a sharp mind. Together, they discussed the news, played word games, and completed crossword puzzles.

When Deja arrived for her shift, Shelby greeted her with a warm smile, eager for the conversations that seemed to brighten her day. Shelby's family members and lifelong friends were already gone. She had no one left.

Inside her ranch house, faded photographs on the walls and tables captured moments from Shelby's past. Amidst the photographs, one took center stage. It featured Shelby, her late husband, and their only child, who had already departed this world.

What secrets and stories lay concealed behind their smiles? Deja didn't want to know. The fear of what she might uncover kept her curiosity at bay. Deja didn't require any further knowledge about Shelby to provide the care she required and the love she deserved.

CHAPTER 61

Present Day - Victoria

Victoria grabbed her bag and headed out of FBI headquarters. With the evidence gathered and the alleged killer apprehended, her work on the case was done. Now the legal system had to do its best with the complicated aftermath of the investigation.

Will thought he was getting away with murder. Victoria knew better. His mother might have helped him evade a conviction for Phoebe's death, but detectives were quietly building evidence and a case against him based on his victim in Miami. He was going to prison, probably for the rest of his life.

Agent Rivera approached. "Good work," he said. "This was all you."

"Thank you, Rivera," Victoria replied, knowing there was still a long road ahead to ensure complete justice for Phoebe and it was out of their hands. "See you on Monday."

At home, a cacophony of wagging tails and excited barks greeted her. The dogs' joyful presence never failed to make her appreciate the simple and innocent joys in life.

Victoria planned to enjoy the lack of urgency that existed between cases, however long or short the time might be. Yet she was already wondering what lay ahead, because the end of one investigation also marked the beginning of the next.

"Welcome home," Ned called from somewhere within the house.

"Missed you," she yelled back.

She glanced at a stack of mail on the counter. A thick envelope with the FBI's seal caught her attention. She plucked it from the pile.

"You wrapped up the investigation today?" Ned asked, entering the kitchen.

"Yes."

He reached out to take her hand and noticed the letter she held. "Do you still feel like going out tonight? Or is there something else you need to take care of?" There was no judgment in his voice, only understanding.

"Give me fifteen minutes to change my clothes," she answered. "And then I'll be ready to go."

Victoria tucked the letter into her desk drawer, saving it for later.

She didn't know what it was, but it could wait. There would be other women like Catherine. Other men like Will.

Fortunately, Victoria also had people like Ned in her life.

One night with her favorite person, no criminals to pursue, and no corpses to haunt her thoughts...that's all she needed to lift her spirits and recharge for her next case.

THE BAD NEIGHBOR

In the idyllic Mountain Meadows neighborhood, a fresh start can quickly become a fatal ending.

For newcomers Chris and Zoey Hamilton, the affluent community seems like the perfect location to build a life together. Instead, history repeats itself when Zoey vanishes without a trace—just like the previous homeowner five years ago.

Enter FBI Special Agent Victoria Heslin, known for her relentless pursuit of the truth. Her investigation uncovers a history of lies and betrayal festering beneath manicured gardens and picture-perfect smiles.

The more Victoria digs, the clearer it becomes: the secrets in Mountain Meadows run deep, and the greatest threats aren't lurking in the shadows...they're hosting dinner parties, attending parent-teacher conferences, going to yoga, and waving hello from behind their perfectly trimmed hedges. One of those polite, smiling individuals will stop at nothing to keep the past buried.

Keep reading for the first two chapters of Victoria's next investigation.

CHAPTER 1
Zoey - Then

After a week of driving from California to Virginia, Zoey Hamilton parked her Toyota in front of 6613 Mountain Meadows Road. She stared up at the white colonial with a mix of nerves and excitement. Her new home. A fresh start. A chance to leave the past behind her.

As thunder rumbled in the distance, Zoey climbed out of her car and got her first in-person look at the place.

The house had lingered on the market, its "As-Is" condition a deterrent to other buyers, but her husband had loved it at first sight. From California, Zoey had pored over online photos, committing every detail to memory, and finding a strange charm in the imperfections. Now that she stood in the driveway, the weathered exterior, the cracked, peeling paint, and the missing shingles were all expected flaws. But an ominous energy seemed to emanate from the house, something she hadn't sensed from the pictures. Zoey forced herself to shake off the strange feeling. Too late for second thoughts, anyway. The good outweighed the bad. The house had five bedrooms—five! If she and Chris got lucky, their first child would occupy one of those rooms next year, with more little ones filling the others in time.

Aside from the necessary renovations, the house was great, though not without a tainted past. Unfortunately, a criminal one. Not the kind of crime that left physical stains. No one had died within the walls. Nothing gruesome had occurred there. The crime was a white-collar case of embezzlement. The former owner had fled, taking millions with him. He was long gone, and Zoey wanted to forget he ever existed, so why was she even thinking about him now?

The front door of the house opened with a loud creak, and Chris emerged on the porch. In jeans and a t-shirt, he looked as handsome as ever. She'd missed him so much.

"You made it!" he called as he jogged down the front steps to join her.

After a celebratory hug and a deep kiss, their first at their new house, he helped her get their Labrador Retrievers, Finch and Wren, out of the car.

Zoey and Chris strolled around the yard, gusts of wind pulling at their hair and clothing as their dogs sniffed the unfamiliar territory.

The front garden was probably a showstopper once, before an entanglement of weeds took over. Zoey planned to tidy it up in the spring, introduce new plants, and put up birdhouses and bird feeders.

There was a lot to do. That was becoming more apparent with every passing minute since she arrived. But Zoey was good at getting things done. She liked to stay busy. With some help, they'd whip the house into shape while making it their own. She planned to write, paint, take long walks, and expand their family. Zoey pictured a future of laughter echoing through the home's hallways and children playing in the massive yard.

She squeezed Chris's arm, and he turned, offering a smile that seemed to touch her soul. In that moment, despite her weariness, her heavy eyelids, and the ache in her back and shoulders, her heart soared with a new energy.

When the first raindrops fell from the sky, Zoey and Chris ran inside together with their dogs.

Little did they know their world was about to fall apart.

CHAPTER 2

Victoria - Now

At 6020 Mountain Meadows Road, FBI Special Agent Victoria Heslin stepped out onto her porch and pulled her blonde ponytail through the back of her cap. Inhaling the crisp fall air, she surveyed the yard. Fallen leaves and twigs littered the grass from last night's storm. As Victoria propped her leg on the porch railing to stretch, the distant whine of a chainsaw cut through the morning stillness—neighbors already at work clearing debris.

Veterinarian Ned Patterson, her fiancé, emerged from their house ready for their run. "I'm glad HR gave you the nudge to use or lose some vacation hours," he said, planting a kiss on her cheek.

"I know it was last minute, so thank you for switching your clinic schedule and taking some time off." Amidst their busy careers, Victoria valued the rare opportunity to spend quality time together.

They jogged down the road, past the sprawling estates of their neighbors, each home surrounded by several acres.

Keeping up with Ned always presented a challenge. With his long legs and quick turnover, he set a demanding pace; one she could barely match, but a reason she loved running with him. Staying in top shape was crucial for her job. She never knew when she might need to outpace a suspect.

"What do you think about driving into the city to visit a gallery this week?" Ned asked.

Victoria scrunched up her nose. "They're always so crowded. I mean, unless you really want to." The thought of staying home and doing nothing was far more appealing. "I have a list of books I want to read, and movies I think we'll both like. We can hike. You can do your cooking experiments."

"A staycation sounds good to me," Ned said, speaking as effortlessly as if he were at home, reclining on the couch rather than running. "We could have a barbecue one night. I'll grill. Invite friends. Your dad. The neighbors."

Victoria shook her head.

"No to which part?"

"The invite-the-neighbors part. I don't really know them," Victoria answered.

"Neither do I. It's been months since I moved in with you, and I haven't met any of them yet. That's the point of having them over. Or...is there something you're not telling me about the people who live here?"

"They're probably all nice," Victoria said with a resigned shrug. "And as long as I don't have to spend much time with them, they get to stay that way."

The words slipped out with more conviction than intended. As an introvert, she actively avoided unnecessary social situations, always finding excuses to avoid going out. On the rare occasions she had to make an appearance somewhere, she handled it well enough—or so she told herself. But the interactions never failed to leave her drained.

"Face it, Ned." She shot him a wry look. "I'm just a bad neighbor."

Ned shook his head. "No, you're not a bad neighbor at all. You don't do anything obnoxious or disruptive. No all-night ragers blasting music or letting the dogs do their business on other people's yards, right?"

"Well, no..."

"Exactly. Like I said, you're not a bad neighbor." He grinned. "You're just...not a particularly good one."

Victoria's lips twitched to contain her smile. "Ouch. Way to sugarcoat it."

Victoria had never interacted with her neighbors aside from the occasional wave from afar, but she had researched them before purchasing her house. She wanted to avoid any unwelcome surprises, especially the awkwardness of discovering she lived beside someone under a current FBI investigation. Or worse, someone she had investigated in the past.

Ironically, her neighborhood didn't get the all-clear she'd hoped for. The FBI was looking for Steve Johnson, who had lived on her street until he embezzled money and disappeared with it. His wife remained, living alone for years before moving away, leaving the house abandoned. The FOR SALE sign had come down just a few weeks ago. Victoria didn't know who had bought the house or if they had moved in yet.

Perhaps Ned's idea of hosting the neighbors wasn't so terrible after all. It seemed important to him. Victoria wouldn't raise the subject of the barbecue on her own, but if Ned brought it up again, she would agree and go into it with a good attitude.

They had reached the front yard of the recently sold house. Bright spots of color came from bird feeders and birdhouses that weren't there before. The new owners must have settled in. Victoria had been working so many hours recently, she'd missed their move.

"I think the new people might be the offenders that email mentioned," Ned said.

"I'm not sure what you're talking about. What email?"

"The one we got from the HOA recently. It was about the pond and toning down the lawn decorations for the sake of our neighbors and property values."

"Hmm," Victoria said. "I must have missed that one."

"If it's this house, it's not like they've gone overboard with plastic flamingoes or anything. The new folks must think we're a bunch of uptight sticklers."

At the common area at the road's end, Victoria and Ned veered onto a five-mile pine-scented trail that looped through the mountains. Leaves, damp from yesterday's heavy rainfall, swished beneath their running shoes as their conversation focused on post-run plans and the blueberry pancakes Ned promised to make.

They finished their run at the neighborhood pond. The sun cast dappled shadows on the still wet grass and glimmered across the water's dark surface.

The world seemed to have quieted to a gentle calmness, and Victoria took a moment to appreciate the beautiful morning.

A sudden commotion came from the woods, and Victoria whipped around.

Two yellow labs bounded toward them.

"Whoa, hello guys." Victoria laughed as the dogs pushed their noses against her legs and wagged their tails. They wore cute collars, one plaid and one with flowers, but no tags.

"Sit," Ned commanded.

Both dogs sat at his feet, looking up at him, tails thumping the ground.

"They listen well," Ned said.

Any second, Victoria expected to see the dogs' owner, but no such person appeared. The surrounding forest remained quiet.

Facing the woods, Ned shouted, "Anyone missing two dogs?"

No one answered.

Ned cupped his hands around his mouth and shouted louder this time. "Hello! Anyone there?"

Again, no answer.

"I've got a scanner at the house," Ned told Victoria. "If they'll follow us, we can see if they're chipped."

"Come on dogs, we need to find out where you belong," Victoria said. "Your owner must be wondering where you are."

"Let's hope so, or you'll want to keep them." Ned gave Victoria a side-long look and a grin.

Despite his teasing, she knew Ned wouldn't hesitate to expand their large pack of animals if it became necessary. He loved animals as much as she did. Yet, Victoria was confident it wouldn't come to that. The dogs obviously belonged to someone. She and Ned just needed to locate that person.

You can order THE BAD NEIGHBOR from any of your favorite retailers.

NOTE FROM THE AUTHOR

If this is your first Agent Victoria Thriller, you might not know it's part of a series. I wrote the books so readers could read them alone without confusion. Each features a unique crime investigation which resolves at the end. Victoria's personal stories continue from novel to novel. There is a list of her adventures and my other thrillers in the front of this one if you're reading a print version, in the back if you have an ebook.

I also want to thank you for choosing to read my book. I'm an indie author, which means I alone am the writer, the publisher, and the marketing department. Please consider leaving a review and recommending this book to others. Your continued support is appreciated more than you'll ever know.

Yours sincerely,
Jenifer Ruff

JENIFER RUFF

USA Today bestselling author Jenifer Ruff writes suspense novels, including the award-winning Agent Victoria Thriller Series. Jenifer grew up in Massachusetts, has a biology degree from Mount Holyoke College and a Master's in Public Health and Epidemiology from Yale University. She adores peace and quiet, animals, and exercise, especially hiking. Jenifer lives in North Carolina and Virginia with her family and a pack of greyhounds. If she's not writing, she's probably devouring books or out exploring trails with her dogs. For more information you can visit her website at Jenruff.com

amazon.com/stores/author/B00NFZQOLQ

facebook.com/authorjruff

instagram.com/author.jenifer.ruff/

tiktok.com/@jeniferruff.author

http://bookbub.com/authors/jenifer-ruff

COPYRIGHT

THE ONES THEY BURIED
An Agent Victoria Heslin Thriller, Book 8

JENIFER RUFF
Copyright © 2023 Greyt Companion Press
ISBN ebook: 978-1-954447-29-5
ISBN paperback: 978-1-95447-32-5
ISBN hardback: 978-1-954447-31-8
Written by Jenifer Ruff
Cover design by Rainier Book Design

All the characters in this book are fictional. Any resemblance to actual people living or dead is a coincidence.

All rights reserved. No part of this publication may be reproduced, distributed, or transmitted in any form or by any means, including photocopying, recording, or other electronic or mechanical methods, without the prior written permission of the publisher, except in the case of brief quotations embodied in critical reviews and certain other noncommercial uses permitted by copyright law.

Made in the USA
Coppell, TX
26 October 2025

61811667R00173